Window on Pike Place

A Novel By

Martin F. Sorensen

Copyright ©2014 Martin F. Sorensen

Published by Sand Hill Review Press
www.sandhillreviewpress.com
P.O. Box 1275, San Mateo, CA 94401
(415) 297-3571

Library of Congress Control Number: 2013934204
Library of Congress Cataloging-in-Publication Data
Sorensen, Martin F.
Window on Pike Place / Martin F. Sorensen

ISBN: 978-1-937818-18-0 Perfect Bound

Cover design by Backspace Ink.
Photo of Pike Place © Matthew Torrie, Dreamtime.com

Window on Pike Place is a work of fiction. Its characters, scenes and locales are the product of the author's imagination or are used fictitiously. Any similarity of fictional characters to people living or dead is purely coincidental.

SHRP
Sand Hill Review Press

For Charleyne

Chapter One

Naked under her black Kristi Vosbeck wrap dress, Rachel stood before the window of her office, fascinated by the late evening Seattle thunderstorm. The lightning bleached the public market on the opposite side of Pike Place.

She untied the wrap and shrugged her left shoulder to let it fall. Her reflection in the window betrayed the ceiling light that shone on her exposed breast. Pulling the dress up, she walked across the soft pile of the rug and turned the switch off. Then she let the dress slip barely open as she strode back and stood before the window in red high heels.

Cool air passing over her breasts contrasted with the hot flush of embarrassment. She worried that the lightning might soon be over, and then her plan to show all of herself to Joshua, her Joshua, across the street would not work. She moved left, out of sight next to the windowpane.

The large half-circle picture window of her office faced the Public Market sign, looking down on the fish market. Joshua's apartment faced hers. His window looked in on a large room. The brilliant red scarf of a Toulouse-Lautrec poster dominated the back wall.

Rachel searched all the other windows across Pike Place and saw nothing but empty black squares. And the people down below on the shiny wet cobblestones could not see her. So she stood there for Joshua alone.

She wanted Joshua to be just as excited. They had a date this evening, the most important evening of her life. She knew Joshua felt the same anticipation, because she had seen him walking back and forth.

Rachel reached back and felt the cool, slick plastic of the phone, fumbled for the speaker button and pressed it, then found the first speed dial button and touched it. After two rings, she heard Joshua's wonderful voice.

"Hello?"

She stepped out before the windowpane, her abdomen tightening as if she stood before the open door of an airplane. Rachel took a deep breath, let the dress fall and sent a smile out into the darkness to search for him.

He looked out his window, so tall, with his wide shoulders, poised and graceful. Yet he frowned. Warmth spread all over her and her knees weakened.

"Don't you see anything in my office, Joshua?"

"No, sweetheart, it's pretty dark out there and...".

Another flash of lightning like a strobe light. A broad smile with those white teeth of his took over his whole face. "Oh, Rachel, you are beautiful!"

"Just for you Joshua, just for you." She smiled back and clicked the speakerphone off. Then she stepped out of sight, pulled the dress up, and tied it at the waist. She walked around her desk to the futon and sat, smiling and breathing hard. She had never done anything this brave outside of Afghanistan. But how thrilling! A hot blush burned on the back of her neck as she imagined her future with Joshua.

She stood, lifted her tan leather jacket off the hook and swung it around her shoulders as she opened the door and left the office. As it clicked shut a second click sounded down the hallway. The elevator doors stood closed, quiet, without the whir of movement up or down.

Rachel walked the few steps to the janitor's closet and opened it. The smell of ammonia hit her nostrils. A large box of industrial paper towels right by the door still had packing tape on it. Nobody could hide in it. Shelves of cleaning supplies took up the rest of the room. She shut the door and went to the stairwell and headed downstairs. Why worry about every little sound? Especially tonight. Maybe she wouldn't even be renting this office space much longer.

With a jaunty step, she went down the stairs and swung herself around at the landing and strode with confidence along the hallway to the street door. Once outside, the cold air cleared her head. The rain still fell in rare little drops. She raised her head and searched across the street. Joshua's apartment looked dark and empty, but Rachel knew he waited inside for her. She rushed out, careful to keep her heels from catching on the wet bricks. A cool mist sprinkled her face as she hurried across the street. Hugging her jacket close, she jumped up on the curb on the other side.

A young fishmonger with a dark crew cut and messy apron smiled and held out a wriggling red and white Alaskan king crab toward her. "Hey, Rachel, fresh in today."

She smiled back, shook her head and waved to him without moving her elbows away from her sides. She continued past Down Under and the grocery store, with its rows of neat green lettuce, to the stairwell.

She took the steps two at a time, feeling an anticipatory pleasure in using her long muscular legs. Then she stood on the landing at Joshua's white front door with its ornate etched glass windows. The door, ajar just an inch, invited her in. She pushed it all the way in, smiling, encouraged. The warm air from inside flowed across her face at the same time as the wet breeze of sea air cooled the back of her neck. She leaned in and peeked left and right into the empty front hallway. An exciting treasure hunt lay before her.

She looked left into the living room with Joshua's wide blue architectural drawing of Frank Lloyd Wright's Fallingwater on the far wall. It contrasted with the dark blue in the overstuffed brocade sofa with matching pillows, and square pure glass dining room table. Above the sofa, the Toulouse-Lautrec. Joshua, the architect as artist. But the room itself showed only furnishings. He had obviously hidden himself. Fine. At the end of the trail, the thrilling surprise.

The first door on the right opened to his workroom, with his architect's drawing table. A model of his current work rested on the table, a conference center on Portage Bay, extending out over the water. Little plastic trees and cars littered the table as if Godzilla had recently passed through. Joshua had been making the finishing touches for his presentation tomorrow morning to the mayor at the Lake Union site.

She waited and looked around with a self-satisfied smile to see if he would appear. Her leather jacket felt hot, so she took it off and then let it drop to the floor in a show of sensuous abandon.

Only one more door left on the hallway. The bedroom. Of course, the natural place for him to hide. A few minutes ago he saw her whole naked body in the flash of lightning. Where else would he be hiding? And waiting.

Rachel put her hand on the cool brass knob and opened the bedroom door enough to peek in, nervous excitement pulsing, expecting to see him languishing across his bed. Not there. The reflection in the dresser mirror against the wall on the other side of the bed showed only the black comforter and a swirly abstract charcoal drawing.

No Joshua, but the familiar warm male scent of Knize Ten cologne permeated the air. She turned around, about to go back and check out the kitchen, when a pair of hands came from behind and covered her eyes. The Knize Ten became more intense.

Then his whispered voice. "Not so good for a private detective, Rachel. You didn't look behind the door." He kept his hands over her eyes as his warm lips rested on the nape of her neck.

She smiled, reached up, and took his hands. She put them behind her. Then she turned around in a slow dance and held both his hands before her. She loved his arms. His arms, and his hands—so surprisingly long-fingered and delicate for a man his size. An architect, Joshua. And a swimmer, with a swimmer's graceful, strong body. Underneath his bathrobe, that swimmer's body still hid from her, but her smile reacted to the smooth skin of his face and his shining hazel eyes. Rachel put her hand on his warm cheek. He had shaved very, very well.

His face lifted in pleasure at seeing her.

"I think you got enough looking for both of us," she said.

Now he smiled. "I know you think I should do something similar. Don't worry, I won't disappoint you. For now, how about having something hot to drink on a cold evening?"

"Sounds nice." She followed him into the small kitchen. He already had two large transparent Irish coffee mugs steaming on the gray tile counter top. They read, "T.S. McHugh's".

"I've never seen those. You? Irish?"

Joshua laughed. "Yeah, well, the best Irish coffee is made with Italian coffee. The Irish part is whiskey as an afterthought."

When he turned to pick the mugs up from the counter, she put her hands around his waist, and pulled him tight and laid her head against his back for a moment. Turning around, he held his arms out wide holding the coffee mugs, then handed her one as he took

11

a sip out of the other.

"Come on," he said.

She followed him out to the living room, her silk wrap rustling as she moved over to the sofa. Joshua wandered over to the window.

"Be careful," she said. "You never know who's looking and you look very casual."

He turned back to her and flashed his big, wide smile, then gestured with his mug, embracing with a sweep of his hand the panorama outside the window. "I feel sorry for people who walk by themselves down the street, who seem to wander aimlessly." He looked out and pointed with his mug down toward the street. "There's a young boy, looking in windows as he goes by. All by himself. It's so lonely. Don't you think?" He turned and looked over at Rachel, anticipation on his face.

"Maybe," she said. "Could be he's on his way to a party and taking his time."

He put his hand on the windowsill. "Yes, but not this young man. It's the way he looks at things in store windows, the way he studies them." Joshua turned and leaned against the window and waited a moment. He nodded as he spoke, as if a memory came up out of the past, and he turned to Rachel with an impish smile. "Maybe he wants a comb for a girl's hair, and she's out searching for a pocket watch chain."

She found Joshua endearing, because he cared about people. He had genuine warmth, she thought, as she crossed her legs and sipped the drink. Hmm. Wonderful coffee, not too much Jameson's in it. Too bad you couldn't get something like this at Pike Place Starbucks.

The thought distracted, and so annoyed her. But the combination of the warm Irish coffee, and Joshua highlighted by the darkening light from the window warmed her soul. His reflection across the dining room table doubled his height.

He stood, and held up his finger in a signal for her to wait a moment. He walked with careful footsteps, with an air of mystery, around the table and back out to the hallway and into his workroom. Rachel sipped again and listened for sounds of his movement as he returned. One minute later he came out, looking puzzled, even somewhat sorrowful. "I misplaced something. I'll look for it later." He caught himself and looked over and smiled at her, then walked with soft steps to the sofa and sat beside her.

He put his coffee down on the coffee table. "I have something I want to discuss with you," he said, looking at her with a seriousness she had never seen before.

Of course, she had never felt this serious herself. Her heart began to beat faster. "I'm ready." When she heard herself say the words her confidence left her. A sudden worry surfaced. What if he wasn't ready? She dismissed it with an internal laugh. Instead, she focused on his eyes, the windows. "There's just you and me and the wind, darling," she said.

Joshua leaned forward a bit, looked in her eyes and at her lips, then closed his own eyes, and moved in toward her mouth. He stopped an inch away, then continued on and gave her a very gentle, hesitating kiss. As if he were kissing a girl for the very first time.

She responded by moving to him and feeling herself go all soft, barely opening her lips. He let his lips rest on hers for several seconds, then pulled away so they were barely touching. He put his hand on her hip, and leaned back so he could see her clearly.

"When I make my presentation tomorrow morning, you know, before the mayor, the whole city council, I want to be the happiest man on earth." When he continued, his voice sounded low but clear. "Rachel, I love you, and I want to spend the rest of my life with you. I think you are the most wonderful person I have ever met. ... Will you marry me?" Then he waited, his eyes, opened wide, on her.

She jumped up and put her arms around him and held him so tight she felt like she might smother him. Then she let go, and between breaths whispering yes, gave him a long, tender kiss, his lips and hers a fusion of whiskey, coffee and lipstick.

Joshua studied her face and frowned for a moment. "I have to tell you, the ring, I..."

Rachel put her hand on his mouth, then moved it to his cheek. "The ring can wait, Darling. I have all I need if I have you."

She smiled and pulled the belt of his bathrobe. "Of course, but there's still tonight—I have been waiting for you long enough. We will have forever after your presentation tomorrow. We can go to the cabin for a couple of days."

Chapter 2

Rachel woke in the silent early morning darkness of the bedroom, feeling Joshua's warmth next to her. As her eyes adjusted she watched the silhouette of his chest rise and fall with the slow cadence of his breathing. She lifted the covers off and the cool air of the room wafted over her legs. She sat upright in a slow arc and waited, then turned and watched him, at rest, peaceful. Her Joshua, forever. She pushed herself off the bed and heard his groggy voice behind her.

"Are you okay?"

She turned back and leaned over and touched him on the shoulder. "Yes, I'm fine." She looked at the alarm clock on the bedside table. "It's four o'clock. I'm going to go over to my house and..."

"What?" He lifted himself up on his elbows. He blinked his eyes and rubbed them with the back of his hands. "Why?"

Rachel wished she had been more quiet. She whispered, "I need to go pack, get ready for our trip. Then I'll come back and organize my office so I can get away."

"Come back to bed. It's too early."

"No, you go back to sleep. You know you didn't get enough work done last night."

He laughed. "Yeah, whose fault was that?" He fell back down on his pillow.

She gave him a kiss. "I'm happy to accept blame." She took hold of his hand. "I'll be back in a while. Go to sleep so you can work in the morning." Rachel pulled away and let his hand drop, but he held her fingers, and pulled her back. She knelt on the bed and gave him another kiss, then gently pushed herself away. "I love you."

"I love you, too," he said as he turned over on his side and pulled the covers up.

Rachel, on tiptoe, took her clothes out to the hallway, dressed and picked up her keys by the door. Her throat felt dry and scratchy, so she walked to the kitchen and drank a glass of cold water. Still on the balls of her feet, she went to the window in the living room and opened it wide. The cool sea air filled her lungs. At first she worried that noise from the market or birds would wake him, but then she thought it would help him to get up on time.

She hesitated about going to her house. Maybe she could help him in the morning. She wanted to help him, be there with him, but then rejected that idea, too. He didn't need distractions on this most important day of his career.

She drove in the darkness over the empty streets from downtown to Capitol Hill and her house across from Volunteer Park. The windows high up on the Water Tower in the park glared in orange light like sentinels. Rachel parked her car and took care to be quiet as she opened the door to the house and walked in. She didn't want to wake her housekeeper Irene in the basement apartment.

She found the small suitcase in the hall closet. No searching around or seeing how clothes looked in the mirror. She just filled it with enough for a short trip. Then she put on her white Adidas track suit, put the pepper spray in the pocket, and went back outside and down E. Prospect for her run on the Volunteer Park outer loop. Back home, she took a long hot shower, got dressed and drove downtown.

Only the industrious delivery trucks populated Pike

Place outside her office window. On the street she saw a red and blue Pepsi truck and a man pushing a handcart full of green apples. Forms moved past the brass pig inside the marketplace. Someone in an apron piled ice around fish. She focused on Joshua's window across the street, still open even though the morning air cooled the neighborhood. She waited and watched, but he did not appear.

A moment of concern gripped her, but then her imagination moved easily back to the night before, to the bedroom she had shared with him. The bleeping of a truck in reverse interrupted her reverie.

Joshua had to be in his workroom, getting ready for putting the final touches on his model, rehearsing for his presentation. Or maybe he left early to take all his material down to Portage Bay and didn't think about the window. Rachel wanted to call him on his cell phone, but knew it would be a distraction.

Later in the morning, his project would surely dazzle them. He had an unbeatable idea, a conference center extending out over the water, where you could see the boats going back and forth between Lake Union and Lake Washington. He had even prepared a virtual tour, with a 360-degree panorama view from inside the main conference hall.

A minor worry surfaced. What if the mayor's people would not let him get away today? She sighed and thought it didn't matter. She could wait a couple of days more. She could still see him and they would be so happy with his success. She wanted nothing more for him. For them.

She shaded her eyes with her hand, and ducked down below the sign on her window to see if she could see anything farther back in Joshua's apartment, but she saw only the red and blue of the drawing and the sofa.

Rachel smiled to herself, then turned back around and sat at her Navy-surplus metal desk, the window at her back, and surveyed her one-room office, with her desk, a file cabinet and a futon. She leaned forward in her chair and put her head in her hands and closed her eyes. She imagined a breeze cooling her face and Joshua holding her hand at the railing of a ferry across the sound.

Boom! Crash! A gunshot exploded from the hallway. The window in back of Rachel disintegrated, shards of glass falling outward to the street.

She fell down to the right, put her arms out and landed on the floor. The fall pushed the air out of her lungs and her muscles tightened. Her left ear rang. Then she started breathing hard and her heart beat faster.

She twisted her head and looked out under her desk. She could see the bottom of the file cabinet and part of the beige carpet of the hallway beyond the door. The only legs she could see were those of the desk, and the futon frame along the left wall. Nothing human.

She kept her head down, reached up and fumbled around her desk drawer desperately searching for her gun, but found only the pint of Hennessey cognac and her Zippo. She grabbed them. For a second, she stared at the polished metal lighter with its gold and black 272nd MP logo of crossed pistols. But how had she misplaced her gun? She had put it in her desk. Hadn't she?

Quiet now. First the big bang, then nothing. No metallic click. No footsteps. Not with the plush carpet out there. No breathing except her own, fast and heavy. The gleam from the clear plastic dish on the hyperbolic microphone in the corner caught her eye. She could hear the quietest movement out in the hallway. But she would be an easy target if she tried to get it. He lurked out there. He hid in the hallway, pupils enlarged and ears tuned, eyes shining from adrenaline, both hands on his gun, waiting for her to stand up so he could surprise her with a quick jump into the room and several rounds into her heart.

Cold air came in through the now-empty street window and shivered down her back. She pushed herself up on her knees and then stopped, quiet. Still no sound. She had to figure out something to do before this dull gray office turned into her tomb.

If he were still around, the shooter would be in the hallway to the right of the open doorway. If she called 911, he would hear her and know where to aim his gun. If she stood, he could simply lean in and unload a semi-automatic up and down her body. But next to the doorframe she could surprise him. Where the hell had she put her gun? She had no answer. She had put it in her desk a long time ago.

She opened the bottle of Hennessey. Then raised her hand but kept her head down, and stretched her arm as far out to the middle of the desk as she could. She twisted her wrist and upended the bottle and heard the whisper-gurgle of the liquid as it emptied on to the surface. The strong dusky smell filled the air. More stillness.

She pulled the bottle back down and laid it on the floor. Then she reached over to the trash can, picked up a small piece of paper between two fingers, opened the lighter top with a deliberate quiet movement of both of her hands, and lit the paper on fire. She threw it on top of the desk.

A deep, loud whoosh erupted with a tower of red-yellow flames. Black acrid smoke hit the ceiling and fanned out.

Rachel stood halfway up, keeping her head down, and ran over to the far wall. She hid for a moment behind the file cabinet, then went around it and stood next to the empty doorframe. Now she'd show him the power of a real combat veteran.

She stood still and tensed her abdominal muscles to control her breathing. The fire died down but the thin black haze still covered the ceiling. The smells of cognac and smoke made her nauseous. No one appeared. She looked in the hallway. The empty stairwell and the open elevator door posed no threat. She shrugged and walked back into her office.

The fire hadn't taken hold on the metal desk, but the black smoke billowed out the window. The smoke alarm in the ceiling screeched its hell. She knew the Seattle Fire Department sirens would pierce the air any minute now, and Seattle Police would be right behind them.

Rachel stepped over to the desk and looked through all the other drawers for the gun. Not there. Next, all the drawers of the filing cabinet. She opened the small number of folders in the top drawer, reflecting the state of her business, and below that the other drawers. No gun there, either.

She had now searched everywhere possible. It had been in the top desk drawer. That's the only place it had ever been. He must have come in during the night and taken it.

The sound of sirens came through the empty window, growing ever louder. The sound came around a corner, down Pike Street, and then stopped outside the window.

The cavalry would be arriving up here any second now. She imagined Detective Diane Scanlan coming in the door, arms out straight, gun tight in both hands, sweeping left and right. Seattle Police could get started on the search for whoever recklessly fired a shot through her window.

The clamor of voices grew from the street. Rachel stopped for a second and listened. The jagged edges of the glass pointed in from the window frame. Why wasn't anyone coming up the stairs?

Her hand rose to her mouth. A pang jolted Rachel's chest when she looked through the empty window. In Joshua's apartment paramedics moved something.

Chapter 3

Rachel ran for the door. Once in the hallway, she ran over to the stairwell, jumped down the first few stairs, then grabbed the newel post and swung herself around. She crashed head and torso into a woman. Rachel and the woman both let out a scream. They tumbled hard down the stairs to the next landing. Rachel's head hit the wall, and bright lights flashed. She found herself lying on her back, looking up at the ceiling. A sharp slash of jarred nerves settled on the back of her skull.

Diane Scanlan, lying next to Rachel, looked upset, disheveled, and at the same level on the floor. Diane concentrated on slow breathing. Her twisted face showed the hurt inside her. She put her hand behind her neck and pulled hard as she massaged it. Then Diane grabbed the railing, pulled herself up with a grunt and stretched out her hand to Rachel.

Rachel reached out and pulled herself up. She held her head in her hands for a moment and steadied herself against the banister. "You okay, Diane?"

"A headache, but it'll be okay. You?"

"Yeah. Why were you coming up here?" Rachel said.

"Somebody called in a gunshot, and when I heard the address I came over. The paramedics are across the street. Your window was out and smoke was coming out of your office."

"Come on, let's go."

Diane nodded and put her hand on Rachel's back and nudged her down the stairs. "What was burning?"

"My cognac."

"Cognac?"

"Yeah, I set it on fire to distract the shooter."

Diane stopped for a second and held Rachel by the shoulder. "The gunshot came from your office?"

"From the hallway, but I looked out there and couldn't find anyone." Rachel pulled away and went to the hallway exit.

They hurried out to the street and shoved their way through the crowd. A cool breeze blew across the back of Rachel's neck. Joseph from the fish market looked up and saw her coming. He took a step back and put his hands behind him, but managed a forced smile. "Rachel, what's going on?"

She gave him a quick look on the run and waved him off. They ran around the ambulance and up the stairs to Joshua's apartment.

Through the back hall Joshua's bed still showed the white rumpled sheets that she'd been in last night. She stood still and stared at them for a second to assure herself the sheets were not bloody.

Turning to the living room, she gasped and held her fist to her mouth.

Paramedics were lifting Joshua onto the wheeled stretcher that had been collapsed down almost to floor level. Deep red blood oozed onto white gauze around his head. They had stuck an IV into him and covered his face with an oxygen mask. She ran over to the stretcher, kneeled and put her hand on her heart. As tears ran down her cheeks, she touched his arm.

His arm moved toward her. Rachel squeezed his hand, but he didn't react. Her heart sank. She squeezed his hand again, with more strength, and held it with both her hands, remembering her fingers entwined with his before she left last night.

A warm hand pressed on her right shoulder. She turned and looked up at the concerned man in the paramedic uniform. She looked back down, put her palm on Joshua's head, and moved out of the way.

A small pool of blood coated an irregular circle on the floor in front of the window. Rachel stooped down and studied it, then looked up and across the street. She mentally followed the trajectory back across the street and saw that the bullet couldn't have been meant for her. The line from the hallway to Joshua's window missed her desk by several feet. The killer had aimed at Joshua, not at her.

Why would anyone want to kill him? There could only be one purpose, to get back at Rachel. It didn't make any sense. Why not shoot her while she sat alone and unsuspecting at her desk? Why kill someone else? She would have seen anyone who stalked Joshua. Then it came back to her: she had thought of vetting Joshua, but it seemed so brutal, as if she couldn't judge character. Now she regretted it. She might have discovered the killer before it happened. Shards of thoughts.

Her own empty window frame looked back at her with black smoke trailing upwards and feathering out in the wind. Clues were waiting over there, things small and forgotten. A blue-white bird flapped its wings close by in a blur past the window. A bus rumbled as it started.

Rachel turned back into the room and put her hand on the arm of one of the paramedics. He frowned and pulled away.

"Sorry," she said, "I want to know where you're taking him."

"Harborview."

Rachel shook her head and shrugged. "But Virginia Mason is closer." She looked over at Diane, who came over, stood by her side, and touched Rachel's shoulder.

"Neurosurgeon. Would you mind getting out of my way?"

"Wait. Is he going to be okay?" The question came up out of her gut. She had to ask it.

"Vital signs are stable now. We gotta go."

She took one last look at Joshua, already in his little emergency room of oxygen and solution, and then turned to her old partner in war and peace. "I'm going over there, Diane." Rachel waited for the paramedics to negotiate the stairs. She followed, with Diane behind her.

On the street, she instinctively looked around for anyone who didn't belong there, but she immediately felt the uselessness of it. Business owners stood on the sidewalk watching the day's sales disappear. Vendors in aprons, arms crossed, seemed like palace guards.

Four black and white sedans parked at crazy angles on the street, red lights flashing, voices squawking from radios. A fire truck and an ambulance blocked most of the street. Men in dark blue unrolled yellow tape, and down the street a Channel 12 news van elevated a dish antenna.

Rachel turned to Diane. "Give me your keys."

"What?"

"Give me your keys."

"No way, it's a police vehicle." Diane cocked her head to one side and backed away.

"Shit, Diane." Rachel shook her head and then ran up the street to Diane's unmarked car. She reached in through the open window, picked up the red magnetic light off the floor, and jogged across First Avenue to her car.

The ambulance started its siren going up Pike Street. Rachel put the red light on top of her car, turned the ignition on and drove down First and through every stop sign and stoplight until she got up to James and the Harborview emergency entrance. Spotting a free section along the curb, she made a quick u-turn, grabbed the space, and ran inside.

"Where's the man they brought in, the one with the head wound?"

The triage nurse in a rumpled green uniform kept her head down, lips pressed together. The nurse finished shuffling papers on her desk, then turned her head toward Rachel. She folded her arms across her chest and settled back on her heels. Rachel took out her wallet and held up her investigator's license.

Behind the nurse, two orderlies pushed Joshua's gurney down the hallway. Rachel watched as his body moved from side to side, he looked like he attempted to escape from his neck brace. The wheels squeaked against the linoleum as it moved away from her. But then the orderlies turned a corner and disappeared with Joshua. She made a quick step toward the hallway, but hit her knee against a low barrier.

The nurse raised her voice to get Rachel's attention. "Are you related to him?"

"I'm his fiancée." The sound of her voice shocked Rachel as she heard the word for the first time out loud. More shocked that she heard it first here, in the emergency room.

"I see." The nurse studied Rachel. "Has his family been notified?"

A second shock. Rachel thought of saying she didn't know them, but realized she could not bring herself to say it. She shook her head. "No, there hasn't been time; I came over here with the ambulance. I'm a private detective. You saw my license. His parents are dead. He has a sister down in Portland, but I don't know her number."

"Let me take down your number. I'll be right back." The nurse moved sideways over to her desk and picked up a pen and pad, then looked over and studied Rachel's license and wrote the number down.

"Excuse me," the nurse said, her voice softened. She stood for a moment and studied Rachel, then turned away and waved the little slip of paper as she walked through the double doors.

Ten seconds later, the nurse came back through the doors in a rush. "Mr. Todaro has been taken to the third floor for surgery. Dr. Neil Golden, the resident neurosurgeon, is operating on him. If you take the elevator, there's a waiting room up there. I will let them know you're here."

Now he fought for his life up in an operating room. She wondered whether she would see him again. A sharp cramp broadened to a sickening feeling.

She took the elevator up and sat in the waiting room, empty and sterile as the operating room itself. Empty seats below meaningless art lit by industrial lamps. Cognac would have been good right now. Her cell phone rang and focused her attention.

Diane. "What's happening, Rachel?"

"Joshua is in the operating room. They won't tell me anything. They said neurosurgery. I'm scared, Diane. "

"I wish I could be there with you, Rachel. But you couldn't be at a better place than Harborview, you know."

"Yes, I do know that. Tell me what's going on there." She didn't really care about anything that happened anyplace else in the world.

"Crime Scene is here and I'm waiting to find out who's in charge."

"Let me know as soon as you do."

She closed her cell phone. She stood and walked to the end of the room, then walked back. She slammed the phone against her thigh. A combat medic, now helpless.

Or maybe not. She held her head high, marched to the double doors, and banged them open. A surprised half naked man pulled covers over himself and fumbled for something on the little table next to the bed. Nurses turned and looked at Rachel as she stomped in, shoes clacking, and walked past several alcoves with curtains pulled back. She pushed through another set of double doors and found herself inside a clinical room with stainless steel doors on all sides.

A large woman in a green gown, mask and rubber gloves came over to her. "What do you want?"

"I'm here to observe surgery on Joshua Todaro for the police."

"They've already started in there," the woman said, shaking her head, mouth turned down."You're not even clean. Get out of here!" The woman pushed Rachel backwards with her elbows until Rachel felt the door give way. "Get her back to the waiting room!"

A big male nurse came up and put his massive hands on Rachel's shoulder, turned her around, and pushed her the rest of the way out to the waiting room. Before he disappeared, he stared back out through the little window to make sure she wasn't going to break the sterile field again.

Rachel walked around the waiting room, desperate to be closer to Joshua, trying to figure out if she could get in there some other way. Going back to the double doors, she looked into the window, searching around the room for an unused gown and mask. But she could see them, watching, ready to intercept her, so she walked back to the waiting area and sat on a black and chrome lounge chair. Rachel took out her cell phone and called Diane again, but she didn't get an answer.

A tall man with glasses dressed in operating green came out and looked around, pulled his mask down to his neck and came over to Rachel. She straightened up, looked over to him, at his dark eyes. She took out her key chain, her hands tight around Joshua's bullet, then pulled her arms around her chest and waited for the sentence of life or death.

"I'm sorry to say that Mr. Todaro died on the operating table. We were not able to stop the cerebral hemorrhaging. He never regained consciousness."

Rachel's heart stopped. Her head drooped. Then she looked up. "Are you the doctor who operated on him?"

"Yes. I'm Neil Golden." He took a deep long sigh, then looked down at her hands with white knuckles, clenched together.

Rachel felt a sting sucking her insides. "I'm his fiancée." She looked up again, pleading. "Please forgive me...I'm sorry, but tell me... did you try to save him? I mean, did you have a chance?"

Neil Golden looked at her with sympathetic eyes. He hunched his shoulders and shook his head. He opened his hands. "We did everything we could. I'm sorry, but the bullet did too much damage."

Rachel put her hands out as if she were going to pray. "How long did he live?" Inside her heart she also meant, how long did I have him to myself.

"I can tell you this, he was a fighter. He did not give up easily." The doctor stood, put his hand on her shoulder, and continued, "Are you all right?" She nodded and the doctor went back in, looking back at her before he went inside the doors.

Rachel sat there with her head in her hands. Joshua, the man she had saved on the battlefield, her Joshua, the man who last night made a solemn commitment to be her husband, who promised her that he would fly away with her today, lay now on a cold slab in an operating room and they were taking tubes out of him and running around with hardhearted efficiency.

Joshua had talked about being together forever. Joshua and she didn't put any time limit on it, because they felt like they were going to live that long, forever. They had laughed, and she for one laughed more than at any time in her life. The laughter that came from happiness that would never go away.

If only she had stayed that night, if only he had canceled his presentation the next day, if only she had left the window closed, if only...

For a moment she felt like she could call him up and tell him that everything will be okay, I'll come get you and we'll go away and...

Rachel sighed and ran her fingers through her hair. She felt the cold silence and emptiness of the room. As empty as her soul. She got up and walked out to the elevator. The words the doctor had spoken to her sounded meaningless now, something they practiced to tell everyone when the patient died. Joshua had gone far away from her and she could not get them to bring him closer.

Inside the elevator the reflective walls showed blurred images of her solitude. It took her a long time to think of pushing a button. When she did, the elevator waited, then descended in silence as if into a grave. The bright light when the doors opened shocked her, and an old woman with a cane stared at her, waiting for Rachel to move. She hurried out and nearly knocked the woman over.

The red light still flashed on Rachel's car out on the street. She kept it on. Halfway back to Pike Place, she called Diane and let her know Joshua had died.

Chapter 4

Yellow police tape blocked off Pike Place corner. White vans with antennas from all the major TV stations crowded the street nearby. Most of the neighborhood huddled close to the yellow tape. They talked excitedly. The men in blue were busy. Flower vendors, grocers, fishmongers stood outside surveying the activity and gossiping with one another. Rachel parked on First Avenue.

One of the policemen saw her as she walked closer, and waved her forward and even gave her a little salute, which she did not return. Kara Moreno, in a bright red dress and pearls, and a scrubby cameraman behind her, came over to her car and held a microphone with a big 13 on it up to Rachel's face and started yelling questions before she even got out. Out of nowhere came still cameras, recorders, and notebooks. She could hardly move.

"What the hell...?" she waved her hands and swung her head back and forth, but that only made them more aggressive.

"Why are the police looking in your office?"

"Do you know anything about the murder?"

Her fiancé just died and these people came on like animals, trying to get anything out of her, no matter what her feelings were. All the flashes accentuated her headache. Rachel sickened inside, wanted to scream out that she knew the killer, he's here, look around you. But she carefully controlled herself, determined not to react at all. She didn't want to do something she would regret. She remembered that on the battlefield the wrong emotions could get you killed.

Rachel pushed her way over to the other side of the car. Her action doubled the number of reporters closing off her path. "Hey!" she yelled as loud as she could. "Get out of my way." She called over to one of the other officers she knew. "How about running interference for me, Tom?"

The tall, thin guy came over, pushed the press out of the way, led Rachel over to the yellow tape, and lifted it for her to go under.

"Thanks," Rachel said. A hand on her shoulder made her turn around. Diane moved closer to Rachel to give her a hug. Rachel backed away, knowing inside she had to keep herself strong and in control.

Diane stared at her, but seemed to understand Rachel's feelings. "I'm really sorry, Rachel. I've called Michael, too. We both can't believe this has happened. He will want to talk to you as soon as you can." Michael, Diane's husband and Rachel's friend. Joshua's friend as well. Until today.

"Thanks, I know it hurts you, too," Rachel said. Diane always encouraged her, and had made her see Joshua for the terrific person he is. Was.

Rachel shook her head and looked at the sidewalk. Then she looked back at Diane. "Where have you been?"

"They called me off to go look at some break-in on Western. I was actually behind you for a while. Now I know where my light went."

"It's not illegal to have a red flashing light," Rachel said.

"Yeah, sure. Until they catch up to you. You don't have many friends around here as it is."

"Diane, that's enough. Let's go see what they've found."

Rachel pushed over to the public market and Joshua's building. A large crowd pressed against the window inside Lowell's Restaurant. She and Diane leaped up each stair to the second floor.

At the top of the stairs, still in the hallway, she could see investigators working in Joshua's apartment. Someone dusting for fingerprints appeared momentarily, disappeared, then reappeared. But they couldn't get far enough in to see anyone else inside the apartment. When Rachel and Diane started to walk in, an officer came out of the woodwork and stopped them. He had sergeant stripes, a thin man with a wide forced smile.

He gave Diane a friendly shake, but moved his head back and forth. "Sorry, crime scene. You know the rules, Detective Scanlan."

"Who's in charge in there, Officer?" Rachel said, her stomach churning as she waited to hear the name.

The man hesitated before replying, rearing his head back and looking at her as if she were impertinent, making it obvious he'd been forewarned. "Detective Phillips."

"Brian Phillips?" The news disappointed Rachel. Brian functioned as Ted's gofer. Not the real thing.

"Yes, Ma'am." The policeman nodded formally to her.

Rachel turned to Diane and whispered. "If Brian's here, that means Tourville is across the street covering his tracks. We're on the wrong side of the street." She turned back to the officer and said, "Let me talk to Detective Phillips."

He looked at Diane's badge and back to Rachel. "And your name is?"

"Rachel McAlister."

He nodded, as if he knew something, as if he remembered the events from a year ago, then went inside for a few minutes and came back out. He sounded artificially apologetic. "I'm sorry, he's right in the middle of a particularly important evidence detail right now and can't come out." The officer turned, then looked back and said, his voice carrying the disdain he heard from inside, "He said if you wanted to talk to somebody, go across the street."

Rachel's heart started to beat faster. "C'mon," she said to Diane.

Diane turned around and followed her down the stairs. Rachel saw a red laser light looking like a high wire going out from Joshua's window and passing through light fog toward her office. They were checking trajectory. The red line led through the open window frame, through her office and on to the hallway door. So they had closed the door. That would make it easier for them to assume that the killer, Rachel, fired the gun from inside the room. They were setting this up already.

Rachel heard the policeman calling someone on his cell phone. He jotted something in his notebook.

People were walking around inside her office, but she couldn't make out who they were. Rachel and Diane crossed the street, walked in and up the stairs. At the top, a man in a perfectly pressed blue uniform held up his hand. Rachel could tell that he knew Diane. By his service stripes and name tag, she could read his status as a fat veteran named Fred Schuler. He politely touched the bill of his cap.

"Hi, Diane. I have to caution you that there's still an investigation going on here. There's glass on the floor, so you aren't going to be able to go inside."

Rachel walked up to him, crossing in front of Diane. She planted her feet and pointed. "That's my office inside there, Officer."

"That may be, Ms. McAlister, but I can't let you inside. Strict orders." Another notation in the notebook.

"I don't know you, Officer. How is it you know me?"

He shifted back and forth on his feet, then bobbed his head up and down and blinked several times before he answered. "We all know who you are."

She swiveled around and looked at Diane, tightened her lips, then came back and faced the veteran. "And who gave you those strict orders?"

"It was the detective in charge, Ma'am, Detective Tourville." He tried his best to act nonchalant, but his face betrayed a smirk.

She twisted her head back to Diane. "He's hard at work already." Then she faced the cop again. "Tell the detective that Rachel McAlister wants to see him. Before he eliminates too much evidence."

The man in the blue uniform walked into the office and came back a full minute later to the doorway and stepped aside.

Rachel saw Tourville's eyes first. Beneath his huge black eyebrows, they were dark, unblinking, and intense with hate. His mouth turned down, ready to spit venom. His huge knotted hands rested on either side of the doorway. His head moved up and down in a slight but continuous motion, his resentment straining against the need to be professional. Rachel started to lunge forward, but Diane grabbed her shoulder firmly.

Ted put his hands out. "You don't have balls, McAlister. Don't act like you do." His nasty smile showed his nicotine-stained teeth.

Rachel felt her spine stiffen and needles of heat spread down her back. She pointed her finger at Ted Tourville. "You have the murder of Gil Hamilton on your conscience, and now you've killed my fiancé." She raised her voice, shaking with rage. "I know you're in there covering up."

Ted moved his tongue around his mouth like he prepared to spit, then gave a short mocking laugh and took two steps back to the office. Then he looked back over his shoulder and pointed at her. "No escape this time, Rachel." He disappeared inside and slammed the door shut.

Rachel shrugged Diane's hand off her, reached for the doorknob and pushed it open, but the policeman and Diane grabbed her shoulders and held her back.

Diane turned Rachel around to face her. She stared at Rachel, eyes glaring. "You don't want a confrontation at a crime scene."

Rachel backed up a step and put her hands on her hips. "I'll have a confrontation any god damn place I want to. Get out of my way."

Diane took hold of Rachel's arm. The large hulk of Ted Tourville showed inside the door.

Rachel wrestled her arm free and lunged toward Ted. Ted's face became red and he moved to her, but Officer Shuler put his hand on Ted's chest and held him back. Ted pushed the arm out of the way with a grimace and continued forward.

Alan Berg came out of nowhere and stepped in front of him.

"Alan, what are you doing here?" Rachel raised her eyebrows. "Prosecuting already?" So, they gave this to Berg. To help him when he came to run for District Attorney. City power obviously generated this so-called investigation.

"Hello, Rachel. It's nice to meet you again."

He held out his hand but she didn't take it. Diane gave Rachel her look of caution and shook her head.

"We are here because it's a crime scene," Berg said, "not because it's your office, Rachel. Don't start accusing people."

"Alan, I want to be in there. I don't trust Tourville."

"You can't go in. You know that."

Rachel let out a caustic laugh, straightened and pointed toward her office. "Yeah, and that bastard is in there contaminating it now."

"Be very careful. I'll make sure that it's handled professionally."

Rachel turned away from Tourville and Berg. She stared at Diane, who tightened her hold on Rachel and pushed her back to the stairwell. Rachel knew Diane had it figured right, they weren't going to get inside anyway, so she walked over to the stairs and started down. When they were on the street, she stopped.

Diane walked right behind her. "Okay, Rachel, you've got to stay calm."

Rachel pointed to her window. "Yeah, he's up there going through my office."

"Hey, take it easy. He can't find what's not there."

"Yeah, and Alan Berg is up there, too. They're all in on it."

Diane opened her eyes wide and looked at Rachel and waited a moment before speaking. "You're going overboard. Alan Berg is doing his job. If there's a conspiracy, it's not the district attorney's office. Ted would have to be working with someone else."

Rachel wasn't listening to her. "Ted can easily find something that he has put there. They should be looking for Joshua's killer," Rachel said, raising her arm high. "Not ransacking my office."

Diane frowned. "Think about it. Chew will get the bullet and do the ballistics. Then they'll know it wasn't you. That's what's important."

Rachel thought Diane too easily accepted Tourville's professionalism. "He's not going to wait for the damn bullet, Diane."

"Well, from what you told me, somebody shot something through your doorway. There might be a shell casing up there."

"No. I looked at the hallway before I went downstairs. Probably a revolver." Rachel looked around to make sure they couldn't be heard. She leaned close to Diane. "But I'll tell you something else. My gun is missing."

"What do you mean by missing?"

"It has always been in the top drawer of my desk. Someone took it out of there."

Diane widened her eyes in disbelief. "How long has it been gone?"

"I don't know," Rachel said. She remembered back to the moments after the shot rang out, when she looked in her drawer. "After the shot, I went to get my gun out of the drawer, but it wasn't there."

"Maybe you brought it home, Rachel."

"No. Someone took it, and they used it to kill Joshua. You know it was Tourville."

"Don't implicate him yet. Don't complicate things. Let him rut around. It's his time he's wasting."

Diane looked up Pike Place and Pike Street. She took three steps away and then turned back and pointed at Rachel. "I've got to go and finish what I was doing. You shouldn't be alone now. Go over and see Michael."

Rachel ran her fingers through her hair, tried and failed to force a smile. She waved Diane off with, "Not yet. You go ahead. I'm not finished here, either."

Diane put herself squarely in front of Rachel. "All right, this is it, Rachel. If this is what you think it is, go look for a lawyer."

"The hell. Shit, Diane, aren't you way ahead of yourself here?"

"No. Trust me."

"Trust you? I need to look out for myself." Rachel touched her chest with her finger and held it there. She waited a few seconds, looking at Diane.

"I mean what I say, Rachel." Diane touched her on the shoulder as she waved to a couple of the police officers on the scene, and walked out past the yellow caution signs.

As Diane moved away, Rachel saw her walk, and thought back to the way she'd walked down the street in the villages in Afghanistan. Diane Scanlan. Fearless in war, too cautious in peace.

Chapter 5

Sand. Under your collar, inside your shoes, jamming your weapon. Grit in your aching soul. Rachel McAlister, Military Police Medical Specialist, slammed her fist against the door of the Humvee. She rode shotgun on the last of three Humvees that rattled east from Bagram air base for traffic control.

Rachel took a swallow of cool water and turned to her driver. "Hard to get lost on a damn straight road with nothing but dirt." The endless brown rocks and gray scrub flew past her window. She switched on her mike. "Hey, you okay up there, Cock Robin?".

Lieutenant Diane Scanlan, the group's leader, responded. "Fine. Same old road, same old rut."

Farther ahead on the right, Rachel saw the familiar mud farmhouse. A small orchard and green field led up to the road. Several bearded men in long robes watched the convoy as it moved in their direction. They kept chopping at the ground. Two more looked like they might be picking fruit from the trees. The two stopped moving. They stared.

Rachel stiffened and tightened her grip on the carbine. She hit her driver on the back.

"What?"

Rachel pointed at the farmhouse fast approaching, then heard the lieutenant's voice in her earpiece.

"You ever see more than one person at that farm?"

"Never."

"Be sharp, everybody," came Diane's voice again. "Show your weapons."

Rachel reached down and picked up the grenade launcher. With a strong audible click, she attached it to her carbine. Eight more grenades went in her vest pocket. She pointed her carbine out the window and adjusted the medical bag hanging from her shoulder. The wind heated her face.

Thud! An explosion sent the first Humvee on its side and threw dust and debris on Rachel's hood and windshield. Oil spilled on the ground in front of the overturned vehicle.

Rachel's driver slammed on the brakes and stopped five yards from the second vehicle. Rachel turned around. "Man the fifty-caliber," she said, pointing to the roof of the vehicle.

He looked at her a second. Rachel had a medic's job. But then he jumped fast into the back seat and up into the turret.

Two men climbed out of the first Humvee down to the dirt in front of it. One clutched his face. The other put his hand on his side and smeared blood. His leg twitched. He grunted and grimaced.

"Get out! Take cover!" Rachel yelled. The driver jumped out the left side, and Rachel crawled across the seat and stumbled down. She raised her carbine above the hood of the Humvee and launched a grenade over the field, loaded another, then looked out from behind the front bumper. The .50 caliber machine gun atop the Humvee cracked fire across the road. Rachel crawled back, reached into the vehicle, and took out the squad automatic weapon and two magazines. She ran and slid down in front of the two wounded men and began spraying machine gun fire into the field.

Diane bolted out from behind the second Humvee and ran in front of Rachel. "I'll cover," Diane yelled. She shot off a grenade, then grabbed the machine gun, lay down in prone position and started firing in a wide arc.

The man who had clutched his face now seemed

okay. He and Rachel dragged the other wounded man out of the line of fire. Rachel quickly put Quick-Clot on the wound, and bandaged it. She rested her hand on his shoulder and he nodded. She gave him an antibiotic shot.

"Thank you, Rachel."

"No problem. I'll see you later, Joshua."

Diane dropped the machine gun, took her carbine, launched a grenade and then hurried back behind the vehicle.

Rachel loaded another grenade, and got set to shoot it off over the hood of the Humvee. But then she yelled "Into the ambush," took off between the vehicles, and ran across the road.

"Cover us," Diane yelled. The fifty-caliber machine gun raked fire into the fields. She got up and ran across the road and followed Rachel into a ditch.

Four masked men were ten yards away from them. The men stared, then fired. Little clods of dirt and dust flew up a few feet from Diane and Rachel. Both women lifted their carbines and started shooting down the ditch. The four men tumbled into the dirt.

One of them held his head as blood rushed out between his fingers. Another lay still. A third looked up and fumbled around for his weapon. Diane aimed a red dot from the laser pointer on her rifle on the center of his forehead and pulled the trigger. He opened his mouth and fell back. The fourth got up, running toward the house. Rachel shot a grenade ahead of him. He flew apart in pieces.

Machine gun fire and grenades from the Humvees strafed the field and the orchard. The top half of a tree fell over. A man hiding behind it stared in surprise, then raised a rocket-propelled grenade. A laser red dot and a rifle shot put him down. Another man ran over to try to pick up the weapon. Red splotches appeared on his chest and an instant later there were shots and he fell screaming. He lay there twitching, then he stopped.

The scene fell quiet. The loud wind kicked up dust. Rachel put her fingers up and felt her parched lips, still observing the scene in front of her. Another burst of fifty-caliber fire to the farm window. Someone inside yelled and then fell out and hung hands down outside the window.

Diane turned around and looked at Rachel, who put her hand up and shook her head. The pop of gunfire had quieted, replaced by the bass chugging of a helicopter as it landed near them. They hunched down to protect themselves from the whirling dust. When the blades of the helicopter settled down to a slow grinding revolution, they helped raise Joshua on to a stretcher and get him aboard and ran a few yards away to watch. They put their hands over their faces to protect them from the gritty dust as the helicopter lifted upwards.

Diane put her arm around Rachel. "You were fearless. My god, you saved us all."

Rachel pulled away and hit Diane on the triceps. With an impish grin and a bit of an air of superiority, she said "They taught us to go toward the ambush, not away from it."

Diane grabbed Rachel's hand and held it tight. "They didn't teach us to do it alone."

Rachel smiled and said in a very serious tone, "I wasn't alone, was I?"

Chapter 6

Two months later, Rachel and Diane walked smartly out to the ceremonial mall inside the Pentagon. A multi-service color guard carried the flag of the United States behind them, the Army flag with 183 battle streamers, the two Afghanistan streamers topmost. Then came the guidon of the 272nd Military Police. As they waited, Rachel turned to admire Diane's dress blue officer's uniform with its MP green and yellow piping on her service cap.

They stiffened to attention when Army Secretary Abbott came out of a door, followed by a coterie of high-ranking officers. Then came Senator Hillsdale of Idaho and Senator Manchester of Washington. Photographers from the Idaho Statesman and the Seattle Times were off to the side.

While this large group filed in, Diane, puzzled, looked quickly at Rachel, who smiled discreetly back, then returned to stiff attention.

When all the dignitaries had settled in place, and the photographers were ready off to the side, Senator Manchester nodded to the group behind Rachel and Diane. A soldier came forward. Rachel felt a thrill in her heart when Joshua stepped up to her right.

The Provost Marshal, Brigadier General Eileen Brannon, read the citation for their bravery, as the Secretary pinned the red, white and blue Silver Star medal on Rachel and the red and blue Bronze Star medal on Diane. After the Secretary offered his congratulations, Senator Hillsdale congratulated them and posed with each of them for the photographers. Then Senator Manchester came forward and pinned the Purple Heart on Joshua's chest.

The Provost Marshall stepped forward and pinned the silver Combat Action Badge on all three of them. More congratulations and more photos followed. Finally, they all posed for a group photo, and the generals and politicians departed into the Pentagon. Then the photographers took photos of the three of them.

Diane turned to Rachel and Joshua. "What was the little smile about, Rachel? You didn't seem as surprised as I was at the size of the ceremony."

Rachel laughed and nodded. "I admit I was in on it."

Diane frowned. "In on it?"

"When I knew this was happening, I called up Senator Hillsdale's office. They thought it was a great idea, to be here. Another helpful photo op for the Senator. And they agreed to get Joshua and the Washington state senator involved."

Joshua shook his head. "So that's how it works. They said in the hospital I was going to get my badges out here. It didn't make any sense to me, but I follow orders." He turned to Rachel and took a key chain out of his pocket. A bullet dangled from it. He gave it to Rachel and said, "Here's a souvenir out of my bone. You know, I cannot thank you enough for what you did for me back there."

She looked at the bullet, turned it over in her hand, then gripped it tight and laughed. "It's pretty beat up," she said, looking at Joshua, her eyes gleaming.

"Yeah, I know," he said, smiling and winking at her. "It's a lot more beat up than my pelvic bone. But it has great sentimental value for me. You saved my life out there, Rachel. I hope I can do something for you someday."

Her heart beat a little faster. "You know what,

Joshua, maybe you'll be able to." She held out her hand and Joshua took it in his own and squeezed it, then let it go as the three of them walked, back military straight, eyes ahead, out of the Pentagon.

Chapter 7

Rachel stood for a moment on Pike Street, hands on hips. The wind whipped her hair back and forth. She watched her old partner walk away. Diane, the best, the most trusted of friends. Anytime. Anywhere.

Then Rachel turned her back to the wind for a moment and saw her reflection in a glass door inside Pike Place Flowers. Alone. Without Joshua holding her in his arms. She looked up and followed the line of the architecture back to the Pike Place Market corner. The window of Joshua's apartment screamed in blackness out to her. Joshua. She had not seen him since they took him away to the hospital. Since he died.

His face peered back at her from the reflection in the window. It hit her that he was still there, at Harborview. She had to see him. She didn't deserve a medal for running away from the hospital.

Rachel ran to First Street and found her car. She got in, closed the door and started the engine. One last time, she couldn't help herself, looked down the street at his window, waiting for Joshua's face to appear in it, beckoning her to come and be with him.

Rachel closed her eyes and shook the thought away. She put the car in gear to drive out to Harborview, but someone banged on her right rear window. She slammed on the brakes and opened the passenger window halfway.

"Nothing to say. Get the hell out of here!" She yelled, hoping in vain to scare away the hordes, her foot on the gas pedal. Instead of reporters, one ugly face appeared.

Ted Tourville, pointing at her. "You're not going anywhere, McAlister. Stop the car and get out."

An impulse told her to put the car in reverse and step on the gas pedal. But she took a deep breath as she felt the cold gearshift lever. "Leave me alone!"

"Be careful, Rachel. It's a well-known fact that murderers are dangerous and irrational." He took out his handcuffs and walked around her car.

Rachel followed him with her stare. She kept her foot on the pedal while he came around the front of the car. She pressed down on it enough to be ready, still gripped by the dangerous impulse, and felt her heart pounding, her throat dry. Ted stopped in front of the car, put his hands on the hood and loomed over her. Ted in his black leather jacket and blue jeans and All-American muscles. A cameraman came running toward them. She turned the engine off and got out of the car.

Ted Tourville stood more than a full head taller than Rachel. Still, she could slam her fist into his solar plexus, and he would feel muscle spasms he never thought existed. It wasn't for nothing that she worked out at the Y three times a week.

She stood rigid, feet apart, waiting for him to get completely around the car. He came over to her with his handcuffs. Rachel put her arms out to him, wrists together, mocking him, as if she were surrendering.

When he opened the handcuffs, she raised her arms up, lurched forward and pushed him off balance. He fell backwards two steps and stopped himself. "Bitch!"

"Bastard!" The thunder of turning helicopter blades became louder. "You be careful, Ted, they've got you on TV, too. It's a great shot from overhead."

Ted shielded his eyes with his hand and put his head back and looked up. Then he turned his head aside and drew his lips down tight, defeated.

Rachel heard footsteps behind her on the pavement.

The Assistant District Attorney himself came running up. "Ted, come over here. Let's talk for a moment," Alan Berg said in a voice loud enough that it could be heard by everyone on the street. He didn't look happy. Ted put his handcuffs away.

So Berg didn't trust Ted to be left by himself, Rachel thought.

"You wait here, Rachel." Ted pointed at her. She pointed back.

Tourville walked with a reluctant gait. He had an animated conversation with Berg, who shook his head as he made his point. The cameras held steady on them as they argued back and forth.

Rachel got back in her car, pulled the door in with only the slightest click, turned the key, drove past them, going south on First Avenue. Driving with slow, deliberate speed, she opened and shut the door tight. Then she kept going until she reached James, then turned left up to the hospital.

The huge sand-colored brick building loomed over her. She drove around to the south entrance and found a parking spot in front of the King County Medical Examiner's office.

Her reflection in the glass doors showed her striding confidently forward. Joshua lay only a couple of hallways farther in, and she could hold his head and give him one last kiss, no matter how cold. One time to let her tears fall down her cheeks and land on his face.

Rachel pulled hard on the heavy gray door and entered, took the long set of steps down to the basement, found another set of doors and pushed through. The young woman at the desk stood and smiled. She wore a black uniform, but not that of a policewoman. The shoulder patch read King County, but didn't give any information as to what department. Generic. Her hair fell in great dark brown billows over her shoulders.

The small foyer had only some standard waiting

room chairs, two side walls with photos of Mt. Rainier, and a dark wood-panel back wall with a single unmarked door on it. Completely plain and innocuous. You wouldn't know it led to the place where human beings ended their lives.

"Hello, may I help you?"

"Yes, I'm here to view the body of my fiancé."

"I see." The woman sat to her computer, pressed several keys, then looked up at Rachel and smiled. "Could you give me his name, please?"

"Joshua Todaro."

"And your name, please."

"Rachel McAlister."

The woman stared at the screen, her face in a pale light. She looked like she concentrated on trying to figure something out. She turned to Rachel but waited a moment before she spoke.

"I'm sorry, your name isn't on here." She said it in a quiet voice.

"Excuse me?" Rachel straightened up and put her head forward.

"Your name. It isn't on the list."

"What list?" Rachel had been here many times as a detective, and had never heard of a list. She took a step closer to the desk and looked down at the woman.

"The family has requested that the body be kept private," the woman said, still in her quiet voice.

"The family? This is the coroner's office."

"I'm sorry, I have to go by what it says."

"You listen to me—" Rachel looked for a name badge, but the woman's uniform didn't have one. "I'm his fiancé and I'm going to see him. I will be right back and I will be going in there."

The young woman sat back in her chair and folded her arms across her chest and waited, looking around for someone to come to her rescue. She sucked in her cheeks and buried her face in the computer screen, the blue glow making her look alien.

Rachel turned and went back out the doors and up the steps. She walked with determination to the corner and turned down to the entrance to the West Clinic of Harborview Hospital. Once inside, she put her gold and silver badge on her belt. Even if she wasn't officially authorized to show one, hospital staff weren't going to question her about it.

In the ambulatory surgery waiting room, only a few people reading magazines. They were quietly absorbed. Rachel walked past them, smiled at the receptionist, and went into the cafeteria. She kept going, turned to the doors marked "Hospital Private" and waited. Finally, a man in a white lab coat came through, and she held the doors open and stepped into the hospital corridor.

At the end, the arrow to the left pointed to the operating theater. To the right, the King County Medical Examiner's office. She had been here before. Stupid not to have come this way in the first place.

Rachel hurried down the hallway to the right and put her hand on the cold steel door. She waited two seconds, took a deep breath, then pushed it open two inches, waited another second, then pushed it all the way open. Another small hallway, with doors on either side, but no one visible.

She knew the last door on the right opened on an anteroom to the morgue. And that there would be more than one person in there working on reports. She determined to go on, whatever happened.

Rachel walked to the last door, opened it, took a step inside the room and stopped, her hand still on the door. Her nostrils were filled with the smell of antiseptic cleaning products. Two familiar faces looked at her.

Jenny Kress showed a blank face, then looked quickly down at her shoes, looked back up and smiled.

Peter Crowley scowled. He sat back in his chair and folded his hands over his chest. "Rachel," he said. He waited a moment, gave an exaggerated nod, and spoke in the somber tone of an announcement. "You are not supposed to be here. You know that."

"Hello, Peter." Rachel looked over at the woman. "Hello, Jenny."

Jenny forced a continuation of her smile.

"So, what do you want?" Peter asked, hands in the air, palms out. His face said assistance, his voice disdain.

"I'm here to see the body of my fiancé."

Shaking his head back and forth, Peter stood. He measured barely up to Rachel's height, a huge stocky man. "Fiancé." He frowned. "I don't know who you mean, but you can't go in there."

"Joshua Todaro. He's my fiancé."

He nodded and put his hand on his desk and moved a paper around. "I see. I'm sorry about that. I truly am. We weren't informed of anything similar to what you're saying. But it doesn't matter whether we were or not. You can't go in there, Rachel."

Jennifer swiveled away from her desk and stopped the chair, staring at the two of them.

"Peter, I'm going in there," Rachel said. She wished she could run into the ambush, but not here in the hospital.

Peter came over to her. "No, you're not. They are in the middle of the autopsy and no one goes in there."

Rachel felt a sting in her heart. She moved to his side, but he blocked her.

"Do you want me to call security, Rachel? You know they are not far away. I suggest you go out the way you came, or if you prefer, I'll have them escort you out the front. And anyway, if he is your fiancé, you don't want to see him the way he looks now. You should know that, too."

Rachel let her shoulders fall and sighed. She knew he had defeated her. She looked over at Jenny in a vain hope of support, but Jenny's face showed the clear embarrassment of Rachel's presence. After nodding silently, Rachel went out to the corridor, through the cafeteria and to her car on Ninth Street.

Ted Tourville leaned on the fender of his car, smirking, smiling, satisfied with himself. Feeling clever. He jumped up. "This is it, Rachel." He cocked his head and nodded at the same time, a demeaning gesture. "No more games. Get in and come downtown with me."

"No way, Ted. No way in hell."

He stood and moved toward her. Rachel moved several steps away, got out her cell phone and called the District Attorney's office.

Rachel held up her hand to Tourville, waited for the receptionist's voice, and said, "I need to speak to Alan Berg."

Tourville put his hands on his hips and looked to the sky in melodramatic exasperation, then threw his hands up and tried to appear amused by Rachel's attempts to avoid him.

The voice on the phone responded. "He's not here right now, may I ask who's calling?"

"Rachel McAlister. He will speak to me. Transfer the call to his cell phone." Rachel walked a few more steps away from Ted, who now leaned against her car with his hands in his pockets, looking up and down the street.

"This is Andrew Berg," came the answer in an irritated voice.

"Mr. Berg. This is Rachel McAlister. Detective Tourville is trying to get me into his car and I'm not going. I'll come to the West Precinct, but I'll come in my own car. I'm going to hand him the phone, and I want you to tell him that."

Berg waited a moment, then said yes.

Rachel gave the phone to Tourville, who listened for several seconds, then closed the phone and gave it back to her. "Shit," he said, looking down, then went back to his car.

Rachel got in her car and started the engine to go up Ninth to Virginia and her interview with Tourville. But she turned the key off as she watched Tourville drive away.

Tourville had been biding his time, waiting in the sewers for his chance, in the year since she had been exonerated in the killing of Councilman Gil Hamilton.

Chapter 8

Rachel felt a cold breeze whip by her face. She found herself against the fender of her car, absorbed in memories of that night in Broadmoor. When she looked up, Ted Tourville had gone out of sight.

Rachel drove down Ninth and pulled up to the curb a few yards before Virginia Street, then parked and walked the block down to Eighth. The familiar black and whites lined up in front of the West Precinct.

Two men in blue standing outside looked at her as she walked up. Yeah, they knew she would show up and had been told to keep to themselves. They turned the other way when she walked by and engaged in low conversation with each other.

But when she walked in the door everybody stared at her. Not one of them said hello or waved, some of them turned their backs, and one of them showed her a piece of paper he held so that only his middle finger showed.

After the death of Gil Hamilton, she had been transferred temporarily to West Precinct. The last time she had been in the station, she'd been walking out at the end of her career in the Seattle Police Department. She got the same kind of looks and attitude from them then. The same shaking heads, looks of disgust and quiet disguised laughter. The same identical finger.

Danny Rogers, still in his newly starched shirt, the kind he wore every morning, that always became a sweaty mess at the end of the day, saw her and looked down at his desk and fidgeted in his chair when he saw her. Anything to avoid a conversation. How many times had they met, even worked together? He knew her, he knew that she dedicated herself to her job. To the protection provided by the Seattle Police Department.

They pretended to ignore her as they heard the sound of her footsteps. But they gave each other knowing looks.

Jack Kurtz, she had actually come to his rescue a couple of times when calls to investigate gunshots related to sour drug deals threatened to end his life. He turned away, too, opened a cabinet drawer and fished around in there for nothing, deliberately making shuffling noises as he flipped folders while he looked at the wall. Then she looked at Danny. She could only see half his face, but enough of it to see that he had turned away in embarrassment. Or shame.

The fan in the corner rumbled away. It, too, ignored her.

Ted Tourville, wearing a clean white shirt, newly shaven, came out of an office and swaggered on down to where Rachel stood. He looked around right and left past every desk and cubicle, making sure that no one missed a chance to observe his triumphal moment. As if they all thought Dirty Harry had come back. "Come on in, Rachel. Let's go on down to the interview room. You must know where it is."

Nothing had changed. The same old smell of male sweat and disinfectant when you walked in. The room shouted sterility, windowless, except for the door, one table and two chairs. One bare light bulb at the center of the ceiling gave out a sterile glare. A chilling feel. The stuffy air dried her face, despite the cold noisy draft coming from the vent in the corner of the dirty ceiling. Rachel couldn't count the number of suspects she'd grilled in a room like this.

Ted made a grand gesture toward one of the chairs, rocking back and forth on his heels. The look on his face.

One shot and he killed Joshua, and then he thought he could frame Rachel for it.

She understood why Ted would want to destroy her. She didn't understand why he would want to kill Joshua. She had thought if she were alone with Ted in a room, it would become clear to her, but it didn't happen.

More revenge? Why hadn't he killed her instead? No. He couldn't have done that. He would not have been in the spotlight. He didn't want revenge alone. He wanted publicity. He wanted public revenge. He knew how to frame someone. Maybe the SPD had exonerated her before, but this time a jury would not. He would make sure.

She sat and put her hands on the table. She looked straight at the man who had killed her fiancé, and she could do nothing about it.

"Good morning, Rachel, thank you for coming in. It saved us the time of going after you. There is nowhere you could have gone, you know. We would have caught up with you. All your medals won't save you now."

He wandered around with his hands in his pockets. She understood what he wanted to do. Provoke her. His plan had a second part, to get her into a position where she would lose her cool and bring destruction down on her own head. He didn't know about her self-control.

"I have a mess to clean up back at my office," she said. "Let's go through the motions as efficiently as we can, so I can get back to something more important. At least I have a medal, and I earned it. All you have, Ted, is no career."

Another smile, a face like a fake puzzle. So cocky and sure of himself. She half expected him to tell her to go ahead and make his day.

The smile left his face. "Let's assess the situation, Rachel. We have a 911 call with someone saying they heard a gunshot. We had a potential victim in the hospital, and now that victim is down in the basement in a drawer with a police lock on it."

He paused for effect. "Said victim is your boyfriend. As if you thought we didn't know that." He leaned on the table on his knuckles like a gorilla. He stared at her for thirty seconds. She kept her head up and stared right back at him. Unblinking.

He spoke louder. "We have a window broken in your office and the break is in the direction of the victim's body when it was found." He walked around with his chest sticking out. He went back to the wall and leaned against it, looking at her as if he were so intimidating that she would fold and try to cop a plea right then and there. "We're getting started, Rachel, and we're going all the way to the finish. Sooner or later. The evidence is piling up. It's going to be overwhelming."

She gave him nothing. He didn't have the power he thought he did.

"Rachel, you can't play dumb now."

She shook her head in disgust.

"We need to talk about why you did it."

She looked at his eyes and could see they were full of nothing but questions. And she had the control to not give him any answers.

"I can help you, Rachel. It will be much better for you to accept it. I'm the one who can do the most for you. We have our little history, you and I, so I'm the one you can lean on."

She nodded her head, crossed her arms in front of her chest, put one leg over another. She wondered about his interpretation of the move. But he took care here, with everyone around. He put his hand under his chin and nodded as if he'd won, that he had cornered her and he could make her spill everything. He smiled once again.

"Don't get defensive, Rachel. Listen, denying it is not an option. You weren't on the moon, you know." His face reddened. "Come on, Rachel. You know the game.

You've done this a thousand times. You're not some whore," he said, emphasizing the word, "we dragged off Market Street last night who doesn't know what the Shinola is."

She glared at him, then went around the table, stood on her toes and put herself an inch from his face.

"You know what, Ted? If you want to charge me with a crime you go right ahead."

"When I charge you with a crime, Ms. McAlister, ex-SPD McAlister, you will stay charged until you rot in hell." He said this in a soft voice, trying to make her feel as if he knew everything, that no one could find a flaw in his plan.

"Well, until you have charged me with a crime, Mr. Tourville, you're wasting your time. I think you should go back down to Market Street where they know you."

She guessed rotting in hell meant he had gone as far as he could go. He didn't have the brains to go any further. "Ted, why don't you play good cop, bad cop the way you usually do as dumb and dumber." She stood, went to the wall, leaned against it, put her hands in her pocket, and waited.

From a detective's point of view, he had nothing concrete to tie her to Joshua's death. Except the anguish in her gut when she thought of Joshua lying there on the floor or standing in his window when the bullet hit the back of his head. In fact, Ted would not know anything about Joshua's death until he received the medical examiner's report and who knows how long that would take. Sometimes weeks. And it wasn't going to have anything to do with her.

He might believe in his own mind that he had framed her red-handed, except she didn't have any blood on her hands. And she didn't have her gun. He did.

The bastard didn't ask Rachel her location when the killer fired the shot. It didn't matter to him whether she had an alibi or not. He didn't ask her anything about her office. For all he knew she worked across town somewhere when the bullet killed Joshua. But then he didn't need to know exactly, because he had her gun.

He didn't need to know the truth about her. Since he knew she had not killed Joshua, and he knew she would not give in, he didn't really have a plan on how to deal with her. He brought her in because it looked good.

"Ted, since you obviously have nothing better to do, and I'm getting ready to go, why don't you do the gunshot residue swab so I can leave?"

He gave her a nasty look. He looked like the complete fool.

"Well, you haven't forgotten everything, Rachel. Stay put."

He went out the door for a few minutes and came back with another guy. "This is ex-officer Rachel McAlister. Would you do me the favor of wiping her hands for residue?"

The young man smiled, but his smile betrayed his insecurity. Rachel didn't know him, but he must have heard everything they had to say today, including all the history. He came over, she held out her hands, he took his swabs, and then he got out of the room as fast as he could.

"Ted, it's way too late, you idiot. If they find any gunshot residue on my hands, it came off you or maybe this room, or maybe somebody put it on the swab to start with. Keep that in mind. I know how it works."

"Rachel, let's get one thing clear. Swab or no swab, you know what it's going to look like. You had a motive to kill your boyfriend, and we are going to find out what the motive is. Cheating on you? That it?"

Joshua. Cheating on her. She put herself as close as she could get to Tourville. She put her finger on his chest. He took his hands out of his pockets and shifted his feet. But he wasn't sure exactly what she wanted to do. She waited half a minute, staring at him.

"Hey, Ted, what do you have?"

He said nothing. Now she had her turn.

"Has forensics finished their work? Or do you even have to wait for that?"

Still no answer.

"Is there a medical examiner's report? Or do you need that?"

More silence.

"Get me some water, Detective."

"Sure. We can accommodate that." He nodded and went out the door. A minute later he came back with a paper cup of water and gave it to her.

Rachel took a sip, looking at him. Then she spoke. "There's no weapon, is there? Except the one you stole."

"There's no crime lab report, is there, Theodore? And you don't need one."

More nothing. She hit him in the chest with her finger. "You did this. You killed Joshua to get at me." She put her feet wide apart.

He moved out of the way. "You're crazy, Rachel."

"Am I, Ted? You're the one with the motive. You are the one who has always wanted to get me. You know what? I'm through with this. And you." She threw the rest of the water into his face and walked out toward the exit door.

Tourville clenched his fist and grimaced, but he did not move.

Before she went out the door of the building, she turned and looked back at the men in the room. "You guys are a bunch of bastards, you know that? You sit there all smug and satisfied and think you know what you're doing, but you don't. Ted Tourville is a killer, he's killed my fiancé, and now he's trying to frame me for it. But he won't get away with it. You should all watch your backs." She stopped for a moment for effect. Then she looked at Danny, who did a little startled jig. "You're starting to sweat already."

Not one of them laughed. They didn't turn around and pretend to be busy. They sat or stood and listened until she finished. Rachel opened the door and started to walk out, then stopped and turned back to look at them again. They all remained silent. She came back in and went to Danny's desk. He slid his chair back when she stood over him.

"Fuck you, Danny. And fuck your Rolodex." She looked around the room, raised her arm as if she were going to knock it off the desk, but instead gave them all a good view of her middle finger and walked out.

Chapter 9

Rachel got in her car and turned the key. Her phone rang. "Yeah. What?"

Diane's voice. "Rachel, how are you doing? Where are you? I thought I would hear from you by now."

"I'm on my way back to Pike Place. I had a short talk with Tourville."

"Short talk. What does that mean?"

"He swabbed for residue at the precinct. Made him feel good."

"You think so? A bit late wasn't it?"

"Yeah, but he didn't have much choice."

"You could have refused, Rachel. He had no right."

"I know, but there's nothing to find. And it makes him look stupid doing it."

"You let him do it. You let him treat you like a criminal." The hard accusation in Diane's voice stung.

"Not at all. If I'd said no, he would have made a lot of noise about it. As it is, he has wasted time. It's no good, Diane. It was long after the gun was fired. Ted Tourville was a fool."

"I hope so. Why are you going back to Pike Place?"

"I tried to see Joshua's body at the coroner's office. They wouldn't let me, said they were doing the autopsy. But, Diane, I need to go back to see his window. I need to remember that. Today. Now. Listen, I'll call you later."

Rachel hung up without waiting for good-bye. She turned the cell phone off, started the car again and headed back to Pike Place. When she arrived, she found the normal commercial activity. One lone reporter stood on the corner of Pike Place and Pike Street.

When he saw Rachel he extended his microphone and motioned the cameraman to follow him. "Ms. McAlister, how do you feel about today's events?"

She looked at him, then his camera, then back to him. "What's your name?"

"Evan Figueroa."

"Mr. Figueroa, a wonderful person was killed today. Seattle lost one of its most promising architects. The Seattle Police Department is hunting down the killer and will soon have him in custody."

"They were searching your office, weren't they? Wasn't Detective Tourville in there? Weren't you and he implicated in the killing of Councilman Hamilton?"

She cocked her head and smiled a long time. "Slow down, Mr. Figueroa, that's a lot of questions. Let me repeat what I said. They will find out who did this. It has nothing to do with Detective Tourville or me." Rachel wondered if the camera would betray her.

"Weren't you taken away in a police car?"

"No. I went downtown to clear up some facts about the victim. Evidence about Joshua Todaro."

She felt that now-familiar agony across her abdomen and wanted to leave. But she continued. "There was a shot from my hallway and I needed to help them with that. You can't very well do everything right here on the sidewalk."

"But crime scene investigators, they were in your office."

"Of course. They were in front of the flower market, too. That's their job. Let's let them do it."

"Are you going to get a lawyer, Ms. McAlister?"

"You know what, Mr....what's your first name again?"

"Evan."

"Maybe you should get one, Evan."

"Me?"

"Yes, of course, you're here at a crime scene. You know how perpetrators often come back to take a look."

With that, he turned around and made his good-byes to the TV world.

Rachel stood silent for several seconds, looking down at the red brick, steadying herself. Then she raised her head and looked up at Joshua's window, now closed. A sudden rain squall pelted her face and cold drops went down her collar. She didn't care.

She forced his image to appear in the window, pale, looking out across the street to her office. He disappeared when she tried to focus on him. She turned away. In her car she sat for a moment, feeling the cold loneliness, then started off, headed toward Volunteer Park and home.

Beautiful big Seattle Box homes, those giant square cubes facing the park, surrounded Rachel's home. She had a smaller home in the center of the block just opposite the Water Tower. The elegant filigree work on the porch, everything off-white, showed off her hard work. She had put just as much work into the interior. She had removed layers of paint and sanded, cleaned, and oiled woodwork and floors back to the original.

First she called the landlord for her Pike Place office and told him what had happened. He said he already knew.

She once did a little industrial espionage for him that saved him a bundle on some construction. He knew for sure they were overbilling him, but he couldn't prove it.

Rachel put in a few hours of discreet work with a telescope, her parabolic mike and her camera and she gave him enough information. He took it to the owner of the construction company. As it turned out, he did the owner a favor by keeping him out of jail and got some good work done on one of his properties at better than wholesale.

Her voice choked as she told him that someone had killed her fiancé. He said he felt sorry, his voice warm and sincere. He promised her he would get the windows fixed as soon as they let him back in there. He would call her when they completed the job so she wouldn't have to think about it. He asked her if she held up okay, and she responded with the control she had managed all morning.

The conversation reminded Rachel that she still didn't really know for absolute sure the location of her gun. With all that happened, she hadn't had a chance to look thoroughly around her office. Tourville had already done that for her. But now she took a good hour to search her house. Drawers, closets, cupboards, shelves, behind furniture, shed. Nothing.

She didn't remember the last time she put her gun in the drawer where she kept it along with the Hennessy cognac. The cognac. At least it did some good. If someone stood in front of her desk making threatening gestures, she had planned to pull out the bottle and put it on top of the desk and announce the label with pride and a smile, offer a drink, reach back into the drawer and pull out one glass with her left hand. And then with her right shoot them through the desk.

She didn't keep the gun lying around. Never at her house. But she felt stuck, just trying to think of any possibility at all, maybe something she had forgotten.

She ended up in the kitchen. The back porch, neat, the way she always kept it, everything in order, held no secrets. Jackets and boots and a few garden odds and ends. It could hardly have been back there, but she didn't have many more places to look. Finally, to be complete, she checked downstairs. She opened the door to the basement apartment.

"Sonofabitch. Sonofabitch." The sharp, squeaky voice of Antoinette, Irene's bird, came loud and clear up the stairwell. Always followed by the evil laugh. "Haa. Haa."

"Irene, are you down there?"

No reply from anybody. She closed the door.

Irene kept house for Rachel and lived in the basement. The previous owners had created a small apartment out of it, enough for one person. Irene, a widow, had transplanted herself from Britain. Once upon a time, she had been a member of the staff in the manor. Now, she stayed home most of the time, which made Rachel feel good that somebody could answer the door.

Irene cleaned the house every other day. Rachel found that acceptable. Today the house looked in good order. If Irene had found the gun, she would have come running the moment she heard Rachel come in and given a lecture on public safety.

Rachel took a glass of sauvignon blanc out to the front porch to take in the sunset as it shined a subdued yellow on the dark brick Water Tower, a view she had shared many times with Joshua. She automatically moved her arm out to touch him, and felt the shock of cold, hard wood.

The light on the Water Tower made her feel even more intensely alone. She turned around and walked inside to her bedroom, put her wine on the dresser, lay down on the bed, stared at the ornate plaster detail on the ceiling, and remembered the hours she had put into restoring it.

Joshua had been very impressed with it. He said she had designed the room to make love in. Once he even mentioned she should change her career and they could set up their own architectural business. He'd do the outside and she'd do the interior decorating. As soon as she remembered that, she felt the pang of knowing it would never happen.

Rachel slowly drifted off with a feeling of him sleeping next to her. She remembered how he sometimes wandered around the house and put his hands on the dark Craftsman molding. He loved to light the old gas lamps still working in the front parlor, and took a bath, long and slow, in the copper bathtub. Said it made him feel like a lonesome cowboy after a hard day's ride on the range.

He had once wanted to put candles all around the tub, saying how romantic it would be. But he knew Rachel worried the house would burn down. Once he said he wished she were a firefighter. He could have the tub, the candles and her, like a Mississippi river boat suite.

The honk of a car interrupted the quiet of the neighborhood and knocked Rachel out of her reverie. She looked around the room. The teak dresser, the white chair, the closet. She went to the closet and moved the clothes back and forth. Nothing hanging there belonged to Joshua.

In the guest room, she looked in the closet for something of his, on the dresser, but they were empty.

In the bathroom, she opened the medicine cabinet and moved aspirin and cosmetics around, but could not find anything of his. He had shaved here. He had brushed his teeth. Why nothing? Did he know it would never be permanent?

A premonition? Coming back to the bed, she saw their photograph on the nightstand, a close-up on the ferry with the lights of downtown Seattle behind them. Joshua, frozen forever, never getting older, always the same. Like the concrete buildings in the background of the picture.

She imagined herself getting old and gray and tired in the picture while he kept the same handsome, energetic eyes and face. Like the ferry sailing away from the city, her life now moved away from him.

Now she started searching back over their conversations, trying to remember everything he said, all the nuances. Trying to find the times he gave her a hint. It took too long, but they did eventually talk direct and straight to each other, even if it only happened on the last night of his life.

She tried as hard as she could, but she couldn't remember that he said anything that she should have taken as a hint. Something that she should have responded to, that would have let him know she wanted him to ask her to marry him. That would have let him know she needed him. Would have, should have—

She had failed to understand him. He wanted to ask in as dramatic a way as possible, so happy when he finally got the chance. He let her know with great emotion how he felt. He had been waiting a long time. She remembered his eyes when she said yes and he kissed her. For the first time as betrothed, and the last time forever.

Now, for him, everything she remembered would always be about the last time.

She went back to the living room, turned on the gas lamps and rested in the useless romantic glow.

With a long sigh, she realized she should not be resting. She should be getting a good lawyer to keep these people out of her face, so she could concentrate on what's important—going after Joshua's killer.

Chapter 10

Roger Chadwick had risen to become one of the senior partners at Denny, Boren, Terry, Low & Bell. He lived not too far from Rachel, in one of the most dramatic of the big Seattle Box houses, white with pale blue and dark grey accents. Inside the antiques were befitting a man of Roger's standing in the community.

His house had once been a consulate, and later, a famous grunge band had tried to destroy it. Roger, like Rachel, had turned a fixer-upper into a gem. Hers looked nice, but Roger's stunned people who came to see it. Photographers sought out his house, and it appeared in travel magazines.

Rachel and Joshua had been to two parties at the house, given by Roger and his much younger roommate, Ulrich, who had a sculpture gallery on the east edge of Pioneer Square. There had been parties at the gallery, too, but Rachel hadn't been invited to those.

She had worked on several cases with Roger, and he had been very complimentary about her work, so she didn't hesitate to call his home.

Ulrich replied to her greeting. "I'm sorry, Rachel, but Roger is tied up at the moment." He let out a little laugh. "Oh, I don't mean that the way it sounds. You know, he would ask me to find out what the nature of your call is."

"I'd like an appointment with him. Tomorrow morning if possible."

"All right, let me go talk to him." Another twenty seconds and he came back on. "Um, well, Rachel, he said, uh, that you would have to call his secretary in the morning and see where she could fit you in."

"I see, yes, thank you, I appreciate that. Would you ask one more thing?"

"Yes, of course. If I can help. What is it?"

"Ask Roger if he will tell his secretary that he will see me. Will you do that? I'll wait."

Another second of silence. "I'll be right back." Ulrich came back on the phone and said, "Roger said he would be happy to do that Rachel, as long as you did not expect too much time."

"Oh no, it won't take time." Only a few minutes of his time and maybe a couple of phone calls, and Ted Tourville would stop and think a bit before he started harassing Rachel.

The next morning, Rachel stepped out of the elevator on the 23rd floor and walked into the plush foyer of Roger's firm. The beautiful young woman with a beige St. John knit suit and pearls too expensive for her position at the receptionist's desk told her that Roger awaited her to the right at the end of the hall, in his corner office.

She reached out to her console and pressed a button, then looked up at Rachel with a gracious smile. "Eleanor will escort you."

The older woman, dressed in a formal black suit, also with pearls, asked Rachel to follow her, then opened the door and announced her arrival.

Roger's office had the standard picture postcard view of Puget Sound and the Olympic Mountains in the distance. A couple of bright red and orange Chihuly seaform loops dazzled from the corner. He came around from his huge Italian glass desk to greet her.

"Rachel, how nice to see you. Ulrich told me you wanted to discuss something with me. I'm sorry he didn't invite you over last night. It would have been simpler for all of us. I didn't want you to have to come all the way downtown to see me. Have you been working more on your house?"

"That's not why I came to see you, Roger."

He motioned her to sit. "I was very sorry to hear about Joshua Todaro," he said, putting his hand on his knee. He leaned forward and looked into her eyes. "I believe I met him at one of our Christmas parties. I'm quite sure of it."

She stared back into his eyes, "Oh yes, that's right, last year. I'd forgotten about that." Rachel remembered Joshua, wine in hand, working the room, framed by yellow drapes and the brightly lit Christmas tree. She shifted in her chair. "How did you hear about his death?" When she spoke the word, torment gripped her body.

"It was Ulrich. He mentioned it when I came home last night. He was the one who remembered Joshua, actually. He has a real eye for style. Went on quite a bit about him, the architecture. Ulrich was quite impressed with some of Todaro's Craftsman renovations."

Roger leaned back, placed one leg on the other and adjusted his cuff links. "Ulrich always has three televisions going at the same time. One turned to some artsy channel. He doesn't want to miss anything. Tapes it 24/7." He looked down and smoothed his tie. "But I digress. Tell me, what can I do for you, Rachel? We'll have to make it quick. I did find a bit of open time, but not much." He checked his watch.

"Thank you for fitting me in."

"Billable hours, you know. But go on. My secretary said you were seeking representation. Is that true?"

"Yes, I am. Not from the firm, you."

He lowered his leg and settled back in his chair, making a steeple with his fingers. "You know, as the managing partner here at Denny, Boren, I take on only certain types of work of substantial consequence for the firm. And a small amount of pro bono cases. Work that

70

is not through the firm is out of the question. You have done some work for the firm, so you should be aware of that." He smiled and took a long breath. "It's in my contract, Rachel, and beyond my control. I'm sure that's not what you're asking."

"Yes, I was thinking your involvement would be minimal, but very effective." She knew very well he could do anything he wanted to. Especially something like this that wouldn't distract from his lucrative business.

"Involvement? In what, Rachel? Be more specific."

He lost his air of warmth and sincerity. She noticed he had a silver pot of coffee on a side table, with cups by it, but he made no effort to offer her any.

"I think, because of my closeness to the victim, and my experience with Ted Tourville, I should have personal legal representation."

"I see. But as I indicated, I don't take on cases of personal representation, Rachel."

"Okay, how about..."

"I have discussed this with my partners, and quite honestly, we all agree that it would not be in the best interest of the firm to take on a criminal case of this nature."

"But you do take on criminal cases."

"Rachel, we don't represent criminals."

She pushed herself up out of the chair. Suddenly the glare from the window made her shield her eyes. "I am not a criminal, Roger." She started to feel hot.

He stood too, smiled and frowned. "I'm sorry, I didn't mean to imply that you are. In no way at all." He laughed quietly with an insincere smile, and a condescending one. "We don't take on criminal cases unless it's one of our large corporate clients. You know, help them out a little on the side, if a kid has a DUI or something. Helps earn our retainer. Now, if you will excuse me, I'm sure that you can find adequate representation, Rachel, if you absolutely feel you need it.

Which I really doubt. They haven't charged you with anything. I would know about it if they had. You need to cast a wider net, that's all."

He would know about it. So he kept informed. He followed it, Ulrich taped it 24/7, but Roger had no time for her.

"Perhaps you could give me a recommendation, Ro..."

"Rachel, with your background you must be familiar with good criminal attorneys in Seattle."

She nodded, feeling caught. "Of course, but your recommendation means something to me, Roger."

He put his hand on her upper arm and held out his hand. "You're thinking corporate, and you should be thinking one of the smaller firms. Someone who can give you more of the attention you think you need. Make the effort and you will find someone appropriate." He turned his wrist and touched his watch. "Now, please excuse me, Rachel. And the best of luck to you."

He gently prodded her in the direction of his door. She didn't move. A prickly sensation moved up and down her spine. He smiled at her like he would smile at a small child.

She wanted to swing her arm out and hit him hard in the gut.

His assistant opened the door for Rachel. Roger saw the look in her eyes. "I know you're upset Rachel. This is a sign that you really need help. I suggest you get it. And soon." He gestured silently to the door as the woman opened it wider and stepped aside

"Ms. McAlister is leaving. Would you please have my next appointment come in." The two of them looked at each other as if it were all prearranged.

Rachel turned around and went out the door, past the young woman, who jumped out of the way, and kept on going all the way to the elevator and down to the ground floor and out to Fourth Avenue.

She leaned against the building in the shade and watched traffic going by, wondering about her next move. Roger had gotten the better of her. How could she have misread him? Images came to her of the last Christmas party at his house. Joshua seemed to get along really well with Ulrich. Both were interested in art. That ought to have made a difference to Roger. And the discussions she had had with him about redwood and ceilings? And the work she had done for him? Didn't that all count? Obviously not. She felt foolish thinking about it.

Now, she thought, why hadn't she made the effort to do more with Joshua? One more thing, if she had done it differently, they would have been at a different place, and a different time and...but she had enough experience to know that a determined killer can always find another time and another place. Especially if he's a cop.

Roger had not shown any sympathy, but he said something true. Another attorney would do as fine for this simple task. She called the law offices of Alexander Stewart, and a receptionist put her through to him.

"Rachel, is that you?" He paused. She heard some indecipherable noises in the background. "How are you?" His voice did not have the ring of sincerity.

"I'm fine, Alexander, considering." A city bus spewed oily smoke and rumbled past. She turned away from traffic and cupped her hand over her ear.

"What is it? Wait a sec." Another pause. "What's up?"

Rachel didn't feel like he gave her his full attention. It irritated her following so closely after her experience with Roger. "Yes. I'm sorry for the interruption. Could I have a few minutes with you?"

"I'm sorry. Appointments all afternoon."

"Couldn't you fit me in for something very short?" She wasn't asking for much. After all, she and Alexander did have some history together. The wind blew her hair in her face. She swept it out of the way. The traffic stopped and she turned back toward the street.

"No, no, Rachel, everything's tight. How about this? What do you say we get together, say, oh, I don't know,... um... Oliver's,... in the Mayflower, around six? Can you do that?"

"Yes, I can do that."

"Okay. I'll see you there." He hung up before she could say good-bye.

She called Keith Gockenbach, who answered himself. That seemed odd. But at the moment it didn't take much anymore for something to seem odd.

"Keith, it's Rachel McAlister."

"Rachel, how are you? What's up? I'm sorry I haven't called you in a while, but to tell the truth, nothing's come up lately that needs your many talents." He said it too fast, obviously embarrassed.

"Keith, I'm not calling to get work from you... although I'm glad our relationship came to mind. I'm looking for personal representation."

"Oh." His voice receded.

"Keith, are you there?" The silence grew longer for her.

"Yes, yes of course... Representation. Hmm. What kind of representation? You're not in any kind of trouble are you?"

"No, I'm not. But my fiancé has been murdered, and the police are..."

"Oh, yes, what was his name... give me a moment... Joshua Todaro, wasn't it? All over the news last night. Quite a topic of conversation over the water cooler this morning. I'm awfully sorry about it. Must have been devastating. What's this about you and the police?"

"Ted Tourville. He's out to get me because of his own failure and he's running the investigation. I thought if I had a decent attorney representing me, they would have to watch their step." Rachel stomped her foot down when she heard herself say "out to get me". She knew other people wouldn't necessarily share her sense of menace.

"What's that supposed to mean?" Keith obviously didn't share her sense.

"You know, aggressive. They don't have any other suspect, and Ted Tourville has it in for me, and..." There again, that quick untested assumption that people were on her side. Even though she had a year's experience with it not being so.

Click. She looked down at her phone as if it would tell her something. Keith hung up on her? She let the phone down by her side and exhaled, her mouth in a straight line. A man walking by in a blue suit and red tie turned to look at her. She turned away. Her phone rang.

"Hello? Rachel? Sorry, I don't know what happened. I was in the, you know...well, anyway, and the phone quit on me for no reason. So, where were we?"

"I need representation. I thought you..."

"No, no. Not me. Not now." He wanted to sound defensive, no doubt, but his voice betrayed more than that. It dismissed her.

She let out a sigh. "Why not?" She frowned at the aggressiveness of her own voice, at a time when she needed help.

"You gotta be kidding me, Rachel." A pause. "I'm sorry, didn't mean to be rude, but honestly, I have to do business with the city, and I don't want to mess that up. You understand, don't you?"

"What's there to understand? I'm not asking you to go before the Supreme Court. Keep the police off my back for a while so I can get some work done."

"I guess you didn't hear me, did you?"

She didn't understand the anger in his voice. "Hear you about what?"

"I said, Rachel, I have to do business with the city. I don't want that business to dry up. I can't go around keeping the local police off your back without rubbing them the wrong way..." He went silent again, and then his voice came back whining. "Surely you understand that. I know it's a difficult time for you right now, and I'm sorry about that, but..."

"Your business is not going to dry up because you did a couple hours of work for me." Rachel pointed her finger in the air to punctuate her little lecture, then felt stupid, knowing he couldn't see her. She turned around in a circle while she waited.

"Rachel, listen I'm going to have to go. But, hey, good luck with that." The phone clicked off.

So that's how they were all going to treat her. She looked up and down the street, hitting the phone against her thigh. An old man shuffled by, bent over. Another bus stopped a few feet away and the acrid smell of exhaust filled her nose.

Alexander Stewart would be different, she hoped. Meeting him at the bar meant he would be out of the pressure cooker of the firm. He could be more honest, and they'd figure something out.

Shortly before six, she arrived at Oliver's. Alexander appeared comfortably ensconced at a polished oak table with luxurious leather chairs facing the paned glass windows.

He raised his drink to her. His eyes showed he'd been hard at work relaxing. "Rachel, Rachel, sit down. I'm having a black devil. Do you know it?"

"No." Who gave a damn what drink? Not a good sign.

Alexander continued. "I try to stump the bartender. Wait. Listen. Is it quiet in here? Love it. Anyway, as I was saying, tonight it's the black devil. From the sixties. Rum and vermouth. I always win. Tried to get him to do a blue blazer, but he was just afraid of the fire."

He let out a little self-satisfied laugh as he looked over toward the bar and raised his glass to the bartender, who paid no attention to him. "But enough of

76

that. Please sit down, Rachel. Let's talk. It was great to hear from you."

Rachel sat opposite him, but remained upright facing him. Alexander put his drink on the table, and made a great effort to partly get out of his chair and lean forward and shake her hand. His eyes showed more disdain than Roger had. Rachel fought back the urge to slap him in the face. She sensed he wanted to waste her time.

"Alexander, can we speak openly?"

"We certainly can, my friend. What is it? Is it this nasty mess with that young man being murdered? How sad. And from your office, too, isn't that where the shot came from? Of course, I don't mean to imply anything about you." He waved one arm about while trying to keep the drink steady in his other hand. "Did you know the man? I thought I heard something about that. What a tragedy for the city, for Pike Place. I hope it doesn't hurt their business. How are you making out?"

"That's what I came to see you about. That young man you mention was my fiancé, Alexander. So let me get right to the point."

A waiter came over and Alexander waved him over to Rachel, but she shook her head.

"What, nothing to drink at all?" Alexander said. He squinted up at her as if he were looking into bright sunlight.

"No. Not tonight."

"I guess you're serious, then."

"Serious as can be."

"Serious?" He leaned forward again, exaggerated frown and grimace. "My god, don't tell me they have charged you with the crime? Have they?"

"No, they haven't. But I don't want to deal with them. I have my own work to look after. All I need is someone to run a little interference for me, let them know that they can't be too aggressive."

"Sounds like a good idea. Sure you won't have a drink? Phil can make anything you want, he's the best in town."

"No, nothing to drink." She hoped the frustration in her voice got to him.

"So who've you found to represent you? I bet you want to get my opinion of the guy. Go ahead, shoot."

"Actually, I was hoping that you would represent me. You know, call them and let them know, so they can't go around unhindered. They can make things look incriminating when they really aren't and you can put a stop to that."

"You used to be a cop, didn't you? Well, never mind that. I'm an honest guy, Rachel, you know that. Straight shooter." He looked down and licked his lips, then looked back up at her. "I'll tell you flat out I won't represent you. And to be honest once more, you won't get anybody in this town who's worth his salt, either. Or her salt. I know you feel bad right now. It's tough, what you're going through. But you ought to face reality."

"I know very well what reality is, Alexander." She felt heat on her neck.

"It's quite simple. You killed a councilman, and you didn't have to."

"I was exonerated, and you know it." Rachel could feel the muscles tighten on her forehead, and her lips closed in a straight line.

"Listen to me," Alexander said in a confidential tone. He took another long drink, and held up his empty glass for the waiter. "That has nothing to do with it. Seattle is a small town, really. Downtown, everybody knows everybody. Besides, you killed a councilman."

"Will you stop repeating yourself." Rachel lost patience with him and had to make a conscious effort to control herself.

"Well, the truth bears repeating. You'd better wake up and smell the reality. You need to get yourself somebody from out of town."

She stood, stiffened her back, and looked around the room, then back at him.

"Now, Rachel, you shouldn't be showing off your famous temper. It will only get you in more trouble."

"Thanks for nothing, Alexander." She shook her head.

"That's all right." He slurred his words. "But let me recommend Herb Brooks to you."

"Herb Brooks? Who the hell is he?"

"Oh, he might be quite good, actually. He just finished a stint with AA and I'm sure he could use the work."

"You're a son of a bitch, you know that. A real son of a bitch." She stood and went over next to him and looked down at him with his damn drink in his hand and his eyes looking too moist, and clenched her fist. He pulled himself down into a hunch and looked at her with wild eyes. She straightened, looked at the bartender and raised her voice. "On second thought, how about a vodka martini on the rocks, fast as you can."

The bartender smiled, as if she had finally caved in. Alexander relaxed and sat back in his chair and pointed for her to sit down.

"I'll wait a moment," Rachel said.

The bartender, smiling like he knew Alexander had won the day, brought the martini over. Before he could put it down Rachel took it off the tray and threw it in Alexander's face. It dribbled down his cheeks and chin and onto his tie.

She enjoyed, for the moment, the surprise on his face as he shook off his hands, looked for a place to put his glass down, took his precious handkerchief out of his breast pocket and began in vain to dry himself off. He looked at her with anger in his eyes. "Goddamit, Rachel."

"No, God damn you, Alexander."

Rachel went to her car, and sat for a moment before turning the engine on. She put the key in the ignition, but turned it off when her cell phone rang. Meredith Rawlings.

"Rachel?"

"Yes, Meredith, Hi."

"You remember, me Rachel, you worked on two cases for me?"

"I do, Meredith, yes, of course."

"That's good. I'm calling because I heard of what happened. I think we should talk about it. I wish you would have called me."

At first, Rachel didn't know what to make of that. But then she realized she did have experience with Meredith on criminal cases. They had worked well together. Rachel remembered two situations where she worked for Meredith. One a DMV investigation, the other tracing somebody's whereabouts. Meredith had been very happy with her work.

"You have heard of my situation, Meredith, as you put it?"

"Yes, when I heard of the shooting at Pike Place, and the murder, the first thing I thought was that I should call you."

"I'll be honest with you, I am looking for a lawyer, but I have only seen three. I am only just beginning my search."

"Let me be blunt, Rachel. I want to represent you."

"You, Meredith?"

"Yes. I think I know you, and, in effect, you helped me out. So it makes sense that I return the favor. You really ought to have legal advice, Rachel."

Legal advice. Exactly the right tone, legal advice, not criminal defense.

Meredith continued. "Rachel, let me give you my cell phone number. You can think it over, but call me any time. I mean that. As you well know, the police are unpredictable. Oh, and one last thing."

"Yes?"

"Keith Gockenbach recommended me."

"I see. Well, thank you."

Rachel took the phone number and thanked Meredith. I'll talk to some others in the morning, she thought. But at least she had a back up.

Chapter 11

The next morning Rachel stood in her running shoes in her bedroom, ready for her jog when the doorbell rang. Someone pounded on the front door. Irene's irritated voice told them to wait. "I'm coming."

Through the window of the door, Rachel could see several men. Ted Tourville in a black suit stood above the others, who were wearing dark blue uniforms. Not a total surprise. What had they found out? she wondered. She thanked Irene, who went back downstairs.

Rachel held the doorknob tight and turned it a half turn, then another, putting her toe hard against the wood, expecting them to try and cram their way through. Instead they all stood, quiet, Ted Tourville at the front. He smiled. He always smiled as if people were required to believe him.

None of them moved, as if they were waiting for Rachel to put her hands on top of her head and surrender. She could take them all out with one quick lunge forward. They would all go sprawling down the front porch steps and back out to the street. The thought had a lot of attraction. She held it for a long moment, hoping they could see her eyes moving back and forth between them and the street. Each of them shifted a bit.

"Why are you here?" she said. There were too many of them on her front porch. Ted, already trying to harass her. He had caught her by surprise.

Ted widened his smile. "I have a warrant which

authorizes me to search your house and all your belongings for your gun and your cocaine."

"The hell you will." She could stop Ted and his plan to come in and do whatever he wanted. Cocaine? Only Ted could think that up. Now is when she needed a lawyer. She hadn't thought he would act this fast. But she didn't have a lawyer now.

She braced herself against the wall. She looked at the shadowy figures on the porch. Immediately, Meredith Rawlings came to mind. Rachel saw her purse on the hall table. Her foot jammed against the door, she reached over, picked up the purse, and found the slip of paper with Meredith's number.

"All right, you all wait right here." They backed away a step and she closed the door.

"We're coming in, McAlister. With a warrant." Ted yelled and pounded on the glass panel next to the door.

Rachel put her hand against the glass to prevent him from breaking it. "You're not doing anything without my lawyer present." She hoped Meredith Rawlings would come over on short notice.

"We're coming in."

Before he could move, she locked the door. Then she pulled the curtain back and put her face close up to the glass. "You can stand there on the porch until I've talked to my lawyer." Rachel picked up her phone and called Meredith Rawlings. To her surprise, she heard a live voice answering the call.

"This is Meredith Rawlings."

The strength she felt at that moment surprised Rachel. She held the phone and looked at it, then put it up to her ear. "Hello Ms. Rawlings, this is Rachel McAlister."

"Good morning. I didn't think I would hear from you so soon. I was going to call you later myself. How are you doing?"

"The police are here, Meredith, looking for my gun. I

don't know where it is. They say they are also looking for cocaine, although they are not going to find any unless they plant it. I think this would be a good time to have a lawyer."

"This is quite a surprise." A moment of silence. "But I can be over there in a few minutes. Do not say anything to them until I arrive."

"Of course not. Thank you." Rachel resisted the temptation to tell Meredith that she knew how to handle policemen.

"Have you said anything to them already?"

"No."

"Have you talked to them at all?"

"No, nothing. Only to tell them to wait for my lawyer."

"Good. Be quiet and act unconcerned and wait for me, will you Rachel? And keep them out of the house until I get there."

"I will."

"Oh, and one more thing. What do you mean you don't know where your gun is?" Meredith's voice carried a strong note of reproach.

"I mean exactly that. It was supposed to be in my desk drawer in my office, but it's not there."

"It's a registered gun, right?" Meredith said. "I mean, you know..."

"Of course it is. What did you think..."

"I'm sorry. Just felt I ought to ask. Did you look for it someplace else in your office, maybe in another drawer?"

"Yes I did, I certainly did, but it wasn't there. Not in my office. And then Diane showed up and I went to the hospital to see how Joshua was doing."

"Joshua?"

"Joshua is, was, my boyfriend—my fi—he's been murdered. That's what this is all about." Rachel felt the return of the sting of loss. She clenched her fist.

Meredith responded with evident sympathy in her voice. "I am very sorry to hear that." Meredith emphasized the word *very*. "It must be awful. How are you holding up?"

"I'm holding up well enough, thank you."

"Were you there at the hospital?"

"Yes, but he died on the operating table. I didn't get a chance to see him."

"That's even worse. I am so sorry for you. Is anyone there with you? And Diane, who is she?"

"Diane was my old partner in the police department."

"In the police department? When was that?"

"A year ago."

"That's right," Meredith said, "you told me that when we worked together."

"But that's not important now."

"What was she doing there? Diane I mean? Does that not make her a suspect?"

"Diane? You've got to be kidding. She was on duty. She heard the 911 call and came to Pike Place."

"Okay, we'll go over those names again later. What is this about cocaine?"

"There's no cocaine, either."

"Then why are they looking for it?"

"They say they found some on my boyfriend, which is not possible. They planted whatever they found." Rachel regretted immediately not saying fiancé.

"I am sure you are correct about that. All right, I will be right over. They seem to be on a real fishing expedition. Remember, saying nothing is in your best interest."

"I know how to do that."

"Be polite, Rachel, but don't let them in to search anything until I'm there. And one last thing: first names, okay?"

"All right. Meredith."

Rachel hung up. She went back to the front door and opened it to tell them her lawyer would be right over. She instantly regretted the decision.

Ted shouldered past her and almost knocked her over on to the hurricane lamp on the entryway table. She steadied her feet, turned around, and grabbed the table and lamp to protect them.

"You'll be sorry you didn't wait!" she yelled but nobody paid any attention to her. One uniformed officer ran toward the bedrooms, another back toward the kitchen, and Ted started wandering around the living and dining rooms. Someone stayed on the porch and the final man had disappeared.

A moment later, she heard a high-pitched "Crazy like hell! Haa. Haa." and knew someone had started downstairs to Irene's apartment. A warrant sure as hell would not include Irene's private apartment. Another Tourville screw up. Meredith would be able to pursue that.

Rachel went to Ted and held out her hand. "Let me see your piece of paper."

He handed her a document and she saw a judge's signature. The judge authorized the search following the death of Joshua by gunshot wound and the discovery of cocaine on his body.

"So, I see you've already been planting evidence. You won't find anybody who's ever seen Joshua do anything with drugs and you won't make it stick." Rachel raised her voice and held her head up as she said it so everyone in the whole house could hear her.

Ted turned around and appraised her, his eyebrows melted into his furrowed forehead. He said nothing and continued searching through drawers and shelves. But now he did it with slow and careful movements, as if he believed her threat about paying for damages.

Rachel thought about calling Diane. It would have been good to have her old friend with her. But that wouldn't have done her any good now. She just had to wait for Meredith to arrive.

Ted came back to the kitchen, asked her where she parked her car.

Rachel looked quickly through the warrant, then looked Ted in the eyes with disdain and shook her head. "Nothing in here about my car."

The doorbell rang, and she went to the door and could see Meredith's outline through the glass. First names, to let Ted know there had been some history between attorney and client.

When Rachel opened the door, Meredith smiled at her. She wore a blue tailored pants suit with a pearl necklace and earrings, and carried a large briefcase. Her white blouse was buttoned up to her neck. Large-framed black glasses made her look like a serious lawyer.

"Hello, Rachel, it's good to see you again. Let me tell you again, how sorry I am about your loss." Meredith leaned forward to give Rachel a hug, but Rachel pulled away, looking puzzled.

"Thank you. Please come in, Meredith. Actually, it's good of you to come over so soon." The intense rose fragrance wafted over Rachel. She wondered if the woman herself sensed the strength of her perfume.

"Not at all, Rachel. Where are the police?" Meredith looked around the hallway and into the living room.

"They are somewhere."

"You should not have let them in without me."

"You're right. But I was not careful when I opened the door. I did tell them they had to wait until my lawyer was present. Those were my exact words. They pushed right past me. I expected you to come over right away as you said."

"I understand, Rachel. Let's see what we can do. That's already something to go after them for."

Ted Tourville appeared out of nowhere.

Meredith didn't wait. "How do you do. I am

Meredith Rawlings, Ms. McAlister's attorney." She put her hand out and gave him a cold professional smile. "And you are...?"

"Detective Ted Tourville, Ma'am."

"I see."

She attempted to move farther into the house but Rachael and Ted were both blocking her way. Ted stepped aside and she walked into the living room. "May I see your warrant, Detective?"

"Certainly. I gave it to Rachel. You'll have to ask her."

Meredith turned. "Rachel?"

"It's back on the kitchen table," Rachel said.

"You may go about your business, Detective. Rachel and I will need a moment to talk about this." Meredith walked ahead into the dining room and took a right at the end into the kitchen.

Rachel liked that. Confident, like she knew her way. When they got into the kitchen, Meredith turned suddenly and almost bumped into Rachel. She backed away, smiled apologetically and said, "Rachel, we need to get something straight. Do you want me to stick around here for a while, or do you want me to represent you? Is that why you called?"

"Yes, of course, why else would I have called you?"

"Oh, people do call and then when they see me, forgive me, but they don't always take me seriously. It has happened, believe me. So I know you think you need an attorney right at this moment, and I will do that for a minimal fee for now. That's not what I'm asking you."

"Don't we need a longer discussion about that?."

Meredith touched Rachel lightly on the arm. "Yes, we do. Of course, you're right. But for the moment, keep quiet."

She walked back out into the living room. Rachel stayed in the kitchen. She heard Meredith loud and clear.

"Detective, I think your time is up here. You haven't

found whatever it is you're looking for. Ms. McAlister will find her gun and bring it into..."

She didn't get time to finish the sentence. A loud voice called out from the back yard. "I found it!"

Ted practically ran out to the kitchen and through the back door.

More commotion came from out back, then several footsteps on the wooden stairs. Ted opened the back door and came into the kitchen with a gun in a plastic bag.

"Let me see it." Meredith demanded.

He looked over at Rachel. "Did you think we wouldn't look behind the bushes?" He held it up in triumph.

"It's not mine."

"Sorry, looks like a Walther P99 to me."

"You put it there, you bastard, you...." Rachel put a foot forward and started to reach for the bag. Ted held it high over her head.

Meredith stepped in front of Rachel, turned and put her finger up to her lips. "I see you found something, Detective, but I don't really know who it belongs to, do I? Or how it got there. Or even what it really is. Don't make judgments before you have done your work professionally. Everything you do is public and under scrutiny. Remember that."

"Give me a little time downtown and I'm sure I'll be back with a warrant for her arrest."

"That's great, Detective, it's a real rush to judgment. I am glad you said that because now I know what your prejudice is."

"Come on everyone!" He yelled as loud as he could. In one minute SPD were all out the front door and the house became quiet. The last person out the door turned around. "You really ought to send that bird to etiquette school."

A second later, Irene came up the back stairs.

Martin F. Sorensen

"Rachel, what was that all about?" Then she saw Meredith and looked embarrassed. She ran her hands through her hair and over her clothes.

"Irene, this is Meredith Rawlings. She's agreed to act as my attorney."

"Attorney? Whatever for?"

"The police are looking for evidence."

"Evidence? Here? That's not possible. Whatever they were doing they didn't search my apartment. They didn't like my little bird, but I can't do anything about that. I'm not going to throw her out because of the way she talks."

Meredith held out her hand to Irene.

"I'm happy to meet you. For the record, may I ask what your relationship to Rachel is?"

"Relationship? I beg your pardon, I would not use that word. I am a tenant and house cleaner."

Irene turned toward me. "I should like to say again, Rachel, how sorry I am about Joshua."

Meredith looked at both of them, then spoke to Irene. "Did you know him well?"

"No, not at all. I only met him once and that was by accident. It was so quiet one morning. I thought I would come up and clean, but when I got to the top of the stairs, he was in the kitchen making coffee. We said hello, that was all, a very short conversation. But I did teach him how to make a good cup of tea. He learned to like Prince of Wales, if I remember correctly." Irene, her eyes misted, looked at Rachel. "I'm sorry."

"Thank you very much, Irene," Meredith said. "What was that about the bird?"

"That was my bird, Antoinette. Some people say she's a foul-mouthed parrot. She's an African Gray Parrot with an educated tongue, picked up before I got her. She only mimics things yelled out loud in anger. And none of it was said by me. Not my idea of polite conversation, I dare say, but then she's a good warning system, and that's most important to me, and to Ms.

McAlister as well."

"There's nothing wrong with colorful language," said Meredith, "especially from a bird." She reached out her hand to Irene again. "Thank you very much for your help."

"Oh, I'm here if you should need anything." Irene shook Meredith's hand, then turned back downstairs. Her door closed and the muffled voice of the bird could be heard saying something unintelligible.

Meredith looked around the house. "Well, Rachel, I must say, this is a beautiful house. Look at all that natural woodwork. It must have cost quite a bit."

"I hope you're not thinking of an extravagant fee. I did all of this myself."

"Yourself? All of it?"

"Yes. All of it. When I bought it, there was paint over everything, nothing on the walls, dirty, ugly soot on the ceiling. It took me quite a few years, but I made it into something."

Meredith rubbed her hand on the dark, rich wood, then turned back. "Yes, it is very impressive. But now, I think we had better talk."

Chapter 12

"You're right about that," Rachel said, "we have a lot to discuss."

Meredith said, "First, let's see who has a window on your back yard."

Rachel walked back to the kitchen and poured two cups of coffee from a carafe, grateful for Irene's thoughtfulness. Meredith stepped out on the small lawn, looking around, touching gardenia and rhododendron leaves.

Rachel, viewing Meredith from the back, thought that Meredith, in her slim blue pants suit and dark brown hair, short and cut in a perfect straight line, looked more like a model than a defense lawyer.

Meredith pointed to a single large white rhododendron in the corner. "I see they picked the gun out from behind that. Not very clever on their part. And I didn't see them with a camera. They should have done a better job of finding a hiding place. It's good to know Tourville isn't so bright after all."

She put her foot out and turned to make a circle to view the neighbors. "This is nice here, a nice back yard, I mean." She pointed up and to the right. "Only that one window looks down over your yard. It's a bathroom and the window is frosted. Not much chance of a witness." She looked at Rachel. "Tell me, how does a nice ex-cop like you get to live in a historical house like this? Inheritance?"

"No. Not at all. You know there were houses around here that were not kept up. But inside they had woodwork from the days when craftsmen created the interior piece by piece with good redwood. I just had to remove the paint. You won't believe I paid $23,000 for this."

"And it's across from Volunteer Park? I'm impressed."

"When I worked out of the East Precinct I got to know the neighborhood real well. So I knew what was up for sale. And what condition it was in."

"Speaking of precincts, you retired early from the police force. Am I right?"

A breeze pushed the leaves of the rhododendron and gardenia back and forth.

"It's getting cool," Rachel said. "What do you say we go in the house." There was no reason to carry on a discussion where nosy neighbors could be listening. And maybe other people. When the police are planning on fabricating a case, they tend to have eyes and ears everywhere.

Rachel led Meredith into a den off the living room. Meredith stopped and rubbed the redwood frame.

"About your question," Rachel said. "No again. I left the police force a year ago. It wasn't a retirement."

"I gather from your reaction to Ted Tourville there's no love lost there."

"Ted is obviously out to get me. He has framed me. The cocaine, pretending he's looking for my gun, that's what he's doing. I don't have a way to prove it right now. Not when he's in charge of the investigation."

"Bear with me for a minute, Rachel. Look at this objectively. Can you do that?" Meredith folded her arms across her chest, and lowered her head so that she seemed to be looking up at Rachel with a new intensity in her eyes.

Rachel stared back at her and frowned, quiet for a moment. "Yes, of course I can be objective." It seemed odd that Meredith framed the question that way.

"You said yourself that the shot came from your

office." Meredith relaxed and sat back.

"There was a shot from the hallway, not from my office," Rachel said. The imprecision on Meredith's part rankled. "There's a big difference."

"Yes, of course, you're right about that. I don't want to sound pushy. But let me continue, if you don't mind. After all, we're just getting started. Was there a second shot?"

Again, Rachel sat silent for a few seconds. She had always questioned, not answered. "No, only one."

"And so the police know that, do they not?"

"Yes, I presume they do." Rachel wondered if Meredith had a plan with all these obvious questions.

"So, Rachel, as a beginning hypothesis, it's not a great leap to think you could possibly be a suspect."

Meredith put her in a corner by making her accept Tourville's point of view. "Except for one thing," Rachel said. "I didn't do it. And he knows I didn't."

"Yes, you and I know that, but you can't become paranoid about the police doing their work."

"Look, he's been waiting for his chance, ever since..." Rachel heard the defensiveness in her voice. She sat back and took another sip of coffee.

"Ever since what?"

"I left the police force because I couldn't work there anymore."

"Why is that?" Meredith looked at Rachel intently.

It made Rachel feel like Meredith sought something incriminating. Rachel wondered if she had misread her. Or mistaken her. She became reluctant to talk. She looked down and studied her feet.

"Rachel, I'm your attorney. We have attorney-client privilege, remember?"

Attorney-client privilege? She talked as if Rachel didn't know about that. Did she forget that Rachel worked on the police force? Did Meredith think Rachel had something to hide? Heat radiated down Rachel's back. She despised talking about that so soon. No, she thought, better to change the subject.

"Yes. I know. Let me ask you something else, Meredith. What about your fee? Isn't that the first thing to discuss?"

"If that is what you want. It's not important to me." Meredith shook her head.

"It's important to me. I'm the one who's paying here."

"There's time to do it in the future. But, if you insist, how about $20,000 up front and $200 an hour? Can you swing that?"

"Twenty thousand? No I don't have that kind of money. I have ten thousand in my savings. Will you take that?"

"Of course, I will. And I repeat I'm not in a cash flow bind right now and I don't want my fee to get in the way."

"And I'll have to get a loan on the house."

"We'll wait on it, then. You just take all the time you want. We'll wait till you get the loan. Let's get back to the situation at hand. Why don't you start with what is between you and Detective Tourville?"

"Before we start, I'd like to ask you a question."

"Of course. Something else about my fee?"

"No, not that. Nobody else is going to do it for free."

"What is your question then?"

Rachel now felt in control. A sense of power again. "It's personal." She focused on Meredith's eyes to get her attention. "You haven't asked me whether I'm guilty or not."

Meredith let out a little laugh and smiled. "No. It's not a question for me. You said you didn't do it. I believe you, Rachel. I don't need to pursue that. I've worked with you, and I know what happened that dreadful day. I don't see you as remotely capable of doing it. Not the way things happened." Meredith got up and walked to the bookcase. "Why don't you tell me about your pictures?"

Rachel and Joshua smiled on the ferry. Michael and Diane pushed their kids on a swing. Joshua and Rachael playing ping pong. Several soldiers with their arms around each other stood in front of a row of Humvees with mountains in the background. A small frame with two military medals half-hid behind the photographs.

"Is that Iraq?"

Rachel stood and went to the bookcase, then pointed back and forth to each picture. "Afghanistan. Diane Scanlan is on the right."

"I admit I am impressed," Meredith said. "I see you don't have a weapon like the others."

"Oh, not in this picture. I was a medic. But my medal was for combat."

Meredith then pointed to the frame with the medals in it. "Those are yours?"

Rachel picked up the frame and looked at it for a moment, rejected the images of Afghanistan that immediately tried to flood her mind, and put it back down, with a slow movement so that it seemed to float back down to the top of the bookcase.

She turned to Meredith, and felt the pride of showing her a medal for heroism in combat. "Yes, they're mine. The Silver Star and the Combat Action Badge. Diane earned the Bronze Star in the same engagement." She imagined Diane and herself running into the ditch.

Meredith looked at Rachel and nodded, acknowledging the heroism. "I think I should congratulate you," she said, holding out her hand. She shook Rachel's hand, then sat down. In a conspiratorial voice she said, "I have seen the way Detective Tourville acted in your house. It's very clear he has something against you. I would like to know what it is."

"Okay", Rachel said, "Let's have some more coffee, and I'll tell you how it happened."

Chapter 13

Damn! The cold wet breeze whipped Rachel's hair around her face as it went by, up from Lake Washington. She pulled her collar around her neck and tried to smile as she finished her investigation.

A severe, frightened woman in a black dress and diamond necklace stood shivering in front of the ornate entrance door to a mansion. The two lions out front had not done their job. The woman pulled her fur coat around her chest and leaned out, looking left, then right, to see if the neighbors were watching. Rachel told the lady to be careful in the future about turning the alarm on. Then she went back to the car to wait for Diane, still inside with the husband.

The open car door provided Rachel a small amount of relief from the wind. As she stood there, her arm on the roof of the car, a call came for a house just a few blocks away. A woman had seen someone sneaking around the garden across the street.

Rachel yelled for Diane, who came outside and looked around, puzzled. Starting the engine, Rachel stuck her arm out the window and waved Diane over. Rachel radioed in that they were going over to the house and made a three-point turn.

As she neared the address she had been given, she turned the lights off. A van about a half a block from the house gave them some cover. She pulled over to the curb. Rachel reached into her holster, pulled out her gun and chambered a round.

Diane turned and frowned at her. "What the hell is that?"

Rachel turned the pistol in her hand. "What the hell is what?"

"That pistol, what is it?"

Rachel humped over in frustration. "What? It's a Walther P99."

"What are you doing with it? Where's your Sig?"

"You like your Sig, take it out. Come on, let's go."

"No, Rachel, you tell me why you got that big thing."

"Anytime, Diane. But not now." Rachel didn't wait for Diane. She got out of the car. She didn't ever wait for Diane. Not back in Afghanistan and not now.

The street lights were a long way off in either direction. The houses were all grand, each with a huge expanse of lawn. There were no pedestrians. Rachel let her eyes adjust to the dark. The full moon overhead created clear walls and deep shadows behind bushes.

There were a dozen hiding places for a sniper. And someone with a night scope could be across the street a little farther away right now, putting her in his cross hairs. He could see her isolation, a simple target, with her backup somewhere way behind her. Her back felt rigid and wide waiting for a bullet.

Maybe someone she had once arrested watched her with a scope. Rachel looked at the shadows for more than a minute, straight ahead. Then she moved her head back and forth, and out of the corner of her eye, as she did in the Army. She didn't see anyone.

Rachel walked until she arrived at the house next door, with a long row of high bushes separating the property from the sidewalk. As she got closer, she stood between two bushes and pushed the branches aside. One of them snapped and scratched her cheek. She jerked her head back. She separated them again and saw that more bushes up, against the walls surrounded the house.

The cold had gone away. In the darkness, there were no distinguishing colors. Rachel looked back. The moon lit the route to her car, but also the shadows watched over it. She could not see Diane.

A tree trunk provided cover where Rachel stood and waited, leaning slightly to look both ways. She watched a long time. Diane finally came toward her, next to the bushes, but still too far away. At least she had her gun up and ready.

Rachel frowned and waved for her to come up, but Diane stayed put and crouched down. Somewhere a small child yelled and laughed. Sirens screamed in the distance. The whooshing of the wind in the trees died down then merged with the rush of cars a few blocks away.

Rachel took a step between the two bushes, pushing with her shoulders. She looked at the stairs leading up to the porch of the house. The yellow rectangle of the window contained the black silhouette of a man.

"Stop where you are! Police!"

He fired a shot, but the bullet didn't come near her. Another shot boomed, whizzing through the bushes to the right of her shoulder. She pointed her gun and squeezed, the shot rang out, and the silhouette fell down like a lopped flower.

Rachel watched and waited, looking to the left. No sound and no movement. She pushed the bushes aside and took a step toward the house. The fallen man did not move.

Two squad cars came to a slow, quiet stop in the street behind her. The officers put searchlights on Rachel, got out of the cars, and ordered her to get her hands up. She backed out of the bushes on to the sidewalk with her gun held visible above her shoulder. As she moved with deliberate slowness to put her gun on the ground, she took four seconds to open her coat completely wide and show them her badge. A nervous cop pointed his gun at her and came up close to look at it. She didn't recognize him and he didn't seem to know her.

"There's a man down over by the window," she said to the short policeman who had his gun pointed at her. He looked around to make sure someone else covered Rachel, then put his gun away, and ran over to the house.

Diane, badge clearly showing on her coat pocket, came up to Rachel, her eyes open wide. "What was that all about?"

Rachel backed away and stared back at Diane. "How the hell do I know? Someone shot at me."

"Why didn't you wait for backup?" Diane shook her head back and forth to emphasize the question.

"Backup? Isn't that just like you." Rachel put her pistol back in its holster, then looked at Diane and waited for a second, to make sure the point hammered home. "Where the hell were you?"

Diane "Where I was supposed to be, waiting for..."

Rachel didn't let Diane finish. "Yeah, waiting for someone else. You weren't like this in Kandahar."

"Jesus, Rachel, this isn't Afghanistan, its Seattle."

Rachel shook her head, then looked up as another squad car pulled up on the street and skidded to a stop. Two policemen got out and came over to them. Then the policemen suddenly changed direction and looked past the two women.

"You! Stop!" one of them called out suddenly, his gun drawn and pointed at a figure walking in the shadows. The man stepped out into the moonlight, then another stepped out and they both showed their badges.

Ted Tourville and his aging sidekick Brian Phillips looked serious. One of those shots must have come from them, but they probably weren't using their SPD-issued guns if they were out here shooting in the dark, behind bushes. Nobody knew they were here. What the hell were they up to? And why wasn't Rachel told they were already on the scene?

Ted came over to her and stood close. "Hey, Rachel, what are you up to?"

She backed away. "Take it easy, Ted, I was just answering a 911 call. Same as you, I hope. I called in and I didn't hear you call in."

"Damn right I did. You must have turned your radio off. You ought to keep it on, Rachel, or you will fuck things up. Especially in this neighborhood."

"My radio was on the whole time, Ted. Watch what you say."

"You were out of your car. Maybe you should have waited longer before you came charging in unannounced."

"Oh, they knew I was coming. But something else is fishy here, Ted. And there's somebody on the ground over there because of it."

"I know you fired at something, Rachel. You're in real trouble."

A captain came over, separated them, and got Tourville across the street.

"It's Councilman Hamilton," Rachel heard from the bushes.

"Get paramedics here now!"

It wasn't long before two fire trucks showed up, and firemen jumped out. One of the police officers motioned them to go through the bushes to the house. Two firemen lugged some equipment past the bushes, breaking tree limbs left and right. They knelt down over the figure. One of them started to lift him up.

"No, you can't do that," one of them said, "he's bleeding from a chest wound. You'd better wait for the paramedics to get here."

An ambulance came screaming through the neighborhood and almost crashed into a police vehicle parked at the curb as it came to a stop. Two paramedics ran over and knelt over the figure on the ground. They put an oxygen mask on his face, and inserted a tube in his mouth. They started to stop the bleeding from his chest wound.

Another paramedic truck arrived at the scene, and two more paramedics got out. This time they took their gurney with them and brought it over to where the councilman lay. The four of them picked up Hamilton and put him on the gurney. Immediately, a policeman with stripes rushed over and told them to put him down on the ground and not to move him.

"This is a crime scene, dammit, you can't move the body!"

"Hell. This isn't a body. It's a trauma victim! We need to get him to a hospital right now!"

Another policeman went and shoved the first one hard, then took him aside. "This guy isn't dead yet. Do you want to be blamed for his death? What were you going to do, pose him for pictures?"

The first policeman shook his head and walked away. The second one motioned to the paramedics to lift the Councilman up to the gurney.

Word got around quickly that a Seattle councilman had been shot, and soon it seemed like the whole city converged en masse on Broadmoor. They arrived in reverse order of importance. The precinct captain, captain of detectives, a fire chief, the police chief. Two helicopters, one belonging to the police, the other from a television station, circled each other overhead like stars in orbit. Even TV anchors left their desk to come to the scene and make sure they got their airtime.

It didn't take long to learn that Hamilton had died on the way to the hospital. Then the long string of official investigations began.

Ted, Brian and Rachel spent half the night and the next day going through interviews with internal affairs, captains, commissioners and anybody else who felt they should get some attention.

So the Military Police Silver Star veteran of Afghanistan killed a Seattle councilman. That event got headlines for days, followed by the hearings that went on for weeks. A criminal investigation followed to determine whether Rachel had authorization to use deadly force, and then an administrative hearing to determine whether departmental procedure had been followed.

Then New York talk show hosts came in, wondering what had gone wrong with the Northwest Coast. Then, a new distraction for the city administration, the threat of congressional hearings to determine if the federal government needed to protect city officials around the country.

In the end they exonerated Rachel from the killing of Councilman Hamilton, but it didn't matter, she didn't have a friend in the world. At least not in this small world.

Ted Tourville admitted under pressure with sweat on his forehead that he hid at Hamilton's residence that night on an unapproved stakeout. He maintained that Gil Hamilton moved illegal drugs and used his City Council immunity to escape investigation. Ted could never have gotten authorization for a stakeout against such a prominent person. Mickey Bauman, Ted's informant, had given him a story and then later retracted everything. So Ted had a story but nothing to back it up. And, Rachel knew, Mickey made it to Ted's get-even list.

From Ted's testimony, it became clear that he thought the stakeout provided him a ticket to the top, so he had kept his plan to himself. Rachel didn't have to read very deeply between the lines to see that he didn't want competition.

Rachel said she killed Gil Hamilton with defensive fire. Ted corroborated that Hamilton fired on her. He claimed it proved the value of the stakeout. Rachel and Diane both testified to a second shot, but the police didn't find any other shell casing or bullet.

Ted's idea that Hamilton functioned as a drug dealer didn't go anywhere. The mayor found a way to avoid a full-blown investigation of a very popular dead city Councilman. He couldn't guarantee the outcome would be favorable to the city. Or himself.

To City Hall's embarrassment, Ted and Brian and Rachel looked like the Three Stooges of SPD. But the mayor, the police chief, the whole police force, and on top of that the legal community, all blamed Rachel for what happened. After all, she was the one who shot and killed a councilman of the City of Seattle.

Rachel stood and looked down at Meredith, her hands out wide. "That's it. Now you know why Ted Tourville has it in for me."

Meredith nodded, and shook Rachel's hand. "Thank you, that helps me understand what happened here today. I'll be in touch."

When Meredith had left, Rachel closed the door and leaned against it. She exhaled deeply and thought back to what Joshua had meant to her.

Joshua honked his horn as soon as Rachel opened the door to the office building and stepped out on the sidewalk. She looked across at him, startled, but now smiling and waving. He focused on Rachel's lithe footsteps as she came across the street in the darkening sunset, checking traffic both ways, wary of the heavy, fast machines hurtling toward her. Not until she came around his car and opened the door did she smile.

"You picked me up, how nice of you. I could have walked back to Pike Place from here." She leaned over and put her am around his neck.

Her breath warmed his cheek just before her kiss. Her arm pressed with too much strength, worrying him. "Everything alright?" When she relaxed he saw the anger in her blue eyes and he squeezed her hand. "How did it go?"

Rachel sat back and fastened her seat belt, her lips drawn tight. "I'm fine, glad to be done with those bastards." She said those words in a harsh, clipped voice, staring past the windshield, seeming to focus on the traffic light ahead. But then she turned to Joshua and cocked her head and said with a half-smile, "Can we go eat?"

"Sure," he said, noting the change in the way she sounded. "I've got some pasta ready at my apartment. Salad, garlic bread, red wine. Okay?" But suddenly he didn't want to force her into something romantic when she had such a tough day. He shrugged. "It'll keep. We could stop at a deli and pick something up. Or eat wherever you want."

"No, I'm sorry," she said, the lowered pitch implying intimacy as she put her hand on his arm. "Pasta sounds great. Nice wine. Take me home, Darling."

Joshua smiled impishly and squeezed her hand. "We'll finish the wine in front of the fireplace. On the bear rug."

She laughed. "Bear rug? Fireplace? Did you remodel today?"

He was glad she was able to show some humor. He smiled but started the car and spoke in a serious tone. "So you're finished with them, right? The Internal Affairs bastards. They're the last ones."

Rachel sighed and shook her head, observing her hands. "Yeah, I'm finished with them. I'm off the hook, the councilman fired at me first, and Ted had no business being there. Blah, blah, blah." The burden of her frustration was obvious. "God, I've been through this with so many people already." She looked out the window at a brightly lit mannequin, then changed her voice to a dismissive tone. "But they didn't like it." She ran her fingers through her hair.

A twinge of worry hit Joshua at that comment. "What do you mean they didn't like it? What's for them to like?" He sensed the adversity of Internal Affairs as dangerous for Rachel.

"There were three of them on the panel. And three of them were shitheads. They read their questions off the paper. In monotone. Without looking up."

"So they didn't show any sympathy, is that it?"

He heard her speak louder as she turned to face him. Maybe he was being too sensitive.

"No, they didn't."

"Yeah, but it's not about sympathy. Did they tell you what they're going to report?"

"That's just it. They said you may go, our report will state you followed procedures, you will be reinstated tomorrow, you can show up for work. But they despised me, Joshua."

"I still don't understand. Despised you?"

"They wouldn't even look at me."

"But tomorrow you go to work? That sounds good to me. You put your life on the line for this city, Rachel." He took his hand off the steering wheel and put it on her knee, hoping she would touch him back. When she didn't, he feared there was a deeper problem.

"Don't you see? Tomorrow, I go back to work tomorrow."

This seemed good news to him, but clearly was bothering her.

"It's what you want, isn't it?"

"Of course I want to go back to work. But it's not up to them, these Internal Affairs zombies. This means they were instructed in advance, before they even talked to me."

"Oh-oh, there's some shit going on."

"Damn right there is."

"I'm sorry, I didn't understand at first. No wonder you're upset." Joshua paused a moment, sensing this was the right time to say what he wanted for her. "You know, Rachel, you don't have to do this."

"What? Not go back to work?" Irritation crept back into her tone again.

He wasn't doing this right so he made another attempt. "You don't have to work for the Seattle Police Department."

"It's my job, Joshua."

"It's your job now. It doesn't have to be."

"I like it. I'm good at it. I want to keep on doing it."

"I'm not saying you have to quit. I'm saying I'll support you if you want to."

"I don't want to."

"Good, but they're shitheads, and something's going on."

She sighed. "Thank you." Now she put her hand on his knee. "I really appreciate your support. It means everything to me. Now let's get to pasta and bear rugs."

The next morning Rachel called Diane to see whether they should meet at the office, or someplace else. Joshua was shocked by her tone.

"What do you mean?" Rachel's face twisted in disgust. "Tonight?" She put the phone down and sat, her lips pressed together with bitterness.

"What's going on?" The vehement way she spat out 'tonight' sent a cold wave through his stomach.

She continued, moving her head up and down to emphasize each phrase as if she hadn't heard him. "Diane's now working out of the East Precinct, and I'm starting graveyard. I'll find out for myself when I get in to work. Goddamn shit."

Joshua knelt in front of her and forced her to pay attention to him. "I'm sorry, this must be difficult for you. If there was something I could do for you, anything, I'd do it. We'll have to see how this works out, it's your call, but I'm with you, Rachel, you know that."

She lay her palm on his cheek and nodded. "Yes, I do. But for now, I'll have to go downtown and see what happens. If I'm working tonight, they won't make me stay long today, and we can have this afternoon before I go to work."

He stood and held her close to him. "Yes, see how things work out." But he had a foreboding.

Rachel left and Joshua opened his computer and buried himself in his design. Three hours later she returned. Her face told the story.

"Well, what happened today?" he said.

She took off her jacket and sat at the kitchen table. "Unbelievable." She threw her hands up in the air. "I could never imagine this happening to me." She looked at him, hesitated and said, "First I got my new gun, a Sig, so I'm going to have to get used to that. I'm going out tonight without ever having fired it on the practice range. I checked the bullets." She stopped again and stared at him. "They were blanks. I had to exchange them, and the goddamn smirks I got. And shit, somebody put a dead rat in my locker."

Joshua put his hand under her chin and spoke in a deliberate, earnest tone while he focused on her eyes. "You don't have to put up with this. Listen to me. We don't have to stay here. We can go anyplace we want. We can go to Idaho, I'll start my architecture business there. I can do homes, commercial buildings."

"No! Don't talk about moving from here. Don't talk about changing your career. You're designing your conference center, it's a big opportunity, Joshua. Don't even think about leaving." She stood and went to the window, looking down on the people milling around Pike Place. "I will not give up. I will live through this." She turned back to him, her eyes shining, and said, "I'm sorry, I don't know what you had planned for this evening. I'm not hungry. Let's rest for a couple of hours, I won't sleep, but maybe I'll doze, and be ready for tonight. Is that okay with you? I'll be all right eventually. It will take a while. I'll find a new partner, and things will work out. Come on and lie down with me for a while."

Joshua took her hand and led her into the bedroom, and they lay quietly next to each other, barely touching, and drifted off into light sleep. When he awoke, Rachel was getting dressed. She came to him and sat on the bed.

"Now you won't sleep well tonight," she said, running her fingers through his hair.

"I'll be fine. I'll spend the time going over my proposal. If things are slow, give me a call."

Rachel kissed him, taking her time, lingering, touching his cheek, pulling his head to her. Then she left. He went to the window, opened it and watched her graceful walk, her hair lit orange by the Public Market sign, her shadow keeping track with her, changing with the light in each store, until she disappeared around the corner.

He went back to his computer, brought up the architecture software, and began to design a realistic landscape around his 3D model of the conference center to match as closely as possible the photograph of the actual site, but he could not concentrate, so he opened the window again, and worried at the shadows on Pike Place, thinking about Rachel somewhere in Belltown or The Jungle, and the dark shadows in those places. Belltown started only two blocks away, he could walk there. The Jungle, those wooded slopes on Beacon Hill, he could go over there and check on her. What an urban hellhole of a farce, greenery an environmentalist would love, birds and animals for an explorer. And the top of the evolutionary chain, humanity, adding only crime and desperation. And danger for Rachel McAlister.

The thoughts didn't bring him any comfort or make her safe. Back and forth he went, the 3D model and the empty streets of Pike Place and Pike Street, watching over her without seeing her, each time passing the phone and wanting it to make her call.

But she didn't call. All through the night he watched Pike Place after the Public Market sign went dark and the pavement was lit by the eerie fluorescent light from empty stores. Then, from around the far corner she came walking, slowly, shaking her head, gesturing.

Joshua called out, "Rachel! I'm coming!" rushed to the door, jumped down the steps, and caught her as she stepped on to the sidewalk. He held her tight in his embrace and led her up the steps to the apartment. "What? What happened?"

"Come on, Darling, you're almost home. I'm here. We're together now."

Upstairs, on the couch, Rachel spoke in spurts and quick breaths. "I went out to the Jungle. They sent me out by myself. Said it was some kid high on meth, got hurt breaking a window during a robbery. When I got there, no other police were around." She glared at him with wild eyes. "They fired several shots at me from somewhere, Joshua. I couldn't see. I called for backup, but no one came. I finally got out of there and came right here. You were right. I can't do this anymore." She grabbed his shirt with her fists and pulled as her whole body shook.

He whispered into her ear. "I'll take care of you, Rachel. Like I promised, we can go to Idaho, and we'll make a new life there."

She breathed deeply, slowly, calming herself. With one last exhausting exhale, she said, "You are wonderful,

Joshua, you really are. But we don't have to leave Seattle. With your help, I'll start a new life."

He smiled. "I've been working on it."

She raised her head, looking at him with curiosity.

"I talked to the real estate guys for the Pike Place neighborhood. They have an office available across the street from this apartment."

The relief showed on Rachel's face. Her eyes shone. She put her arms around him and held him for nearly a minute, breathing silently with him. She asked him to show her the office, and he took her to the window on Pike Place and pointed it out to her, right across from his, above the corner grocery, with graceful half-circle windows. "Office for lease."

She smiled and held his face in her hands. "You'll be able to see me from here."

She put her arms around his neck, and pushed herself against him. His heart raced.

"Into the love," she said.

Joshua nodded. "Into the love." He could feel her relief, her happiness. It was as real a presence as his own heart beating.

Chapter 14

That night Rachel, stunned with exhaustion, her arms impossibly heavy, couldn't fall into a deep sleep. The image of Ted Tourville, walking out of the bushes, walking around in her house, kept her awake. Then fevered reveries alternated between Joshua at the window and Joshua on the couch. Joshua's hand came over her when the corner of the pillow hit her eye. Then Ted would come back.

She could see Ted looking around at the woodwork from which she had removed layers of paint and then finished to perfection. She saw the jealousy in his eyes as he looked it over. More than jealousy haunted his mind. He hated it, because he hated her. She had exposed him for the fraud he is.

She had originally thought that he'd be satisfied with forcing her out of the police department. But she also knew he wanted to destroy her in the most painful way possible. It had to have been him. She saw it in his eyes as he wandered around her home, lording over the scene.

She sat up in bed, her head swimming. The bastard thought this would be the perfect crime. He had a long enough career as a cop. He could get any kind of evidence he wanted, and plant it anywhere he pleased. Her gun, the cocaine. He killed Joshua, and yet he didn't know anything about their relationship except that they had one. Ted saw how easy it would be to kill Joshua from across the street, right from her office.

But of course, the way he did it, he had to know something about their relationship. He had to know what Joshua did, when he did it, and when he came and went. She tried to think back over the last days and weeks, if she should have noticed anyone on the street. But her memory came up empty.

He found it so simple, so easy, the killing and the investigation. He took pains about staking them out and setting it all up, painstaking about cleaning up afterwards. And all of it against Rachel McAlister, the pariah chased out of the Seattle police department. The target everyone would understand.

A breeze flew in through her open window, and the fresh air aggravated her restlessness. Rachel put her feet down on the floor and forced them to stay touching the wood as the cold crawled up her legs.

The dichotomy of Joshua and Tourville stayed with her. She shook her head, trying to shake Tourville loose. In the picture by the bedside, Joshua's face stared at her. She imagined him looking out his window from his apartment.

His apartment. She knew that's where she had to be. That would make her close to him, allow her to inhale his presence, and relieve the loneliness that drained her soul.

Rachel pushed herself up from the bed and crossed the cold floor to the chair where she had thrown her clothes, and put them on. Outside, in the dim light of the streetlamp, she walked to her car, her move followed by the watchful eyes of the orange lights of the Water Tower in the park.

In a few minutes she arrived at Pike Place and parked. She reached into the glove compartment and pulled out a small flashlight, then got out and looked around. The brass pig at the inside corner of the market stood as a solemn, lonely guard in the threatening mist of the night. The neon signs and fluorescent bulbs conspired to mock the emptiness of the marketplace. As she passed the fish stall, the air near the empty beds of ice cooled her face. She turned right and went up the stairs to Joshua's apartment, listening, hearing nothing, putting her foot down one step at a time and making no noise.

They had locked the door, but no SPD seal indicated this as a crime scene under investigation. Of course there wouldn't be anything, because it wouldn't have taken them very long. There had been no need for Ted Tourville to do a thorough, professional search. He knew what he wanted in advance and he intended to get it.

The key that fit this lock lay on her open palm, shining in the glare of the overhead hallway light. Rachel wrapped her fingers tightly around the metal pieces as she remembered the day she and Joshua gave each other keys.

She unlocked and opened the door and went in and shut the door behind her and stood for thirty seconds, inhaling in slow deep breaths, letting her eyes adjust. The reflected lights from Pike Place came through the living room window and created a lattice of deep yellow shadows. She went up to the window and looked across the street at the dark oval of her office window. A dark brown ugly piece of plywood covered it. Her arm and chest muscles instinctively cringed into themselves as she thought of the bullet that came across from her window and pierced his skull. She put her hand behind her head and fell to the floor and knelt there. She waited to feel Joshua, but nothing happened to bring him close to her.

Joshua's presence had been obliterated. He had been stolen from her right here in his own rooms. Too many people had been in here, defiling his apartment. One of them left a trail of hate with forensic chemicals.

She moved down the hall into the bedroom and opened the closet, took his shirt in her hands, put her face into it and saw herself in his arms. The fragrance of Knize Ten overwhelmed her, for a moment, but then the flimsiness of the shirt told her the truth, the truth of his empty arms. She let it fall away. She didn't know exactly why she wanted to be here. She had wanted to feel close to him, but instead he seemed even farther away.

The bed lay unmade, the covers and sheets rumpled up as a hideous reminder of their last love-making. She wondered if Tourville had thrown them around in a rage. She couldn't be in the room any longer. The door slammed behind her as she left. More like fleeing than just leaving.

Down the hall, the open door to Joshua's workroom, pulled her in. She tiptoed in and closed this door behind her without making a sound. As if someone worked in there whom she couldn't disturb. As if she were sneaking in on him for a surprise visit.

On the work table she could see the model he had prepared of his design for the Portage Bay conference center. She put her hands over her face and leaned back against the wall. The beautiful little model glowed with warmth from the light of the window, complete and perfect, as if she were looking down on it with him, from heaven.

She turned on the flashlight and lit up the little glass water surface. The beam reflected on the blue glass and shone on the tiny plastic windows of the sweeping front of the center.

Something inside the glass, in the model room, caught her eye. A box. A dark grey velvet box for an engagement ring.

Rachel's heart stopped. She put her hand up to her mouth for a second and froze, then lifted the top of the model and picked up the box. Her hands shook. The box, she noticed, lay on top of a small black notebook. She picked up the ring box and the notebook.

Rachel felt the notebook, awkward between her

fingers, small, but thick and heavy, an artist's notebook. Joshua had meant for her to look at it. She knew he had put it under the ring. A drawing in Joshua's recognizable neat style took up the first page. A drawing of a house, the location unmistakable, her home town. That curve of the Snake River Canyon near Twin Falls, with a view of Blue Lakes and the Perrine Bridge.

The following pages showed the interior of the house. The living room windows showed the river as it diminished in the distance, the perfect view of a sunset on Blue Lakes. They had talked about a vacation home there, but she hadn't known he completed so much of the design work.

She held the ring box in both hands, closed her eyes and remembered Joshua's proposal and the kiss. And then she remembered his frown when he had come out of his workroom. He must have forgotten where he had put the ring. It didn't occur to him to look inside his architectural model. And now she had the ring.

Now. But without him. She put the box to her chest and felt her heart beating against it. Then she held it in the open palm of her right hand, and lifted the top open.

A box with nothing inside. She imagined Joshua's fingers as he put the ring in the box and closed it, maybe held his hand there for a few seconds.

She screamed, put her hand up to her mouth and inhaled a short breath. Tourville. He had stolen it. She looked down once more at the empty box and imagined the ring inside it. And Tourville's fingers reaching down and picking up the ring. She fought to control the tears. She wasn't going to lose control for something Tourville did to her.

Now she knew why Joshua had frowned when he had come back from his office the night of their proposal. Her heart ached now for him, for his disappointed face, when he came back in the room without the ring. She wished she had been more forceful about telling him it wasn't important. Instead, she had practically ignored it.

At least Ted had left her the notebook. She got to keep something from Joshua's own hand and his own imagination. Ted hadn't understood what it would mean to her.

Rachel held the notebook and box in her hands, clutched them against her chest, and walked backwards, staring at the model, until she felt her back against the door. She slid down the length of the door, and sat, exhausted, drawing up her knees and letting her head fall. Then she pulled her arms and legs as tight as she could and shut her eyes for a long, silent time.

She listened to the quiet, wanting to hear Joshua's voice. But the silence allowed only the brutal ache in her chest.

The sharp corners of the ring box brought her back. She let her legs splay out, rolled over, got up and faced the door. Without looking back, she opened the door, stepped out. The cold sea air hit her face. Outside, on the landing, Joshua remained possible behind her, but then the air shifted and the door shut behind her.

Cold, hard, finality crushed her.

She walked back out to the empty streets, Pike Place and her car. She put the box and the notebook beside her on the passenger seat and started the car. In a few minutes she arrived home and hurried into her bedroom.

In the closet, she pushed clothes aside and picked open a very small cabinet door in the cedar wall. It hid in the corner, without any knob, noticeable only if you knew about it. Inside, a small .38 snub nose revolver.

Rachel didn't operate like some other cops who had an untraceable revolver in their cruiser, in case they had to shoot someone and then find out the dead guy didn't have a gun. She did it strictly to have a handgun at home so she could keep her pistol in the office. No other reason. A gun. If necessary. All legal. Hidden in the closet, away from curious eyes. Especially children.

She understood now why she had kept it, waiting for this moment. Rachel decided that she had to push her chips forward, stand up and confront him.

She stuck the revolver in her coat pocket.

Rachel opened the bedroom door, standing absolutely still to listen for Irene. Nothing in the house and nothing in the street. Midnight. Silent and dark.

The front door opened with a quiet click. She reached over and turned the porch light off. She went down the stairs to the sidewalk and up the street the half block to her car. Looking around and seeing no one, she got in, and started the few yards up East Prospect and on to Queen Anne Hill.

Tourville lived halfway up the eastern side of the hill, below a radio tower, red lights blinking all night. She had never been inside his house, but she knew where he lived. She had known for a long time. Maybe she knew because deep inside she waited for him all this time.

Strange how her subconscious had done its own work.

He had nothing against Joshua. The rot and evil inside him came to the surface and he thought he could strike twice, killing him and framing her. Now, she could do something about it. And somebody had to. Somebody had to stop Ted.

Rachel parked half a block uphill from Ted's house on Queen Anne Avenue. She took the revolver out of her pocket, pushed out the chamber, turned it, and saw that all the cartridges were in place. Sitting for a moment, she made sure of the quiet in the neighborhood. After looking around in every direction, she got out of the car.

All the houses stood in a macabre fabric of light and shadow. Few of them had porch lights on. Below her, the lights of downtown and the Space Needle glowed like an alien civilization. Far above and behind her, the blinking lights high up the tower looked down on her, made her feel centered in her purpose.

She stood in the dark gray of night. Rachel's two shadows on the sidewalk from the streetlights above and below her made her nervous, as if two ghosts were watching her.

She felt the cold steel and saw the glint of the barrel in her hand. She put the gun back in her pocket, but kept her hand on it. The soft rushing sound of the freeway nearby soon blended into the background. Whatever dogs were in the neighborhood were either sleeping or uninterested.

For a moment, she stood still on the sidewalk, listening and watching. Rachel didn't have a plan, nothing but a gun and a heart beating hard against her chest. She started walking downhill past the first house, then the second, then another, until she faced a room at Ted's address, looking at a small window with drapes shut.

She turned to look across the street. When she turned back, she saw the dim yellow light in the window. The blurred dark form of a woman moved across it. Ted's wife, Sandra. She had worked in the department, but quit after she married him. She had always been helpful and friendly. Sometimes Rachel thought Sandra gave her smiles that were more than smiles, looking for a friend or a helper, but something inside kept Rachel from following up on them.

She went down to the corner and looked right, then walked a few feet downhill. They kept the windows on this side of the house closed and dark.

Rachel walked back up and around the corner again. Sandra's silhouette showed behind the curtain now, but only her head moved. Maybe kids slept upstairs. Innocent children.

And then Rachel knew. She had no rot of evil inside her and she could not carry out her intention.

She felt that constant crucible of heartache that

burned inside her so often since she lost Joshua, and sometimes even dizziness, and more, something as close to hatred as possible. But not evil, not for Rachel. She took her hand off the gun.

The lights stayed on a long time, then a dog barked somewhere, and a car came around the corner and continued on up the hill. Once more she saw her long shadow going uphill and a weaker one going downhill and she felt unreal. She had two shadows, like two realities. Like two lives, one still living, one now dead and gone.

She saw her car in the dark up ahead. Rachel took her keys out.

An arm reached around her neck, pulling back hard, and a gun barrel shoved against her spine. She tensed her muscles and held on to a forearm and tried to move it away from her neck, but the attacker pulled harder and tighter. His strength overpowered her.

Next to her ear the raspy whispered voice of Ted Tourville said, "What the fuck are you doing at my house in the middle of the night, McAlister?"

She ducked and tried to escape. He jerked her head back tight.

"Don't." He remained silent for a moment, breathing heavily. "This is the end for you. When I let go, you take two steps away, and then turn around, Rachel. Or you're dead."

He released her neck and held his gun against her back for a long moment, then took his gun away. She looked around the street, empty, no one watching them.

Violence in the quiet darkness of the night. She turned and faced him. He held the gun at his waist, pointed at her. But he didn't do or say anything.

Rachel wished she had left the gun in the car. If he had felt her gun, he would have gone berserk and unloaded his whole magazine into her. But he didn't. Tourville didn't have the courage.

120

And he didn't have eyes in the back of his head, or he would have seen Diane Scanlan coming around the corner behind him. But he certainly heard her cold, hard voice.

"What are you up to Tourville? What's with the gun pointed at an unarmed woman?"

Tourville turned and looked back at Diane, back at Rachel, and back to Diane again.

"What?" He stepped away from the two of them. "McAlister is a suspect in a murder. I'm the one investigating. Here she comes creeping around my house."

"I was out for a walk," Rachel said.

Tourville turned back to her, carelessly waving his gun around.

Diane moved closer so that the three of them formed a small triangle.

"A walk?" he said. "The hell you were. Like you live around here. And what are you doing here, Scanlan? Both of you together? Don't bullshit me."

"One of your neighbors called 911 about something going on over here on Queen Anne. I had my scanner. So I came to see what I could do."

"I'm taking her in. Now."

Diane stepped between Tourville and Rachel. "Let me tell you something," she said. "If you do that, I can make a whole hell of a lot of trouble for you. You know exactly what I mean." She folded her arms across her chest. "I advise you to drop it."

As she spoke, a black and white car came down the hill and screeched to a stop. Now people came out on the porch or leaned on a window ledge.

Diane held up her badge and went around to the driver, who listened and gave her a quick salute.

The cop on the passenger side spoke to Tourville. "Is everything okay here, Ted?"

Tourville looked over at Diane and then nodded. He

had hidden his gun. The driver waved, Diane backed away, and the car went on down the hill and turned the corner, leaving them all once again in the night and the witness neighbors.

"I think this is over," she said.

Ted fidgeted with his feet. Then he looked at Rachel and jabbed his finger toward her. "If you ever come near my house again, it will be the last day of your life."

He turned and stared hard at Diane for a moment, then went back in and slammed the door. Most of the neighbors now disappeared, but a few stayed, watched, and talked. Diane came close to Rachel and put her arm around her, felt the gun in the pocket and backed away, her mouth open in shock.

"What the hell are you doing?"

"Nothing, as you know."

"With a gun."

"I didn't even take it out of my pocket." Rachel wondered if any neighbor had seen her with the gun.

Diane moved her head back and forth in disgust. "Rachel, I'm going to go back to my car, and go back to my house. I expect you will follow me. Is that right?"

Chapter 15

Rachel skidded her car to a stop in front of Diane and Michael's home on Mercer Island. In the early morning quiet the motor pinged as if it wanted to keep going away from this house. She got out of the car. Darkness enveloped the street except for this house where Diane and Michael waited inside.

As Rachel walked across the lawn toward the porch steps, she felt the weight of the revolver in her jacket. She put her hand inside the pocket and held the gun tight. In the darkness surrounding the porch, the glaring white light overhead felt like a spotlight. Images from the street in front of Ted Tourville's house floated in front of her.

The revolver in her pocket became warm. She took it out and turned it over in her hand. Bought for protection, almost used as an instrument of death. Rachel fought back the urge to throw it into the bushes where it could no longer be connected to her killer instinct.

Her arms and legs became tired. She put the gun back inside her pocket. She wanted to turn around and run down the street into oblivion. A gray cat eyed Rachel with suspicion as she crossed the front lawn.

The door opened half way. Diane stood there in silence, immobile, more like a guard than best friend. Not even a smile. In the unforgiving bright glare of the porch light, Rachel kept her hands in her jacket pockets and looked at Diane's eyes. She felt a stinging rebuke.

"You told me to come here," Rachel said, as she backed away a step and raised her head so that she appeared to look down at Diane.

Diane raised her eyebrows. "Yes, I invited you. The door is open." Diane pulled the door open wider and backed out of the way. She kept one hand on the doorknob and the other straight down at her side.

"Is Michael here?" Rachel asked.

"Yes, he's here. He'll be down in a while." Diane waved her in. She did not offer to take Rachel's coat.

"I know you invited me, but I don't feel very welcome."

Diane pointed in to the kitchen. "Silver before bronze."

"What is that supposed to mean?"

"After what you did, Rachel, you're not in a position to ask questions." Diane drew out the syllables in the name.

"I do have a question, Diane," she said, returning the emphasis on the name. "Why are you following me?"

Diane made a little grunt of disdain. "You should be happy I did."

"I can take care of myself, thank you."

Diane shook her head and let her breath out in a dismissive gesture. "It didn't look like it."

Rachel still had both hands in her coat pockets, one holding the gun. "Why did you come to Ted's house? Answer me that, will you? How could you know I was there?"

"I heard a call for assistance. And I knew it was you. Ted's house? Who else but you? I was needed."

"No you weren't."

Diane pointed to a chair. "Sit down, Rachel."

"No thanks. I'm here. Tell me what you want." She held her hands out wide.

Diane moved a step closer and shrugged. "I want you

to trust me."

"Trust you? What for?" Rachel felt heat rising on the back of her neck.

"What for?" Diane put her hands on her head in disbelief. Then she raised her voice. "What for? Jesus. You came so close to premeditated murder? And you ask what for? You keep on like this, Rachel, and you're going to have no one. You should have called me before going over."

"You're goddamn right about one thing. After Joshua, there is no one."

Michael's voice came from the hallway. "What's going on?" He looked at the two women, then focused on Rachel. "Are you all right?"

Rachel looked at Diane, and Michael behind her, and the wedding portrait on the wall behind them. Joshua's face looking out his window flashed in front of her, and then she saw him being wheeled around the corner in the emergency room, and she felt nauseous.

She put one hand on the table, then swung back, and grabbed the counter, and suspended herself there, her head dipping below the spread of her arms. At first she remained bent over and silent, then a terrible sound came out of her. It built to great, ugly sobs. She started shaking and her knees bent, but she held on. The sobs died down and she continued there, bent over, crying softly. Then she lost her legs and fell to kneeling on the floor. She bent her face to her knees and wrapped her arms over her head.

Michael pulled her up. She then put her hands on his chest, looked into his eyes, saw his immense concern, and pushed herself away. She went to the sink and splashed water on her face and dried it. She stared at her reflection, the dark window a mirror in the night. Looking down, she brushed her hair back, wiped the tears from her face, and turned and saw the tears on Diane's face. Rachel took the gun out of her pocket and put it on the table.

"I know," she said, "I have no one now but you two."

Diane put her arms around Rachel and held her tight, but Rachel pulled away after a few seconds. Rachel kept her head bent down, afraid to look Diane in the eye so close. She raised her arm, touched Diane on the cheek and held her hand there.

"What time is it?" She looked up at the kitchen clock. "Three?" She shook her head back. "I'd better go."

"You're sure you don't want to stay here?" Michael said.

"No, but I have a favor to ask. I have a lawyer, and I'd like to bring her over tomorrow. She wants to meet you in person."

"Since when?" Diane said.

"Since this morning. Look, I don't want to go over it now. My head is splitting. Is tomorrow afternoon okay?"

"Of course. But tell me who it is."

"Meredith Rawlings."

"Well, you need a lawyer. I've heard of her, but I'm not convinced she's the right one. We'll see."

Rachel nodded, then picked up her gun.

Michael reached out and put his hand over hers. "Don't you want to leave this here?"

Rachel looked at him, then at Diane, then stared at the weapon in her hand. She nodded and put it back on the table. "All right."

She hugged him for a long moment, then went to Diane. They embraced. Rachel walked out of the kitchen, put her fingertips to her lips and touched the wedding portrait as she went down the hallway. She waved a hand back to them over her shoulder as she closed the door.

But she didn't go home. Halfway there, instead of continuing north toward Capitol Hill and Volunteer Park, she found herself going to Stewart Street toward downtown. Her car followed the dictates of her subconscious.

She drove back down to Pike Place, parked in the

empty street, and walked up to Joshua's apartment and into his bedroom and lay there in silence. Her arm moved over to his side of the bed, wanting desperately to touch him, then withdrew in shock when she felt only sheets.

He had asked her to marry him. At least she had that.

A headache tightened at her temples. She pulled the comforter up and then his presence surrounded her until she drifted off. In the middle of the night she found herself sitting upright on the side of the bed in the dark, waiting for something. She became aware that she waited for nothing. She lay back down and waited, awake, until the morning light came.

The noise of the first delivery truck and the lonely cry of seagulls jolted her and made her conscious of the emptiness of the room. Was Joshua really gone?

Chapter 16

That afternoon, Meredith picked Rachel up and drove her over to the Scanlan house. Even from outside, Rachel could feel Michael's gaze on her. When they arrived, Diane and Michael stood at the open door, both smiling in anticipation. Rachel pushed Meredith ahead up the narrow stairwell.

Michael immediately put out a hand to Meredith, who smiled more than the occasion warranted. Michael smiled back, but more reserved. "Welcome. I'm very glad to meet you."

"The pleasure is all mine." Meredith turned to Diane. "I'm glad to meet you, Diane."

Diane shook Meredith's hand. "Why don't you come in and make yourself comfortable. I'd like you to meet our two children, Sean and Shannon. We just celebrated their ninth birthday a couple of weeks ago."

The always well-behaved Scanlan twins stepped forward and shook Meredith's hand. Michael ushered them all into the living room, watching Rachel as she passed by. She took off her sunglasses when she passed in front of him, but did not say anything.

"Thank you," Meredith said as she gave her coat to Shannon. Meredith ran her hand gracefully over Shannon's long, red, shoulder-length tresses. Shannon looked back at her and smiled, then walked away with Sean.

"Please take a seat, anywhere you like," said Diane. "Meredith, have you seen Rachel's house? It's quite something isn't it?"

"Yes, it is, but you also have such lovely furniture here."

"I love the old Victorian furniture, although we can only afford it for the living room. Now, Rachel's house, that's something else. She refinished practically the whole interior."

"I understand she put a lot of work into it."

"It was a total mess when she first moved in. I tried to convince her not to do it, but she was determined. She's made it beautiful. Quite out of place for a cop."

"Not much of anything at the moment," Rachel said. "Me, I mean."

"Rachel, fill us in on what's happening," Michael said.

Meredith looked at Rachel as if she were expecting some particular answer, but then looked back toward Michael and folded her hands carefully on her lap.

"Ted has made progress."

"How is that?" Diane looked back and forth at both Meredith and Rachel.

"He found my gun, hidden in my backyard. Or that's what he says."

"He what? Why didn't you tell us this last night?"

"I wasn't thinking straight last night. Is that enough?"

Meredith sat up, clearly agitated. She looked at Rachel. "Last night? Did something happen?"

Michael didn't wait for Rachel to answer. "No, nothing special. Rachel was here for a little while last night, and she didn't mention anything to us. That's one of her problems. She doesn't confide enough."

"I see," Meredith said, looking at Rachel, clearly puzzled.

Michael turned to Rachel. "What do you mean, hidden? Did they have to dig it out of the ground?"

"No, they found it behind the rhododendron, in the corner. So they say."

"Which they didn't, Rachel," Michael said, almost before Rachel finished talking.

Diane looked over at Meredith. "What do you think?"

"Without witnesses, there's no way to determine who put it there." Meredith realized the implications of what she said and raised her hand. "Sorry, I didn't mean to get technical. I don't mean Rachel, of course. The most important element is what they find when they do their tests."

"That's not all," Rachel said, "they were also looking for cocaine."

"Cocaine?" Michael said. "Why on earth would they be looking for that?"

Meredith sat up. "They found some, or so they claim, on Joshua's body."

"He was drugged?" Michael said. His face contorted into total disbelief.

"No, they found it in his clothing."

"The police could easily have put it there, I'm sure," he said.

"Actually, it wasn't the police that found it. It was the staff at the hospital."

"The hospital staff didn't do it," Diane said.

"Like I said, the police." Michael said, nodding, as if he were adding punctuation.

"No, of course not," Meredith said. "It's the same as the gun. But, unfortunately, we have nothing we can use to point suspicion at the police."

Michael sat up and put his arms out, palms up. "Rachel, he never used cocaine. It's out of the question." Then he looked around the room. "Joshua was about as straight as they come."

"You're right," said Meredith. "Neither Rachel nor I believe that he was using drugs. It's not just our belief. We know. They had to have been planted. No doubt this was arranged by Ted Tourville."

Diane found Meredith's remark very interesting. She raised her eyebrows as she looked at her. "Oh, you know about him?"

"Rachel has told me the whole story about Ted and

the unauthorized stakeout that led to the death of Gil Hamilton." Meredith's eyes started to mist up. "Excuse me." She looked ashamed. "I have defended people who did horrible things, and I was not as upset at those trials as I am now. This is so obvious a case where the police are determined to put the blame on Rachel, and I know she is innocent."

"I know she's innocent, too," Diane said, looking at her husband. "Michael and I are convinced of this. I'm curious as to why you think so."

Michael leaned forward, waiting for the answer, saying "Not think. Know."

"No," Meredith said. "It's not about belief, or knowledge. She is my client. That's enough."

Michael clearly did not like that answer. He gave Meredith a stern look. "Wait a moment here. Aren't you clear about Rachel's innocence? Didn't you just say...?"

Meredith smiled. "I seem to have a problem communicating today. Yes. Rachel is innocent. I know she is. That wasn't my point. We're not going to have this kind of discussion with Mr. Tourville."

Diane stood and adjusted her jacket, looking around the room. "There's a lot more to talk about, but I'm going to go get the coffee first." She disappeared into the kitchen.

Michael put his hands together. "Please don't get me wrong. Tell me, how much experience do you have? I'm sorry if I sound too blunt, but this is my good friend we're talking about here."

Meredith smiled once more. She hesitated before she spoke, looking down, then back up at Michael. She injected a note of seriousness to her voice. "Certainly, I understand, Michael, and that's again, why I told Rachel she should herself consider another lawyer."

"Wait a minute, Michael," Rachel said, cocking her head. "Meredith is my lawyer. She does have experience, in both California and Washington. In my book, a lawyer who believes in me, and knows the truth, is worth more than somebody who doesn't."

"Rachel," Michael said, "how many Seattle lawyers did you try?"

Rachel looked at him with a face that showed irritation. She hunched her shoulders up. "I already know a dozen who won't work with me, and I could give you some of the biggest names in town. And people I thought were my friends."

"Who exactly?"

"Chadwick."

"That's one."

"Gockenbach. Alexander Stewart."

"What was their reason?"

"You know damn well. Don't act stupid."

Diane returned with a large tray of cups. "Let me put this down and I'll bring out the coffee in a second." She turned and walked out again. This time, Meredith got up and left with her.

Michael leaned toward Rachel and said in a very low voice, "I think you're making a mistake. Seattle isn't the only town with lawyers. She may be good, but you deserve the very best."

"I'm not going to argue with you." She shifted in the chair. "It's my neck that's on the line here, don't forget that."

"Don't make this personal," he said, frowning, adding a tone of great sincerity to his voice. "I want what's best for you." He sat back, lowered his chin, seeming to look up at her. It made his remark more serious. "But I want you to be smart about it. How much do you really know about her, anyway?"

"More than you think." She sat up straight and put her hands on her knees, making sure he saw her looking straight back at him. "She's got good experience. She will be tough with Tourville and whoever else thinks they can mess with this."

Michael looked down, tightened his lips, taking his time to make his statement, then looked up at her again. "Okay, don't get mad at me, but I have made a few contacts," he said. "Robert Anderson in L.A. is interested and could be convinced to talk to you."

"You what?" Rachel's eyes widened. "Anderson? So what? He's from L.A.?" She felt her neck and cheeks flush. "Well, so is Meredith. I don't want any super hyped-up media lawyer making a circus of this."

Diane came back smiling with Meredith, who held the coffee.

Michael said, "Tell me, Rachel, what have they charged you with, anyway?" "You haven't said that." He looked truly puzzled.

"They haven't charged me. Yet. They can't move that fast." But Rachel knew that they could move very fast when they wanted to. If somebody in the police department thought it important.

"They can't possibly find anything on your gun," Michael said.

"Nothing as far as I'm concerned. I've never even fired the thing, didn't even make it down to the firing range. I never got any work that was dangerous enough to carry it."

"So, there you go," said Michael, looking at everyone and lifting his palms up and out.

"Look, if somebody took the trouble to plant it in your garden, they obviously could've used it to fire at Joshua," Diane said.

Michael began to frown again. "Why in the world would anyone want to kill Joshua anyway? He was such a great guy. It doesn't make any sense to me. And from your office, Rachel, how is that even possible?"

"It wasn't from my office, it was from the hallway outside. The shot went through the window in my office."

"Well then, somebody framed you. It's clear isn't it?"

"Until we hear back about what they find out about the gun, or who knows what else they picked up in the house and didn't tell us, we won't know what it looks like to them."

"My god, they are not going to find anything else. Unless, but, how do you know about the cocaine anyway?"

"Because they showed me the search warrant, and it said that Joshua had cocaine on him and so that was the excuse to search my house for it."

"Don't tell me they found cocaine in your house, Rachel."

"Of course not."

Michael and she were having their own private conversation. "Look, Ted Tourville is going after you because he wants to get back at you. But he won't get very far with it. Sooner or later they're going to have to go after the real killer."

"There, you're right," Diane said. "He convinced a judge to let him in your house. Wait until the lab examines the gun. Then the truth will come out and Ted will look like a fool."

Chapter 17

The next morning, Rachel took her cup of coffee to the front porch. The dark red brick Volunteer Park Water Tower loomed high across the street.

But a car at the end of the block at the corner on 15th Avenue piqued her interest. So near to the corner it posed a danger for any driver in a hurry. And parked in front of a fire hydrant.

A woman sat behind the wheel. Ted Tourville sent a woman up to do his spying for him because a couple of guys eating donuts and reading the paper would've made themselves more obvious. She sat there, leaning forward and looking down East Prospect in the direction of Rachel's house. She was somewhat familiar, but Rachel couldn't make her out, not from this distance.

The woman appeared to be fine out in the open. In fact she wanted to be noticed. The more Rachel looked, the more she felt the woman didn't survey Rachel's house, but rather sat and waited for her.

She went back inside and pulled the curtains and drapes closed. In the dresser in her dining room she found her 90 degree lens adaptor. It allowed her to point the camera forward while taking a picture sideways without the target being aware they were being photographed. She put it on her camera.

Rachel knocked on the door to Irene's apartment, opened it slightly, and called down the stairs. "Irene, are you there?" She knew she had no right to open the door without Irene's permission, but she knew, too, that Irene would forgive her.

It took a moment for Irene to respond. "Yes, I'm here. Where else would I be? Do you need anything?" came the muffled voice.

"I wanted to ask a favor. I'm going out for a little while, and I may be back soon, and maybe not, but I want to make sure you go out and stand on the porch every once in a while, so people know you're here. You know, so they know the house isn't empty."

"Why do you want me to do that?" Irene's voice sounded irritated.

"Because there might be nosy cops around and they would take advantage of it, that's all. Will you do it?"

Irene's voice came closer to the stairs and had some warmth in it. "Sure, you know I do everything you ask. I'll help you out any way I can. I'm working on my quilt today, so I have lots of time."

"Thanks, Irene. I'll see you later. I might be back real soon, but I'll be in and out all day."

"Certainly. Is everything okay? I mean, I'll be glad to work all day up there if you want."

Irene's comforting offer made Rachel feel better She closed the door, put the camera strap over her shoulder, donned sunglasses, exited the house and looked up the street. The woman still waited, still watched, still puzzled.

Rachel walked past a few houses, then across the street, and stood for a moment, turning in several directions and taking pictures. Aiming the camera on the wide, light green trees in front of the Water Tower, she looked through the viewfinder and zoomed in on Sandra Tourville.

What? Sandra? That didn't make sense. She couldn't be doing Ted's dirty work. She didn't act that way. At least not up until now. Rachel and Sandra had been good friends when she worked for a brief period out of

North Precinct, before Rachel moved to West. She seemed a little plump, never glamorous. But Sandra showed herself to be a warm and caring person, even if she did make a mistake with her marriage. Sandra had given up too soon on finding somebody who would really appreciate her.

Before Rachel could figure out what to do next, Sandra started the car, drove over, and stopped next to her, the window down. She leaned out the window, her face anxious, her eyes nervous. "Rachel, I need to talk to you. Will you come up to the conservatory in the park?"

Stunned, Rachel waited a moment before answering. She gave a quick look up and down the street. Then she spoke warmly. "Yes, of course, Sandra. I was just a little surprised to see you."

Sandra did not respond to Rachel's remark. Her voice had an edge to it. "Go around the left to the back of the conservatory. The fence to the cemetery."

What did Sandra want? There was only one way to find an answer to this enigma. "Okay. I'll be there in a minute."

Rachel went back to her house and got the car keys, then drove to the fence and parked next to Sandra, who stood with her back to the fence. Behind Sandra the gray tombstones leaned at odd angles. A pockmarked angel dominated this section. The older part of the cemetery. The red, white and blue of small flags contrasted with the ageless gray of the cement.

Joshua, too, would have American flags put on his grave each year, along with a mention of his Purple Heart.

Rachel wondered if Sandra had a gun to shoot her. But the idea didn't make any sense. She had no reason to mistrust Sandra. But still, the idea wouldn't go away.

Rachel saw tears in Sandra's eyes. "I'm leaving Ted."

"Why?" And why, Rachel thought, did she tell me this?

"The last straw. He was going on about you killing your boyfriend, and all I said was maybe you didn't do it. He got all emotional and went on and on about it. Like I was his enemy. Like we both were. He wouldn't stop...crazy... as if I knew something. As if I were talking to you. I really got scared and didn't know what to do. Finally, I decided I had to come see you."

"Why do you want to talk to me?" Rachel said.

Sandra shrugged her shoulders and sighed. She kept her hands on her purse in front of her. Rachel couldn't help thinking it meant something. She looked down at the purse and then up at Sandra, but Sandra did not react to that.

"What in the world were you doing at my house in the middle of the night?"

Rachel didn't answer her for a moment. "I didn't think of it being your house. I thought of it as Ted's."

"I saw you, Rachel. And then Ted, I don't know where he was at the time, but he got his gun and went out the back way. I was afraid. So I called 911."

Sandra didn't mention anything about Rachel having a gun. She must not have seen it.

"Aren't you worried he'd find out about it?" Rachel said.

"No. I used a cell phone he doesn't know about. Not in my name."

"Sounds like you've been prepared for something all along."

For the first time, Sandra looked Rachel in the eyes. "That's right."

"I still don't understand why you want to talk to me now, Sandra. What is it?"

"Because I'm worried for you."

"Why?"

"Ted hates you so much."

"I think I understand that. He's hated me for a long time."

Sandra wiped the tears from her eyes and looked at Rachel. "But I think he wants to kill you."

"Sandra, how do you know that?"

"I heard him on the phone."

"You heard him say what?"

"I heard him say he's going to get you. I've never seen him this bad. It scares me."

Rachel turned to face Sandra directly. "I think it was Ted who killed my fiancé."

Sandra looked at Rachel with a terrified look in her eyes. "Your fiancé? Ted?"

"Well, you think he wants to kill me. Think about it. It's logical. First one, then the other."

"Rachel, I'm sorry." Now she began to cry again. She wiped her eyes with her hands and sat silent for a moment. "I didn't know that."

"You didn't know my fiancé was killed, Sandra?"

"No, honestly. I don't know, I've been so mixed up, afraid. I didn't know he was your fiancé."

"Maybe Ted followed you here," Rachel said. "What if he sees us?"

"He's on duty at the precinct. He can't follow me. I checked before he left, and they said he was there."

"They've probably told him you called."

"That doesn't matter. I left a message about dinner and said to tell him I was going out. And I called again, just when I arrived at your house."

"Maybe he had somebody else do it, follow you, I mean."

"I watched. I moved around. I do know how this gets done, Rachel. I've worked there long enough. There's nobody around. And there's nobody around up here."

Sandra moved her eyes around the park, then continued. "I didn't go over to your house just now to see you, Rachel. Not at first. I went to see if someone else's car was there. I'm nervous about him, too." The breeze lifted her hair. "I hate him. I wish he were dead. I wish I were dead."

"I'm so sorry. I didn't know it was so awful for you."

"No, of course you didn't know," Sandra said. "Nobody did. Not my family either."

"Then why do you stay with him?"

"It's never been this bad. I know that now I'm going to leave him and take the kids with me. We'll be okay. But you need to watch out."

"Sandra, I will watch out. I promise you. I don't need anybody to tell me that."

"We better go now. He doesn't know what I have in mind. And I don't know how he would react if he found out."

"Is there anything I can do for you?"

"No, I have to leave, Rachel. I have to make sure he doesn't know."

"Where will you go?"

"I thought of going to my parents in L.A., but I don't trust him to leave me alone."

"I have a cabin at Mt. Baker you could use." Rachel regretted saying that. She knew you just don't let other people know too much about your private life.

"Thanks, but that's too close. I need to disappear for a while."

"He doesn't know about it. The cabin, I mean."

"Maybe. He's constantly on the phone asking about you."

"It's in my mother's maiden name. He can't know about it. My offer still stands. I'll help you any way I can." Rachel looked out to the park, making sure they were still alone.

"Make sure he doesn't know we talked. I have some old friends I can go to, where I'll be safe, and then I'll decide what to do."

Sandra looked around. Then she touched Rachel on the arm, went to her car, and drove away.

Funny, finding out once again Rachel could talk to

Sandra, even if she found it hard to listen. Sandra had found herself in a bad relationship, worse than that, in a bad marriage, and she did not deserve it.

Rachel waited a long time, looking at the gravestones on the other side of the fence, and imagined Joshua's name on one of them. Once again agonizing sorrow attempted to control her. Once again she straightened up, stiffened, and controlled herself.

Chapter 18

God's Acre lay in the middle of Holyrood Cemetery in Seattle. Rachel had come with Diane and Michael. Diane drove them in as far as she could, and then they walked a long way in silence to the grave site.

Only a few people attended Joshua's burial. Not many at the funeral, either. The funeral announcement came from the undertaker, and didn't mention any family.

When Rachel talked to the undertaker, he said that it had been arranged by a lawyer up in Oregon, that the family didn't want any information to be given out and he wouldn't reveal any more information. Also, there were only three floral sprays, one from Rachel.

The three of them had deliberately come in late to the funeral and sat in the back. Only a dozen people were there and Rachel didn't know any of them.

She had called the coroner to find out if any arrangements had been made. They didn't want to talk to her, but she finally learned they had reached a sister in Salem, Oregon, who said she would take care of everything. A sister. One more thing Rachel didn't know about Joshua. In her mind, it had been something they were going to explore once they got back from that trip the next day, the one that never happened.

The eulogy at the funeral home comforted no one. She, the pastor or whatever, had to look down at a piece of paper every time she mentioned Joshua's name. No one else spoke. The whole thing sounded nondenominational and efficient. That's what happens when it's all directed from out of state.

Rachel understood. At this moment, she, the one who had been the closest to Joshua, sensed her position as the most distant.

She hadn't realized how few friends he had. She recognized a couple of them from a party or a dinner a while back, but she didn't remember their names and they didn't come over to her.

It was odd that Roger Chadwick and Ulrich showed up, dressed in black. Rachel didn't know what to make of it. Roger looked over toward Rachel, but his face didn't give any indication of what his feelings were.

One tall young woman reminded her of Joshua. She seemed bitter, her face drawn, and her mouth down. She could have been his sister, but Rachel was sure that she projected this. If she were Joshua's sister, wouldn't she have tried to contact Rachel? Maybe she didn't even know Rachel existed.

Two women wore dark business suits, and one of them wiped tears from her face, but everyone else seemed only somber, not particularly sad.

Michael looked at Rachel as if maybe he wanted her to go over and say something. But his solemn face seemed to say that right now didn't seem like a good time to do it.

When it was all over, they waited until everyone else had thrown dirt on his casket, and then took their turns, at the end. Each clump landed on the casket with dull finality. The blackness and heavy smell of the dirt, after the rain the previous night, made it seem like the earth was a decent home for him. Home in the earth and waiting for her.

As they moved together to make the long walk back to the car, Rachel turned back one more time to look back at his grave in the distance, lonely, surrounded with ugly artificial green, with a few flowers around it. Joshua, now the enigma. She would never get to know the true depth of his heart and soul.

She wondered how soon they would make this repulsive hole into a grave that she could come and visit. And feel close to him even in her grief.

Michael looked at her several times, as if trying to figure out what she really felt.

Rachel looked at him and Diane. Then she looked back at the open grave again. "Thank you for coming with me."

"You don't give yourself enough credit. Joshua really cared about you."

"Yes, I'm starting to realize that he was the only person who cared for me, apart from you two." She looked Michael in the eyes and noticed how intently he observed her. "I never really gave him a chance."

"Rachel," he said, stepping close to her and holding her by both shoulders, "don't be hard on yourself."

"I'm not hard on myself, Michael." She looked up at him, but looked down before she went on, "I'm coming to see what he might have meant to me. It's me, I didn't make the effort. I took too long to get to know him really well."

Michael took his hands away and folded them across his chest. "If that's what you're starting to think, maybe he could've made more of an effort, too. You were together, after all."

"No, that's not true. It's me." Once more, she looked at his grave. She couldn't see the coffin. It looked like a gaping open wound and she felt the pain in her chest. "He gave himself to me, all of himself, and I didn't see it soon enough."

Michael put his hands in his pocket, put the toe of his shoe out, and played with a pebble, as if he knew this short soliloquy of hers displayed her grief without foundation.

"I'm alone," Rachel said, looking back to him. "I never realized that before. And it's my own fault."

Michael frowned, clearly at a loss for something to say to her, sighed and said, "Rachel, I..."

She interrupted before he could get started. "I don't even know what I lost. Maybe if I had listened to him more, thought more about what he wanted, he'd be alive today." She didn't really talk to them, she thought out loud.

Michael and Diane looked at each other, helpless to get Rachel beyond this moment.

Someone put a hand on her shoulder. The tall young woman who bore a startling resemblance to Joshua. She stared at Rachel, breathing hard, her mouth turned down and closed tight.

Rachel expected a hug and tears, but the woman put her arms out and shoved Rachel. Rachel fell backwards and landed on the gravel. She pushed herself up. The woman threw her down again to the gravel and stood towering over her. Rachel sat, her hands stinging, dazed and bewildered, unable to summon all her combat training.

"You bitch," the woman yelled. "First you give him cocaine, and that wasn't enough so then you killed him." She pulled her leg back to kick Rachel, but Michael rushed over and pulled the woman out of the way.

Diane stood in front of the woman, close to her, eyes on fire. "Who the hell are you?"

A small crowd began to form around them.

The woman wrestled free from Michael. "Sylvia Todaro. Joshua was my only brother. The only one left in my family. I warned him not to come up here, and now it's come true." She brushed off her suit, pulled on her jacket and shrugged to adjust it.

Rachel rubbed her knee then stood. Sylvia Todaro started to move toward her again, but Michael got in the way.

"Hold it," Michael said, "you have this all wrong."

"I don't have anything wrong. She drugged and murdered my brother. I heard his voice message. Look at her, no feelings at all. No tears. She's not even sad. I know why."

Diane looked at Rachel. "What voice message?" she said.

"Don't act so innocent," Sylvia Todaro said, looking first at Diane, then back at Rachel. "You know damn well. He left a message saying he was afraid of you."

"I don't believe you," Diane said, shifting her body toward Sylvia.

"You will." Sylvia, nodding as she spoke, turned to face Diane.

"It can't be, not Joshua," Rachel said. Not the Joshua she knew.

"He waited for you, do you know that? He thought everything of you. He was waiting to ask you to marry him. He waited! I told him to forget it, to leave you. But no, he said you loved each other, you needed more time to let him know. And now he's dead. My only brother is gone. All I had left of my family." She stopped, defeated.

Diane took out her badge and held it in front of Sylvia Todaro's face. "I'm sorry about your brother. We all are. No one more than Rachel. But you've got the wrong person. I suggest you get out of here."

Rachel blurted out, "No, wait. He did ask me to marry him. The last night I saw him."

Sylvia Todaro started to jump at Rachel again, but Michael held her back. She gave Rachel a long stare, eyes ablaze. She pulled free and walked away, shaking her head. Then she stopped, looked back at Rachel, and spoke. Her words came out in a torrent of rage. "Stop talking about him," she said, leaning forward, spittle coming out of her mouth. "You're a murderer!" A man put his hands on her arms and led her away. She looked down as she walked away with a wobble to her step.

Rachel buried her face in her hands. Joshua loved her and she didn't recognize it soon enough. She looked yet one more time at the dark hole of his grave site surrounded by flowers. Along with the soreness of the raw emptiness of her world, came the recognition that they didn't come any better than Joshua Todaro. Now she realized it, and now the time had passed for her.

She could have stayed with him, driven him downtown, saved him trouble finding someplace to park and then waited for him. They could have taken off right from downtown. The list of things she could have done to save him went on and on.

Diane put her arm around Rachel and pulled her away. "Come on, it's best we get out of here before somebody else comes out of the woods."

Michael and she each took hold of one arm and they started back to the car. They walked past tombstones and angels and statues and didn't pay any attention. They arrived at the end of the path and started to turn down the dirt road to where they had parked the car.

A familiar haughty voice came from behind. "Not so fast, McAlister!"

Rachel turned into the face of Ted Tourville, his eyes excited, arms folded across his chest. He'd obviously watched the whole confrontation with Sylvia Todaro. Behind him hovered the court jester Brian Phillips. In the distance were two squad cars, with men in blue standing next to them.

Tourville reached behind, pulled out a pair of handcuffs, showed them to everyone in triumph, and said, "It is my personal pleasure to arrest you, Rachel McAlister, for the murder of Joshua Todaro. And I'm sure you're not going to resist. After all, you're a professional. This time, my handcuffs will go where they belong."

The uniformed officers leaned in Rachel's direction to make sure she took this seriously. Her instinct told her to kick Tourville in the groin but Michael held one of her arms and Diane moved in front of her.

"So, Ted, where are the cameras?" Diane said.

He laughed as he spoke. "Aw, come on, Diane, you know that would be unwanted publicity for all of us. We want to respect everyone's privacy."

"Yeah, we know," she said. She lifted her head up and raised her eyebrows. "You don't want to be seen disrespecting it yourself, Ted."

Rachel struggled in Michael's grip.

"Don't do anything, Rachel. Don't make more trouble," Michael whispered.

Diane turned and looked at her. "Don't let it get to you, Rachel. You go with them and I will call Meredith for you."

Rachel saw the other people from the funeral, looking back at her, shaking their heads, and talking excitedly. What nerve she had coming to the funeral. The perfect exit, her hands behind her, manacled. Joshua's sister looked particularly satisfied.

Chapter 19

Deputy Amy Sheridan put a light touch on Rachel's arm as they entered the elevator inside the Superior Court building. She belonged to the sheriff's office. She worked for the courts, not the city. She didn't belong to the great establishment that Rachel had offended in killing a city councilman. So it wasn't surprising to Rachel that Amy could afford to show some sympathy.

Amy pressed her lips into a straight line and shook her head, a sign that she knew justice had not been served here. Rachel wanted to say something to Amy. She did feel some gratitude for Amy's treatment of her. But she held back because she tired of meeting old acquaintances in her new condition. And deep down, she worried that she misread Amy's behavior.

They were both quiet on the ride up to the sixth floor and administrative segregation for women, AdSeg to the initiated. Segregation from the general criminal population because the people on the sixth floor hadn't yet been convicted.

The elevator doors opened on to a long, gray concrete hallway. For one second, forgetting where she stood, Rachel felt the impulse to march out of the elevator with confidence, head held high, posture straight. She hesitated, then controlled herself. Instead, she walked straight ahead without thinking of how she looked to others.

On the left and right were four interview rooms, each

with a large glass window with crisscrossing wires in the door. Beyond them on either side were six one-room cells. There were no prison bars, just gray doors set in gray walls with a small window. A woman looked out of each one as they passed by, staring with curiosity. One of them looked familiar to Rachel, and seemed to be studying her face as she went by. Rachel didn't try to connect the woman with anything from the past. No one on the floor made a sound.

"Third on the left." Amy pointed to the door, unlocked it and opened it for her, standing out of the way. "I'm sorry about this," Amy said, "you know, around here we don't believe it."

"Thank you."

"We think you were right to go after Gil Hamilton. The police are covering up their own dirty work."

Rachel put her arm up to touch Amy, then thought better of it. But she forced a smile and nodded. "Thanks Amy, I do appreciate your sympathy. But I was there for a 911 call. I wasn't going after anyone in particular."

"Well, I'm sorry. I...we all want you to know that." Amy nodded and then said, "I'll come and get you when your lawyer is here."

"She will come to my cell?" That seemed odd. Lawyers talked to their clients in the interview rooms.

"It's not a cell, it's a room." Amy smiled.

Rachel raised her eyebrows. "Give me a break, Amy. Please." Then Rachel realized that Amy wanted to do her job and didn't articulate it very well. "I see, there are no bars." Rachel wasn't thinking straight and worried for one moment if she ever would. But in the end at the door to her room, she accepted that Amy stood with her, at least. And that meant she could rely on her.

Amy soon returned and knocked on the door without looking in. She stood in silence, a faceless silhouette in olive and khaki. The politeness unsettled Rachel, as if she shouldn't feel incarcerated. Amy didn't move, so

Rachel went out as if it were her own free will until the time when jurors decided her fate.

Amy pointed down the hall to an interview room with the door open. Again she followed Rachel. When Rachel moved inside, Amy closed the door. Rachel saw herself alone and getting familiar with interview rooms from the other point of view.

At first she sat at the small table, then she walked around the room like a caged cat. She reflected on the recent past. Rachel had gone through the arraignment, and pretrial motions, and Meredith had done her best, but to no avail and no surprise.

Meredith had made the standard attempt to get the charges dropped, but Judge Thomas Magnuson had scoffed at the idea.

Meredith had tried to get the venue changed, but Judge Magnuson had said that King County surely had enough jurors who were not obsessed with events from the past. Maybe if necessary, the jury pool might have to be a little bigger on this one. It happened.

Meredith had pointed out the huge amount of television coverage. The judge had said it wasn't something that would deprive jurors of their capacity to reason. At the suppression hearing, observers in the room had the nerve to snicker at Meredith when she made the obligatory motion to have evidence thrown out.

When it came to Rachel's freedom while Meredith prepared for trial, the judge had continued his matter-of-fact decision-making. We have after all, he had said, a murder trial, as if he were speaking for the tabloids. Rachel was a flight risk. Period. No more questions.

Maybe he had wanted to please the District Attorney. And maybe he wanted to appear tough, for future elections. The reasons didn't matter now.

Rachel, sitting on the bed, heard footsteps, interrupting her thoughts, expecting Meredith to walk in the room, and looked up to see Diane come in.

Diane smiled. A smile that Rachel knew meant solidarity but she also knew it came from deep within Diane's heart. "How are you holding out?" Hearing herself, Diane moved her hand up to her mouth, then brought it down. "Sorry to ask so bluntly." She closed the door. "Michael sends his love. We're both worried about you. And you know the kids send their love."

Rachel took her time answering the question, having to digest all the messages from the whole family. "So far I'm okay."

Diane continued. "We know you can take care of yourself. It's been a while since the funeral. You're not alone, Rachel. We're there for you always. You must know that."

Rachel stood and put her hand on Diane's arm. "Of course I know that. I have always known that. You and I have been through hell together."

Diane put her hand on top of Rachel's. Then she reached in her purse and pulled out a keychain. She handed it to Rachel.

Rachel inhaled sharply and put her hand over her mouth. Even though she had known that Diane planned to bring it, her heart skipped a beat. She took the keychain and held it tight in her hand, then looked at it, held it against her chest, eyes closed. The small chain held the bullet, beautiful no matter how damaged. The one Joshua had given to her. She looked at Diane with gratitude and said "Thank you for doing this."

Diane nodded. "No problem. As I said, you know I'm always here for you. But I've got to go. I just wanted to make sure you got it. Irene was very helpful when I told her that you wanted it." Diane's voice became cold and formal. Her face lost its color. "Anyway, your lawyer is here." Diane opened the door quickly and slipped out before Rachel could reply.

As Diane closed the door, Meredith slipped into the

room, nodding to Diane, who looked the other way. Meredith closed the door and leaned on it, standing for several seconds before Rachel, face blank.

Rachel sat quietly with the keychain, eyes closed, looking down. She imagined Joshua at the Pentagon handing it to her. She saw Joshua on the battlefield, bleeding, looking at her as she treated him. This bullet, this poor battered substitute for a wedding ring, could carry her safely through this ordeal.

As she turned it over in her fingers, she pinched it tightly so the ragged edges gave her a small amount of pain. A transfer of Joshua's pain to her.

"Everything okay?" Meredith raised her eyebrows and smiled.

Rachel looked up, but did not smile back. "I haven't thrown a tantrum, if that's what you mean."

"No, that's not what I meant. Diane didn't look happy when she left. I thought perhaps there was some new problem."

"No. Not with Diane. Never with her."

"I'm glad to hear that. The way you put it, it sounds like there's a problem with someone else."

"No, not at all."

"You know she's a witness for the prosecution."

"Who, Diane?"

"So, you've seen her deposition."

"Yes. I don't think it's going to lead anywhere. They're going to ask her about your confrontation with Detective Tourville at the scene of the crime, that's all. You had every right to be upset, so it won't mean anything. In fact it will help us."

"How is that?"

"It's this, Rachel. It will show your state of mind, how upset you were. That's what will impress the jury. So, let's go on."

Rachel understood what Meredith said, but it meant that she wouldn't be able to talk to Diane during the trial. As if she lost her best friend.

Meredith sat opposite Rachel and pulled her hair behind her ear, then put her briefcase on top of the table, and opened it and with great care, searching, selecting, took out a stack of papers and a legal pad. She sighed, and then looked at Rachel. Then she shook her hair and shrugged. The fragrance of roses filled the air.

"Here is where we are. I am going to lay out the whole case against you. It helps to keep you focused." Meredith smiled but her lips did not carry any warmth.

"You don't think I'm focused in my little room?" Rachel took a deep breath and forced herself to exhale all the air out of her lungs.

Meredith cleared her throat and looked as if she were trying to force Rachel to get focused. "No, Rachel, what I mean is that you have to have a good grasp of the whole case now, because we are close to the trial. It will give you confidence. It's about the jury's perception." She patted the top of the stack of papers.

"Please, spare me the legalese," Rachel said as she put her palms on the table.

Meredith narrowed her eyes. "You are going to have to be very honest with me, Rachel. No matter how difficult it is."

"Don't tell me what's difficult and what isn't." Then Rachel waved the comment away.

"Okay. Let's make it simple and clear. Let's go over the basic facts," Meredith said, raising her eyebrows. "To help us focus." Meredith raised her right forefinger in the air. "Number one, they have a bullet fired from your gun that they took out of his brain before he died."

Rachel raised her voice and put a hard edge on it. "He had a name, Meredith." She emphasized the word "name" she spoke.

Meredith spoke with a quiet and sympathetic voice. "I'm sorry." Meredith folded her arms across her chest, then sat up and put her pen down on the yellow legal pad. "This is not a college dorm discussion, Rachel."

Rachel's eyes flared and her mouth pursed in contempt. Her voice quavered when she spoke. "Does this look like a college dorm to you?"

Meredith sighed and spoke in a soft voice. "I'm sorry, we're getting away from our goal, Rachel. Once again, believe me, this is about keeping focused on the essential elements of the trial." She put her hands on the seat of the chair and pushed down, straightening her back and shoulders.

She studied the table, then looked back up and continued in a voice that sought Rachel's sympathy. "The jury needs to see us in agreement."

Rachel leaned back again, defeated in her attempt to make the discussion more sympathetic and less analytical. "The only thing I can say is that I have never fired that gun, ever. As you already know. I didn't even get around to going down to the test range. Whoever fired it wasn't me. You know all that, too."

Meredith fluttered her fingers as if to dissipate the words. Then she stood. "Rachel, we have discussed all this, yes. That's not the point. You and I are now making the basic case crystal clear. We need to focus our minds. I can't repeat that enough. The jury will notice."

Rachel pursed her lips, then nodded.

Meredith sat. "They found the gun in your backyard, wiped completely clean. I inquired of the one neighbor who had a view of your back yard and he never looked out that window. But we still need to tell the jury."

"Tell them what?"

"If you didn't do this, Rachel, somebody else did, and we need to get the jury to think about that."

Meredith ran her fingers down the paper in front of her, then continued. "Now, number two. Your gun killed him, you were in your office when the gun killed him, and the bullet went from your office to his apartment."

"The trajectory didn't go from my office, Meredith, it

155

went through my office. It's circumstantial." If Meredith wanted to be devil's advocate for the state, Rachel wanted to make her feel some resistance.

"The problem is, to a jury it's not circumstantial, it's incriminating. Somebody had to do it. Joshua Todaro was your fiancé, wasn't he? Of course the jury can think it was you. They can believe you did it if they believe the witnesses. The jury will not naturally think it was somebody else. It's up to us to get the jury to think about the other person." Meredith gestured to the notes on her legal pad. "But before we do that we have to look at the prosecution's whole case."

Rachel looked down at the pad and then up at Meredith.

Meredith tapped a line on the yellow paper. "Let's go on. Number three. Joshua's next-door neighbor, Mrs. Moralis. She heard you and Joshua arguing very strongly the night before the murder."

" We stayed in his apartment." Rachel thought for a moment back to the thunderstorm and standing in the window. She wondered if someone else had actually seen her. "We made love." She looked down at the floor, and spoke without looking up. "Then I went home in the early morning. We didn't argue." Rachel sat back in her chair, eyes closed, arms crossed. Her abdomen tightened and she put her hand on it.

Meredith waited while Rachel went through her reverie, then leaned over and pushed her gently on the top of the head. Rachel looked up at her, surprised for a moment to see her sitting there. It felt so easy to go back in time. So often.

"Tell me, exactly how did you break up with him?"

"There was no break up." This irritated Rachel. "Why are you saying that?"

"I mean, how did it happen? How did you leave him that night? Maybe you had a few words, you know, got angry about something. Nothing important, something small, irritating."

"No, I said I...we... I would see him in a few hours, that was all."

Meredith leaned forward, probing. "What did he say to that?"

"I don't know," Rachel said in an agitated voice. "He didn't say anything in particular." She thought back to the moment, resting her head in her palm, but nothing jumped out at her. "Just good night. He went back to sleep when I left." Was Meredith trying to fabricate details? "Is this going somewhere?"

"No, certainly not." Meredith's voice took on a comforting tone. She must have realized that this line of thought hit Rachel hard. "It goes where it goes. Go on."

"There's nothing more to say. I said good night, too."

"Then what did he say?"

"Nothing, I said. I went down the stairs and outside. Before leaving I went out to the front room and opened the window to let in cool air. That was all."

"What was his voice like? Do you remember that?"

Rachel sat back and folded her hands across her chest and waited a few seconds before answering. "My god, it was quiet, like mine. He was going back to sleep." She looked intensely into Meredith's eyes. "For God's sake."

Meredith met Rachel's gaze with a smile. "Yes. All right," she said, raising her eyebrows, "none of the other neighbors heard anything. So there was no argument between you. That's clear."

"Yeah, but let's say we did have an argument. What does that prove? "

"Mrs. Moralis says she heard you yell very loudly that you hated him, and, Rachel, she heard you say you would kill him."

"We didn't argue," Rachel said, shaking her head, her eyes becoming dark. Then she continued in a low voice, and she drew the words out. "We made love."

"Do you know Mrs. Moralis?"

"No, I don't. Never met her. Ask her if she's familiar with Ted Tourville."

"I don't think we need to worry about her. Even an inexperienced lawyer could destroy her confidence."

"You think so," Rachel said.

"I do think so, and I'm not worried."

"What about the voice message on Sylvia Todaro's phone? She mentioned it at the funeral." Rachel let her arms hang loose.

"She mentioned it, perhaps, but she doesn't have it now. There's no way to know."

"So where does that leave us?" Rachel said.

"We have the gun, the bullet, your office. And one more thing."

"Which is?"

"They found your DNA on his body. Hair, fluids."

"Like I said, we made love." Rachel didn't like hearing this from Meredith. She didn't like her talking about it. They had taken away all the privacy in her life. Holed up in AdSeg, nowhere, alone. Now even in nowhere there's no private existence. Nothing personal left. Rachel looked at Meredith. She had to hear this woman talking about Joshua like a specimen in a lab.

"And they found DNA from somebody else, a woman."

Rachel sat there stunned, staring into Meredith's eyes. Another woman? Not Joshua. It wasn't possible.

"Somebody else? Who?"

"They don't know. They know they found DNA evidence from two different women on him when they did the autopsy. Two different blood types."

"So what? Blood types? It's contamination from someone. It was planted, like my gun, like the cocaine."

But Rachel didn't accept her own reaction. Rachel felt locked in a crazy world. She got up and kicked the chair hard. It slammed against the table leg and hit the wall. She banged her palm hard down on the table then stood there looking down at it with both arms crossed tightly on her chest. She could feel her heart beating fast.

Amy opened the door, frowning and concerned. "Everything all right in here?" She looked at both of them, her hands hanging by the thumbs from her belt.

Meredith held up a palm to keep Amy away. "Yes, Rachel is in control of herself. It's just a chair."

Amy nodded, looked over at Rachel, righted the chair and set it next to the table. Then she closed the door.

"They can do DNA testing," Rachel said in a quieter voice, as she sat.

"Yes, but it has to be in a database for identification."

"But we could do something," Rachel said.

"What do you mean?"

"Don't you see? She is the killer. It was she who had the argument with Joshua and she who came back the next day and killed him. There have to be some clues somewhere." As she heard these words coming out of her mouth, Rachel felt a rising panic in her chest. And confusion in her mind, words swirling around and her breathing becoming shallow and fast. She forced herself to breath in and out in a slow deliberative pattern until she felt calm.

Meredith continued, seeming sensitive to the emotional turmoil that tormented Rachel. "But they don't have the other person. And there are some problems with it here."

"Such as?" Of course, there are problems here. I'm in a damn prison, aren't I? My fiancé is dead, isn't he? You're grilling me, aren't you? Ted Tourville is free, isn't he?

"Your gun was used to kill him and the bullet came from your office. You have to explain what the other person was doing in your office, when you know yourself she wasn't there."

Joshua kept coming into Rachel's head. She looked

down at the floor. They never fought. Ever. Of course, because he always did what she wanted and never asked for himself. And he had another life with somebody else?

Meredith touched Rachel's hand to bring her back.

Rachel stared as if she had an epiphany. "It's him, Ted. He stole the gun, killed him, and then hid it at my house."

Meredith put her hand on Rachel's arm and gave her another deep, piercing look. "How are we going to prove that?"

How many times had Rachel prepped prosecutors on the proof they had. And now, where did she end up, with nowhere to go?

"Let's keep the fundamental issue in mind, Rachel. Remember, we don't have to prove anything," Meredith said. "It's their burden of proof, not ours. But if we offer a defense that somebody else did it, we have to either get you an alibi or find the other person."

"The only person who saw me was Diane, and that was on the stairwell after the shot."

Looking at Rachel, Meredith put her hand on Rachel's arm and said, "See, it's a simple reason why they want her as a witness, nothing threatening at all." Meredith took her arm away and sat back.

Meredith sat quietly for a moment, waiting for Rachel to calm down. She talked without looking up, as if she intended to go on with or without Rachel. "The police didn't find any evidence of another suspect."

Rachel ignored her, going on as if she knew where this would lead. She wanted only to exonerate Joshua. "Did they interview anyone else?"

"No. You do have a point, Rachel. That's the key weakness in their case. They were only interested in you. And that is what we have to hammer home to the jury. But for now we've got to concentrate on the fact that you're on trial. They have means, motive, and opportunity. And it all points to you. We have to face reality. Listen to me."

Face reality? Reality was what she knew. Being framed was reality. Being in AdSeg was reality. Joshua was cheating on her. That was reality.

Rachel kept her head lowered. "Yes, I'm listening." But the world was spinning, her heart was beating, her ears were buzzing.

"I have to ask you about a plea bargain."

"What?." Rachel stood, shook her head, and waved her hands around as if she were going insane. "Plea bargains are for killers. Jesus. I guess I really misread you."

"Calm down. I had to do it."

"Bullshit, you didn't have to do it."

"Do you not know about this?"

"I guess you figured out what my answer is. Did you?" Rachel threw her arms up in disgust and looked away, as it dawned on her that she had lost mastery over her own life.

"Rachel, listen. It's time you thought about what the D.A. is doing."

"Meaning?"

"Meaning Berg doesn't want to take the chance you might be acquitted." Meredith shook her head and started writing on her pad. "Don't worry, Rachel, I'll tell him you declined. I've followed the rules. Let's move on."

Move on? To what? There something tightened around her neck. In her years with the Seattle Police Department she never once planted evidence, lied on the stand, forged documents, beat up a suspect, or threatened anybody. And she helped prosecutors win so many cases.

Diane and she both were beyond reproach. Impeccable. They could've written the book on ethics. And all the while everyone else was setting her up. Including Joshua. How soon did it start after he gave her the bullet in the Pentagon? As soon as they arrived back home in Seattle? As soon as they looked at each other on Pike Place?

Chapter 20

Administrative segregation quieted down in the evening. There were no distractions, nothing to give Rachel's mind a target. She had nothing to focus on except whatever floated around inside her head. And everything that arrived she shook away, throwing her hands up in disgust, standing up, sitting down, turning.

Anita brought dinner on a cart with quiet rubber wheels, served on a tray with an aluminum cover. She departed as quietly as she arrived, embarrassed to be in the room. When she came an hour later and picked up the tray, she did it with the same ghostly efficiency. A nod going in and a nod going out, recognition, but also a statement that Anita understood with relief it wasn't her who was locked up, awaiting trial.

Rachel spent the evening imagining Joshua, trying to remember how she felt when she looked into his eyes, looked at his face.

She tried to find the betrayal.

She tried to ponder her fate, the fate of a fool.

Joshua, no longer the person she had known. This fact, now clear, now heavy, now dark, now ominous.

She turned one way. She found it unbelievable to think that you were loved, and to learn the horrible truth that he wore a mask. She turned the other way and missed Joshua. She turned back again and hated him.

She tried to go over in her mind if there were any signs. Joshua did go on many business trips. He went to

L.A. often. But he hadn't gone on a trip for several days before his death. Why should that have any meaning? She knew she couldn't relive life locked up in this cell.

Yet, what did she know? She didn't follow him around. He didn't have to leave his apartment to betray her. How many people were in and out of there? How many women? She could never tell. She assumed they were women in real estate or construction. Or architecture.

She couldn't get clear in her head about Joshua because Rachel had believed him for such a long time. It had been ever since the battlefield in Afghanistan. She believed what he said to her because he looked at her with those big, deep shining eyes and his voice always had the ring of truth to it. It had never occurred to her that he would have been talking the same way to another woman.

She sat down with her elbows on her knees and her head resting on her hands. What was she thinking? Now it had come to this? She had started to imagine the possibilities for infidelity. She began to feel like she had given up, and wondering how much she knew about him at all. It didn't take very long to wonder how much she knew about herself. She couldn't think back to their last two nights together, because every time she saw him in bed he had his arms around someone else.

In bed with another woman instead of her. Each time the image appeared, she pounded her head with her fist as hard as she could, till her skull couldn't take the torment any more. What a fool she had been!

She stood, walked to the other side of the room and leaned against the wall. Maybe she had known it all along. Her own feelings just weren't on the surface. They were buried deep inside somewhere inaccessible. Or not there at all.

Rachel stood in the center of the room, head down, arms at her side, remembering. At the cemetery she felt like she had let him down. Now she knew that she had let herself down. Worse than that. She had let Tourville had tricked her and she didn't even know it.

She remembered when the lightning flashed and she appeared naked in the window. She had done it just for Joshua, no one else. Rachel, the complete sucker. Who else watched her that night? This woman? Maybe even Tourville, behind the curtains, laughing?

The night of the lightning. "Just for you, Joshua, no one else." That's right, just for him. And then, having played the fool, he got the fool's reward, his death. Two fools prowling around in the night. Ted fooled Joshua to fool Rachel. He set Joshua up to die so he could frame me, Rachel thought.

Who was Joshua anyway and what did she know about him? An architect. His marriage proposal. That fake exercise. An excuse to have Irish coffee. He could say anything and bail out whenever he wanted and not feel anything. He and Ted and the woman must have really laughed over that. Except Joshua didn't know that he laughed last because he laughed no more.

How else could Rachel find someone so compatible, so interested, across the street so that she could see him every day and evening through a big picture window. There were unlimited opportunities for Joshua to bump into her, to look at her, to be seen himself.

Now it seemed inevitable, the perfect trap and she the complete idiot. The person in the window across the street. The simple setup and she fell for it. Invisible because so simple.

Here she worked as a private investigator, with every tool possible to find out about someone. They did take a tiny risk that she wouldn't do that. It seemed they had her pegged pretty well. Ever since Gil Hamilton's death they have had time to work out all the details and construct the perfect crime. And she had this amazing confidence she had found her soul mate.

Bedtime approached, but Rachel looked down at the bunk with disgust. Sleep ran away from her. She sat on the edge of her bunk, her head in her hands. Footsteps approached outside, but she paid no attention. Then a quiet knock on her door made her sit up. She saw Amy's face in the window. Wondering what it could be so late, Rachel went to the door.

It opened slowly. Amy backed away and Diane Scanlan appeared. Her face appeared ashen, her eyes red, her mouth tight. Traces of tears trailed down her cheeks. Her hair flopped around in a ragged mess.

Rachel put her arms on Diane's shoulders and pulled her into the room.

"What are you doing here? You're a witness for the prosecution. You're risking your career coming to see me."

"I don't care." Diane said the words to herself, with bitterness.

"What's the matter?"

Diane pushed her away and wouldn't look her in the face.

"Is it Michael," Rachel said, "the kids? Tell me?"

Diane looked at her, then looked down again. She shook. "I have something terrible to tell you. Please sit down."

Rachel sat on her bed, elbows on her knees, hands supporting her head, waiting.

"This is not about my family. I only just found out myself, and I came over here as soon as I could."

"For God's sake, tell me." Was there some new damning evidence, Rachel wondered?

Diane sat and put one leg over the other and crossed her arms over her chest and pulled them tight. Tears started down her cheeks, her lips were trembling. She brought her hand up and smoothed one side of her hair back. She took a crumbled tissue out of her pocket and wiped her face. She fought an internal fight. She didn't want to say it, but she had to.

Rachel spoke in a voice that came from deep within her heart. "This is me, Diane. We've been through war together. There isn't anything you can't tell me."

Diane pushed Rachel's hands away and stood. She went to the corner by the door and turned around. "You are going to hate me."

Diane bewildered Rachel. How could there be hate between her and Diane? Unless... "Hate you? For what?" It suddenly hit Rachel. "What? Are you going to give testimony against me? Is that what it is?"

Diane shook her head violently. "No, no, of course not." She looked up at the ceiling as if pleading for an answer to come down to her.

Rachel stood. Her voice became firm. "Then what is it? Why can't you tell me?" Now the fear had left Rachel and anger took its place. "If you can't tell me, why did you come?" She turned away from Diane and went to the opposite corner of the small room. Sweat began to run down her back.

Diane looked at her in quiet for several seconds, pleading with her eyes. "You know there was DNA from a second person, a woman. They haven't been able to find out who it was."

"Yes, I know that. It's an important part of our defense. There's evidence of a second person, but they haven't gone after that other person." Rachel's voice showed exasperation. "Why are you so upset about telling me that? Does it have something to do with your testimony?"

"No, you know they are going to ask me how long I've known you, and what happened that day."

"So, what's the problem?" Rachel's voice became louder. And hard.

Diane took a deep breath and let it out in a long, controlled exhale.

"Well, first of all, they are going to ask me on the

witness stand if you were the maid of honor at my wedding."

Rachel sighed and gave an exaggerated slump. "I know that already. That isn't very damning, is it?"

Diane looked away toward the wall. "No, not if that were it."

"Okay, I don't see why all this should be so upsetting."

"And they are going to ask me how long we have been friends."

Rachel took her head in both hands and walked back and forth before speaking in a voice too loud for the distance between them. "Of course, Diane, don't you see? I know where this is going. Then they're going to ask you how I killed Gil Hamilton."

As Rachel spoke, Diane shook her head and bit her lip.

She waited several seconds. "The DNA. It's mine."

An ice pick stabbed at Rachel's heart. She screamed, "Your DNA? You killed him!"

"No!" Diane screamed back. "I'm being framed, too!"

Rachel lunged at her. Diane held her hands in front of her face as Rachel landed against her and slammed her against the wall. They crumbled to the floor. The door opened and Amy came in and pulled Rachel off of Diane.

Diane got up and went to the door, but before she left she said "It's not true. I'm innocent."

"Go to hell!"

Amy held Rachel down until Diane had left, then she let Rachel stand. "I should not have let her in here. It's my fault for breaking the rules. But I did it for you." She guided Rachel over to her bunk and forced her to sit. "Are you all right now?"

Rachel nodded quietly.

Amy walked out but kept her eye on Rachel until the door shut.

Rachel slumped over, rested her elbows on her knees, and put her head in her hands. She rocked up and down. Joshua's betrayal. Diane's betrayal. The sickness in her, the burning hurt in her heart. The emptiness of her life. She thought, "Why didn't I die in Afghanistan?"

Chapter 21

Meredith came into the interview room the next morning with a grim face. "Rachel, I spent all yesterday evening and long into the night thinking about your defense. You know, we have a major complication."

"I'm quite aware of it."

Meredith looked surprised. "You are?"

"Diane came to see me last night."

"Last night? She came here? Isn't that a big risk for her?"

"Yes, but she came. She told me that they finally made a match for the second person's DNA. She told me it was hers." Rachel felt the back of the chair pressing against her shoulder blades. A confusing sequence of images of Diane in Afghanistan and at home flooded her mind. "You know, I was maid of honor at her wedding. Alan Berg has a motive."

"I don't think this is good for the prosecution."

"And why is that?"

"Think of her testimony. She is automatically a suspect. We have a potent weapon for the defense."

"I don't see that."

"Listen to me. Let's say she admits to being Joshua's lover. She is in the same position as you. If you are jealous, then she is jealous. She's the second woman and she's a real live person."

"But you've read her deposition. She was in the precinct all night and at the time of the shooting. There will be several police witnesses to back her up."

"Rachel, don't forget your own background as a detective. How hard would it be for her to find somebody to do the job? Remember, Joshua proposed to you the night before he was murdered. It's the perfect motive for her, too."

"So, how are we going to make our case?"

"It's clear. If she testifies about being Joshua's lover, there's her motive."

"What if she denies it?"

"Is that what she's going to do? Deny that she was Joshua's lover?"

"I don't know. I'm asking, what if she does? What then?"

"Then she has lost her credibility. Under cross examination, she will have to admit under oath that she was framed. The same as you. Either way, she helps us. I will enjoy crushing her as a witness."

Rachel listened to "crushing her" and thought, I have no one left but myself.

"But you must believe in yourself," Meredith said, "because the jury will be able to see that. The importance of that cannot be stressed enough." Meredith put her pen down on the table, adjusted her glasses, and focused on Rachel's eyes. "But let's go on." When she had Rachel's attention, she continued. "There are three ways the defense can win a criminal trial. The first way is to impeach the evidence. The second is to impeach the witnesses. The third is to delay. We'll not have to do the third."

Rachel stood and leaned against the wall. "Why not?"

Meredith seemed to want to smile, but held it back. "This is a rush to judgment, Rachel. If we delay, we lose that argument."

Rachel nodded in agreement. Meredith pointed to the chair and Rachel sat.

"Let us begin with the first way," Meredith said. "The

hard evidence is the bullet and the trajectory. I don't see what we can do about that."

Rachel saw this hard evidence as a wall closing in on her. "This is exactly what they think it is. It is a revenge killing except it's not me. It was Tourville."

"Anything's possible at this point, Rachel. But that's not getting us anywhere, is it."

"Maybe they've broken the chain of evidence."

"No. The gun is all properly signed out, taken into custody, put in the evidence room, taken out for testing, put back in order. There's nothing there."

"The chain started in the operating room," Rachel said.

"You are right, but the neurosurgeon took the bullet out of Joshua's head and did the paperwork perfectly. It is the heart of their case that the bullet came from your gun."

Meredith threw her pen down on the table again and put her hand out, palms open. "Notice now, we are discussing the second way to defend. A good defense attorney can get detectives and cops confused on the stand. If Ted Tourville has gotten people to commit perjury, we'll find it out, I promise you."

Meredith seemed really sure of herself. But Ted loved the witness stand. And all the state's witnesses were going to be prepped and primed. Rachel shook her head. "They are not going to leave it all up to a nervous cop on the witness stand."

"It does not have to be a nervous cop, it has to be a cop who has to answer a lot of questions."

"How is that?"

"If the witnesses sound confused, the jury will think there's reasonable doubt."

"And how are we going to get the witnesses to sound confused?"

"A complicated series of questions. Eventually they are going to look and sound confused. Because they will be."

Rachel shook her head and raised her voice, her eyes wide open and glaring. "You mean our defense is that we are going to dazzle them with bullshit?"

Meredith clearly didn't like the insult. "Don't be stupid. Think like me, Rachel. These are jurors, not rocket scientists."

"But the evidence is simple."

"That's not the point."

Rachel threw up her hands in frustration. "Then what is the point?"

"The point is that witnesses, to the jury, start to look confused. They frown. They wait too long to answer, trying to remember what they said before." Meredith looked left and right, searching for more examples. "They look over at the prosecutor. They hesitate, then rephrase things. The jury sees them acting confused."

"I hope you're right." Rachel sat back, her arms folded, eyes down.

Meredith's voice took on a tone of confidence. "I know I am right. It is not an art. It is the science of psychology. Get a policeman on the witness stand and make him answer 'No' three times in a row, and he will lose his cool."

"I still hope you're right."

"We'll get Ted Tourville on the stand. We'll rip him to shreds. We'll focus on his hate. He has completely ignored the possibility that someone else could be involved."

Meredith got up and started to leave, then stopped. "Pay attention to me, Rachel. Think of Ted on the witness stand. Now think of their strategy. Sure, the gun, the trajectory. Have they even looked into the possibility it was someone else? No. Should they have? Yes."

"Okay, and?"

"Okay and, the next question for Ted on the stand is that. Why did you not pursue any other investigation?"

She pounded her fist on the table. "You should have investigated."

She punched the air with her fist. "But you didn't do that, did you? Why not?"

She turned and shook her head several times. "Why did you not round up the usual suspects?"

She pointed her index finger at Rachel. "Because for you there was only one suspect."

Meredith stretched her arms out wide, before an imaginary jury. "That's why he didn't do a complete investigation, Rachel, because he was only interested in you."

She picked up her briefcase and stuffed her documents back in. "And that's what the jury will understand. That's what we'll pound home. And Ted will help us."

She turned back before leaving. "Remember, Ted is the key. He is responsible for the rush to judgment. That's what will trip him up. I will catch him in a lie. The jury will see the witness lie. The case will fall apart."

She stopped, then opened the door. "Tourville will not have his revenge!"

Meredith started to leave, then one more time turned around. "You will be wearing a dark suit, won't you? The continuity of fabric increases your size and makes you look more formal. More innocent." She closed the door.

Chapter 22

On the first day of trial, Meredith wore a dark gray well-tailored and fashionable-looking pants suit, with a simple white silk blouse. She had combed her hair perfectly down either side from a part in the middle. Nothing out of place. Her eyebrows seem bushier and darker than before, and she seemed extraordinarily tall. She wore no jewelry, which made her Rolex stand out even more.

Meredith sported glasses with the label Kawasaki very visible. Her nails were cut short, unpainted but glistening. She appeared intimidating. She nodded approvingly at Rachel's matching navy blue jacket and skirt and light blue blouse.

Rachel looked to the back of the courtroom. Michael nodded to her with a forced smile, as if he could make up for Diane's treachery. Several seats away from him sat a woman in a bright red dress, gold necklace and large gold earrings. The most visible person in the room.

Sylvia Todaro, Joshua's sister, her face bitter and grim. She, too, nodded when Rachel looked her way. Rachel held Sylvia's gaze, and Sylvia glared back at her, not moving, not changing. Rachel kept her stare until she heard the bailiff's voice.

The bailiff told everyone to stand up when the door behind the judge's desk opened, and they all dutifully sat in unison when the judge told them to. No mistake about who owned this room.

The air overhead cooled the room in silence.

Naturally, the judge, Linda Watson, had on a voluminous black robe. And she controlled the thermostat behind her. She could keep her courtroom as cold as she wanted.

Judge Watson knew Rachel. She had been in this judge's courtroom often enough, testifying about the behavior of criminals. Rachel always gave straightforward testimony, well supported, and respectful.

Rachel did not argue with herself or Meredith when they got Watson for the judge because she knew her to be very levelheaded, a no-nonsense kind of judge. She had a reputation for fairness to both the state and the defendants. Very few litigators got away with crap in any trial she presided over.

She talked to the jurors and explained details to them. When there were sidebars, she listened very carefully and made a quick decision. Her decisions landed on the right side of the law and evidence. If you had to be a defendant in a courtroom, you would want her to be the judge.

It was obvious on her face that Meredith sensed the courtroom luck, too, because she felt that her kind of defense would play well and the judge would see it that way. Even though there were going to be objections at every step of the process, Rachel believed Judge Watson would enjoy watching the defense make the prosecution witnesses sound confused. That amounted to keeping the judge intellectually involved. This thought instilled in Rachel some confidence in Meredith.

Rachel turned around to look at the rest of the spectators. Reporters were there with their notebooks, one person with colored pencils and a pad, not many people from the police department. The chief probably kept them all away so that it might look like the police department had no dog in this fight.

The jurors were no doubt the best they could get

when they couldn't get the venue changed. The jurors looked at Rachel, most of them. As far as she could tell they were just curious. None of them had had a serious run in with the police outside of ordinary traffic tickets. They all swore up and down that they could be fair and make a judgment based on the evidence alone, but you never knew what might happen once they went into the jury room.

Judge Watson welcomed the jurors and thanked them for their service. She knew that none of them wanted to be here. She apologized for the inconvenience, for the interruption to their lives, apologized for the delays that had occurred, and always occurred in trials of this nature. She made it clear that she, at least, sat on their side.

Alan Berg, the prosecutor, wouldn't even look at Rachel and Meredith, except for one scornful glance clearly for the jury's benefit. He wore his black suit with red power tie. The suit gave him a little increase in height to reduce the impact of his expanding waistline.

He wanted to make sure that everybody knew that if he had the power, Rachel would already be on the way to death row. He thought this trial would help his career big-time, move him up the ladder, and get him ready for a political race. The whole police department and district attorney's office counted on him to make a spectacle of her. They put him here to make sure it happened.

Put your best foot forward. And your best bulldog.

Berg assumed a professorial demeanor behind the podium. His opening statement sounded straight-forward. Rachel's gun fired the bullet that blasted her window. As she occupied her office. Diane's lipstick would be devastating in showing the motive and Ted Tourville would tell the jury how Rachel's guilt had driven her to hide the gun in her back yard. He said it in a simple matter-of-fact way, with his voice calm and even.

Rachel had watched the juror box as Berg mentioned Diane's name, her hands clenched on her lap. Their faces showed that they had no idea how Diane's behavior had changed from heroic to monstrous.

Of course, he also stated the whole case as if he got it all from stone tablets on Mt. Sinai. He had talked to juries enough times to sound like he knew his material, friendly, turning to them often, smiling, and he put himself in the company of the judge as he ended by thanking them for their service.

Berg didn't have a smoking gun. Meredith capitalized on this. The prosecutor had a number of experts who were going to fall all over each other about very few details. This was the opening she wanted.

Meredith stood, put her arm on Rachel's shoulder and held it there for a second, then walked out to the middle, facing the jurors. She took her glasses off and folded her hands in front of her and stood, quiet, motionless, looking at each juror in turn. Then she put the glasses back on and shook her head for a moment.

She impressed the courtroom with her height. The jurors in the front row had to lift their heads up to her. Eight males, four females. She had to give it to Meredith on that, Berg didn't even see it coming.

"I also want to thank you all for what you're doing. There's nothing more important a person can do than serve on a jury. It is not easy, and it takes more time than we all would like." She took a few steps to the right.

"You have heard the state's case laid out before you. But you haven't heard everything. There's another person in this courtroom, who is invisible. The prosecutor does not want you to hear about this other person. It is the person who killed Joshua Todaro." She walked to the end of the jury box, turned and faced them at an angle and put a hand on the railing.

"The state has told you that my client had the means,

motive and opportunity. But they didn't tell you this, that someone else also had means, motive, and opportunity." She walked back to the center of the jury box and turned and faced them directly.

"That other person is invisible because he or she is not sitting here today before you. Why not?" She shrugged and held her hands out, palms up. "Because the state made a rush to judgment. They investigated only one person. They have a huge staff. They have great laboratories full of sophisticated machines. But they chose to pursue only my client. They didn't look for other leads. They only considered my client."

She came back over to Rachel and stood in front of the table.

"They have chosen a single-minded pursuit of Rachel McAlister. Why?" Meredith shook her head slowly side to side. "You will hear testimony from the officer in charge of the investigation, Detective Theodore Tourville."

Meredith continued. "What you will not hear about it is the reprimand that he received while he was on duty. When you hear about it, it will become clear to you why there has been a rush for judgment. In fact, this is malicious prosecution."

Berg shifted in his seat, put one hand on the table, looking agitated, clearly wanting to interrupt, not sure what he should do. He didn't need to do anything. His body language said enough to the jury.

"There's evidence that two women were involved with the victim. You will hear about the jealousy of the one, but not the jealousy of the other."

Meredith walked out to the middle again and stood in the center of the room facing the jurors.

"When you have heard all of the evidence, ladies and gentlemen of the jury, you will then be able to see why my client is innocent. Why you must return a verdict of not guilty. She is innocent. There's no reasonable doubt about that."

Meredith looked at each juror in turn. "Thank you. I have one more statement to make. The state has a monumental challenge to prove my client is not innocent of these charges. The very wise men who wrote our Constitution and Bill of Rights gave us sacred protections, ladies and gentlemen. It is your duty here not merely to pass judgment on an individual. It is your sacred duty to uphold the Constitution and the presumption of innocence."

Rachel had seen a lot of juries paying attention to testimony and opening and closing statements, and she had a good read on this one. They liked Meredith. She mentioned innocence enough to hit home without overdoing it. There's nothing like a solid professional to make the jury pay attention. In a courtroom where everyone up beyond the railing seemed to be professional, Meredith stood out.

She brilliantly disguised what she planned. As she looked at all her sticky notes that identified the jurors, she thought things that were off everybody else's radar. Meredith walked back to the defense table and sat. The jurors sat still, watching her come back to the defense table, certainly impressed. For now.

Judge Watson waited a few moments, arranging papers on her desk, then leaned over and had a short conversation with her clerk. The court reporter came over and joined them. Then she nodded, sat back, and told Berg that he could call his first witness. He stood and smoothed back his hair, straightened his tie and buttoned his coat like some sort of parliamentarian. He turned back toward the door.

"The state calls Dr. Neil Golden." He said it so loud Rachel thought he yelled at the bailiff.

Dr. Neil Golden walked like a military man through the courtroom and looked like he was receiving his commission when the clerk swore him in. He sat tall and scientific-looking in the witness chair. He dressed in a blue pinstripe suit and striped red tie. His pale skin showed freckles. He wore square-rimmed glasses, which were tailor-made to accent his square jaw line. All the jurors sat up straight, facing the witness chair.

"Good afternoon, Dr. Golden. Thank you for taking the time to provide your expert testimony to us," Berg said.

"You are welcome." Golden showed the same self-confidence he would have shown in the operating theater.

Berg for his part showed great deference to Golden, speaking to him in almost hushed tones. Just loud enough that the jury could hear, but in low, respectful tones. "Could you please tell us where you work and what your position is?"

"I am a neurosurgeon on the faculty of the University of Washington, Seattle."

"Are you a professor, Dr. Golden?"

"Yes I am a professor."

"What do you do as a professor, Doctor?"

Rachel whispered to Meredith to try to get her to object to this useless information, but Meredith whispered back that it would just make the jurors pay more attention to Golden. Better to get this over with. Rachel sighed and shrugged her shoulders. She looked at the jurors. They seemed bored with this testimony so far.

"I am the chair of the Department of Neurology." Golden said this in the most straightforward manner. He didn't think his position needed to be embellished, whatever Berg tried to do.

"Do you have another position at the University?"

"Yes, I am the head of the Institute for Neural Research."

"So, is it correct to say you're on the cutting edge of research, Dr. Golden?"

"Certainly, it is the leading institute on matters of the brain."

Well, interesting. Rachel wondered if Berg gave him a secret sign to start using words the jury could understand.

"One last question about your background, Doctor. Do you perform brain surgery very often?"

"Yes, of course, three days a week."

"What kind of brain surgery do you do?"

Golden sat silent for a moment, thinking. "I don't think that's an appropriate question. Surgery of every kind is complicated."

Chastened, Berg backed up a step before continuing. "Turn your attention to the victim, Joshua Todaro. He was brought in to the emergency room. Is that where you work?"

"No. I saw him in the operating room."

"Yes, we understand that, Doctor. Can you describe the operation for the jury please?"

Golden turned and faced the jury. Head high, eyes clear. "He was brought into an operating room at Harborview. He had a bullet wound in his head. The bullet had entered the back of his head and was lodged in his brain. To give you the basic details, I cleaned the area around the wound, and then I extracted the bullet from the brain. I was in the process of irrigating the tunnel produced by the bullet when the patient expired on the operating table."

"Doctor, can you tell us exactly what the victim died of?"

"He died of a combination of factors. There was major injury from the bone fragments and lead penetrating the skull and brain tissue. And the brain was beginning to swell, leading to intra-cranial pressure."

"Thank you, Doctor. There's then, no doubt that the victim died of the gunshot wound."

"No, there's no doubt. The brain shut down with the

trauma that occurred. As I said, it wasn't the bullet alone, it was the bone fragments, which contributed to the hemorrhaging."

"And this hemorrhaging was on a massive scale, didn't you say?" Berg clearly tryied to act like he knew something about brain surgery.

Meredith finally stands. "Your Honor, I object. We've already heard what the victim died of."

Judge Watson clearly agreed. "Objection sustained. Get on with it, Mr. Berg."

Berg looked over at Meredith, nodding. Then he turned back to the witness. "One final question then, Doctor Golden." Berg went to the evidence table and picked up a small plastic bag. He came over to the defense table and showed Meredith and Rachel. It contained a bullet.

"Is this the bullet you took out of the victim's head?"

Golden took the plastic bag and looked at it. "That's our signature on the label."

Berg then introduced the bullet into evidence and laid it back on the table.

"Thank you very much, Doctor. We appreciate you giving up your time to come here and give your testimony. I have no further questions." Berg sat, looking satisfied.

Meredith stood again. "I have a few questions, Dr. Golden." She walked out in front of the table to the middle of the floor.

"When you operated on Mr. Todaro, did you notice any bruises, any marks on the skull around the area where the bullet entered the skull?"

"No. You must understand, he was brought in under extreme emergency circumstances. When I stepped up to the body, the area around the entrance wound had already been irrigated. I had only one thing on my mind."

"Thank you, Doctor. One other thing. What did you

do with the bullet?"

"I put it into a tray."

"What happened to the bullet after that?"

Golden looked puzzled and frowned at Meredith. "I can't tell you exactly. The tray was taken away. I was doing other things."

"So you don't really know, Doctor, if the bullet you were shown is the one taken out of his head?"

"No, of course not. It looks like it, but I don't keep track of these things."

"Thank you very much. I have no further questions." Meredith came back to the defense table and placed her hand on Rachel's shoulder, letting it rest there for a moment before sitting down. One or two jurors seemed to notice the gesture.

"You are excused, Dr. Golden," The judge said.

Berg stood. "One moment, please, Your Honor. Redirect, if I may."

"Proceed."

Berg picked up the plastic bag again. "Do you recognize the first signature on the bag?"

"Yes, the first one, it's the signature of Helen Robb, the head operating room nurse."

"Thank you again, Doctor." Berg sat down, a satisfied smirk crossed his face.

"Do you have any re-cross?" Judge Watson said, looking over her glasses at Meredith.

Meredith stood, took a sip of water, and smoothed out her suit. "Not at this time, Your Honor."

"Your Honor, at this time the state calls Dr. James Chew to the witness stand."

Chapter 23

The bailiff went outside again, sighing and walking like the whole thing bored him. He returned with James Chew, the head of the crime lab for SPD.

Chew came in quietly, unassuming, you could hardly hear him. His brown herringbone three-piece suit had an impeccable fit, along with his cream button-down shirt and restrained, single color beige tie.

Berg stood as soon as Chew sat down. He walked out in front of his table and paused for theatricality. His head down, he appeared to be thinking, then he spoke. "Dr. Chew, thank you for testifying today," Berg said. "Could you explain your position, please?"

"I am the head of the Seattle Crime Laboratory."

"Could you explain for the jury, please, what the laboratory is?"

"Yes, I'd be happy to."

He took justifiable pride in this lab. Rachel had seen the work he did many times. The lab had been the backbone of the D.A.'s list of convictions. Maybe, just maybe, the bigger they are the harder they fall, she hoped.

"We have a laboratory of about 13,000 square feet, with DNA testing, personal identification devices, electron microscope, and computerized forensics."

"Thank you, Dr. Chew. It's important to know that your laboratory is..." Berg stopped, searching for the right word. "Complete. As a doctor, would you tell us, what is your degree?"

"I have a PhD in criminology from UW."

"Dr. Chew, how big is your staff?"

"We have twelve people working full time analyzing evidence."

"All right, then. Let's say this. You have a very high-tech lab, Doctor Chew, don't you?"

"The latest high-tech equipment."

Berg went and picked up the plastic bag with the bullet it in, and brought it over to Chew.

"Let's get to the nitty-gritty. Doctor, do you recognize this bullet?"

"I see that the evidence bag has our laboratory signature on it."

"So your laboratory has analyzed this bullet?"

"Yes, we have."

"What did you use to do that?"

"We used our Scanning Electron Microscope."

"Could you explain a little bit, not getting too technical?"

"Certainly. The Scanning Electron Microscope can analyze details as small as one millionth of a meter. Nothing escapes the microscope's analysis. Our staff watches on the computer screen while the analysis is in progress."

"Doctor Chew, I have another evidence bag here, which I wish you to also look at." Berg went back to the evidence table and picked up the plastic bag that had Rachel's gun in it.

"Do you recognize this evidence as well?"

"Yes, it also has our signature on it. It is the gun that fired this bullet."

So what did they hope to gain, all that with the microscope? They didn't tell the jury how it related to the case. It served only to impress the jury. Rachel looked at Meredith and opened her eyes to question it, but Meredith smiled and nodded.

Meredith leaned over and whispered close to Rachel's ear. "I'll get it in the closing statement."

"Objections count, Meredith."

"I'm not going to waste time on minor technical stuff." Meredith put her hand on Rachel's arm. "Bear with me."

Berg twisted a little to the left, managing to put everyone's attention on the defense table, as if he were waiting for Meredith and Rachel to finish, then continued. "How do you know that, Dr. Chew?"

"We used our new gunfire tracking system."

"New gunfire tracking system? What is that?"

"It's called Drugfire. Drugfire scans bullets and casings for every make of gun."

"Every test firing?"

"Yes. The Crime Lab fires about 1,500 guns a year, every handgun booked as evidence. The database keeps growing."

"I see, and were you able to make a match?"

"Yes. We are certain that the bullet was fired by this gun."

"How exactly, Doctor Chew, were you able to determine that this bullet," he held up the bullet in his left hand, "was fired by this gun?" He held up the gun in his right.

"It's automatic," Chew said. "Drugfire matched the microscopic marks on the bullet and cartridge cases."

The eyes were glazing over on some of the jurors. But some of the men were paying close attention.

"This is automatic?"

"Yes, completely." Chew nodded in rhythm with his words.

"And this bullet, the one in the evidence bag, was it in bad shape?"

"No, it was very well formed." Rhythm nodding again.

"So you didn't have to do any extraordinary testing

or analysis on this bullet and this gun?"

"No, with our system, we didn't take long to make a positive identification. We test fired Ms. McAlister's gun with a different bullet and used that bullet for comparison."

"Is that always the case?"

"I'm not sure what you mean."

"I mean, can you do this with every gun and every bullet."

"No, not every gun. It doesn't work well with Glock pistols, for example."

"I see. But does it work well with this make of gun, the Walther P99?"

"Absolutely."

Meredith stood in a hurry. This time she forgot to take her glasses off. She opened her arms wide, palms up and slowly shook her head, raising her voice. "Your Honor, I object. There has been no statement that this gun belonged to my client."

Berg looked at Meredith and frowned, then moved toward the judge as if to speak. Chew didn't wait for him. He looked at Berg and held his hand up as if to stave him off. "It was identified as McAlister's gun. And to be sure, I checked the registry myself."

Berg nodded. "You mean, it was all in the chain of evidence?"

Chew nodded back, self-satisfied. "Of course." He looked over to the defense table, making sure everyone saw that he said something beyond doubt.

Meredith sat and whispered to Rachel. "I will bring this up again in cross. They knew it was your gun. They could do what they wanted."

Rachel squirmed in her chair, then thought of the jury and stopped it. This didn't help. The gun supported their whole case and they got it in without a whimper. The jury sat in rapture. Rachel's gun. They didn't need to hear anything else. Her heart sank and she felt very close to Joshua at this moment.

For the first time the thought occurred to her that he waited for her. Somewhere, he watched over her, held her in his hands—

Then his betrayal entered her consciousness and—A juror coughed and took Rachel back to the courtroom.

She thought of Tourville later on testifying he found her gun hidden – that would be his word, hidden, meaning guilty - in her back yard, but now, after this interchange with Chew, Berg hardly even needed that. And this had a solid impact on the jurors over there. She saw it in all twelve of them.

Meredith touched Rachel on the forearm and whispered, "This is about the jury. They need to know the prosecutor is not careful."

Berg waited, again making sure the jury saw Rachel and Meredith huddled together. He turned back to his witness. "You were saying, Doctor, that the process is completely digitized, is that correct? Not touched by human hands, so to speak?"

"Yes, that's right. Completely digitized. The bullet in the evidence bag and the bullet test fired from the gun are separately scanned and digitized and the computer makes the comparison."

"So, for example," Berg turned to the jury and looked up and down the row before proceeding, "let's say somebody in your lab, this is hypothetical, but bear with me here, Doctor. Say someone in your lab who had something against Ms. McAlister, there was no chance that he could make a visual comparison and stretch the evidence. Is that possible?"

Rachel realized the prosecution had anticipated the defense strategy and her body stiffened.

"Absolutely not. We wouldn't even think of that. It doesn't even come into play. A digitized system is beyond human interference. The computer never lies."

"So you can say, Doctor Chew, that the Crime Lab

has determined with certainty that this gun, the defendant's gun, fired this bullet."

"Yes."

"Thank you very much, Doctor." Berg turned, then looked back at Chew. "Thank you, Doctor Chew. I'm sorry to say again. One last question. You analyzed the gun, did you not?"

Chew looked puzzled.

Berg planned on dragging this out as long as he could. Once the jury had connected the gun to Rachel, they would be receptive to all sorts of inferences. And if the defense tried to object, it would only drive the point home. Berg went all offense and Rachel could not see any defense in sight with any power. Certainly not from Meredith. Not yet. It made the cross examination of Tourville that much more powerful. The final impact.

"What I mean is, this particular gun, what make and model is it, did you say?"

"It's a Walther P99."

Meredith started to rise, but Berg hurried on.

"I see. Is there only one kind of Walther P99?"

"No, there are several kinds."

"These several kinds. What are they?"

"There's the Carl Walther German-made P99, and the Smith and Wesson SW99 made in this country."

"And which version is the gun used to kill Joshua Todaro?"

So, there it is. Another chance to let the jury hear about the victim.

"It is a standard German P99."

"Standard?"

"Yes, standard. It is produced at a factory in Germany, without any special adjustments. It is off the German shelf, so to speak."

Another nail. Now the jury saw that Rachel treated firearms with expertise. She might as well have been wearing an Idaho militia uniform. When she bought that

190

gun it was nothing more than a gun, it was a newer model, maybe something more than she needed, but that didn't matter here. Once again, if they objected here it would clearly be a case of protesting too much.

"Any other characteristic, Doctor?"

"It's a quick action trigger."

"Quick action trigger? What's that?"

"The quick action trigger is often used by police tactical units. It's a hammerless pistol. It has a partially preloaded striker. Ready to go."

"Used by police tactical units, you say? Why is that?"

"Because they are often in dangerous situations with little time to react. It works faster, that's all."

"Tell me, Doctor, what use would a private investigator have for a pistol used by SWAT teams?"

"I don't know. You would have to ask the investigator."

The jury now knew Rachel as a trigger-happy cop. The jury followed this carefully. Not too technical. More like a television show.

"Is this common?"

Rachel turned to Meredith and whispered, "Can't you object?"

Before she could respond, Chew continued on. "Not too common. It's the gun used by James Bond."

Judge Watson turned to the defense table. Clearly, she could see that Berg was adding layers of innuendo. Meredith finally stood.

"Objection, Your Honor. There's no relevancy."

Watson turned to the jury box. "Objection sustained. The jury will disregard the last statement."

Meredith sat and whispered to Rachel that the jury could see grandstanding anyway and it didn't amount to much. Berg looked at Rachel with a satisfied smirk. Then he became serious and turned back to look at the effect his handiwork had on the jurors. He stood and waited a long moment while he buttoned his coat.

"I have no more questions, Your Honor."

Judge Watson nodded to Berg and then turned once again to our table.

"You may begin your cross-examination Ms. Rawlings."

Meredith turned to the judge. "Thank you, Your Honor."

Chapter 24

Meredith looked at Chew, then turned and faced the jury, got their attention, then led their gaze back toward Chew. "Dr. Chew, you stated you have a degree from UW. Is that right, did I get that right?"

"Yes, you did." He spoke with his head high and a slight, but slow, nod.

She met his nod with one of her own. "But the University of Washington does not have a graduate program in criminology." She turned her palms up and shook her head. The jury watched this melodramatic act with some skepticism. "I am confused. Can you clarify this for me?"

Interesting, Rachel thought. She knew more than expected. And now the jury also showed more interest, leaning forward, not so skeptical.

"Of course, I would be happy to." Chew smiled, looking very condescending. "I didn't say I have a degree from the University of Washington. It's from the University of Wyoming."

Meredith stopped and took a breath. She brought this on herself, clearly, but she had to continue. "Really? A PhD program in criminology?"

"Well, of course the PhD is in education. It's a self-directed program."

"I see. Where is the program, exactly?"

"Casper. It has one of the best graduate programs in criminology in the country. I'm actually an adjunct faculty member there."

"Faculty member? In Wyoming? That far away?" Meredith tried to keep this going against all odds. She should have given up on it. It wasn't important enough. He had enough machines in his lab to do the job, he didn't need this educational boost that she afforded him. And the jury could see that.

"Yes, sure, but that's why I'm adjunct. My seminar is quite popular with crime scene specialists from Salt Lake and Denver."

"Thank you, I am sure it's a fine school. I am sure they have a fine equestrian program as well."

Berg stood with arms out and head shaking in theatrical exasperation. "Objection, insulting, not relevant, and besides, that's not a question."

Chew laughed. "I don't mind. I get that all the time. I've noticed they have classes in fishing at the University of Washington."

"Please make your statements relevant to the testimony of the witness Ms. Rawlings. Continue," Judge Watson said. She had just demolished Meredith for the jury. Watson wrote something on her legal pad. No doubt she wanted to include this item in her instructions.

Nice going, Meredith, Rachel thought. She wanted to turn and look at Meredith in the eyes, but realized it would not look good.

Meredith took a step toward the witness stand. "You mentioned in your testimony the Scanning Electron Microscope, but you didn't say how it relates to this case. Can you do that for me now? What exactly, precisely, is it used for?"

"It's used for analyzing gun residue left on the skin."

"Did you use this Scanning Electron Microscope on my client?"

"Actually, we don't do it directly on the person. We analyze swabs that the police have brought in."

"Swabs. Hmm. Do you have any of these swabs with you?"

Berg wanted to object, Rachel knew, but those were his swabs, and he didn't look like he included all his own evidence, and he didn't think fast enough to come up with some spin to make it plausible.

"No," Chew said, shaking his head and looking down, then back up, "that's police evidence."

"But you did do an analysis of the swabs rubbed on the hands of my client, did you not? Surely everyone in your lab knew about that, too."

Chew smiled, a defensive smile. "Yes, we did do an analysis."

"And what did that analysis show, Dr. Chew?"

"Nothing." He sat back and smiled. This seemed a bit too smug, even for Chew, as if any answer would do.

"Nothing? What do you mean nothing?"

"There was no gun residue."

The jury looked surprised. Did they realize how this helped Rachel?

"But my client is accused of murdering someone with this weapon." Meredith turned to the jury and stood there, silent, then turned back, arms out, palms up. "How can there be no gun residue on her hands?"

"It's often the case that there's no gun residue."

"Then what good is this big machine, Dr. Chew?" She looked back at the jury again, but they weren't paying any attention to her.

"Gun residue is like fingerprints. When we have them, it helps, and can often be conclusive."

"But Dr. Chew, if there's no gun residue, then my client didn't fire the gun in evidence in this trial."

Berg raised his head. "Objection, not a question."

Meredith looked at him and then back to Chew. "Is that not true?"

Chew frowned and screwed up his mouth. Was he thinking or just confused? Rachel hoped the jury would think he was confused, as Meredith had promised.

Meredith raised her voice but remained polite. "Is it not true that there's no gun residue?"

Chew looked at her quizzically. Berg sounded as exasperated as he could. "Objection, asked and answered."

Watson sustained the objection.

"So let me ask you this, Doctor, do you know for sure that my client fired the gun?"

"No, myself, of course not." Chew became defensive here.

"Then what do you know?"

"I know that this bullet was fired by this gun."

The jury sat back, assured. Rachel hoped Meredith had not forgotten the cardinal rule: you're not supposed to ask questions unless you know what the answer is going to be.

" But there was no residue on my client's hands. In other words, Doctor, you eliminated my client as a suspect, didn't you?"

The crease in Chew's forehead showed he didn't like his conclusions made for him. "It's for others to eliminate suspects."

Meredith cocked her head and raised her eyebrows. "Excuse me, sir, didn't you say you eliminated possibilities?"

"Possibilities, yes...sure...of course. But not suspects."

Rachel wasn't sure whether this made any difference to the jury at all. Maybe it made them confused, maybe it made them eliminate the topic from their minds. She looked at them all and they seemed to have blank stares, like they wished they were somewhere else. Maybe Meredith had figured this right. The jurors may have been thinking the witness betrayed confused.

"Dr. Chew, does your system always match bullets perfectly?"

196

"No, not always." Chew said this with his usual shrug and head shaking.

"Well, when does it not match?"

"When the bullet is too much deformed."

"Was this bullet deformed, Doctor?"

"No, it was almost perfect."

So this had led nowhere and only convinced the jury that the evidence is solid. Meredith struck out.

"So is it your testimony that someone fired this bullet with this gun, but you don't know who?" Meredith's palms were up, and her head twisted back and forth again. "It could've been anyone?"

Chew laughed to make sure everyone knew to take him seriously. "Of course not. I never know. That's detective work."

"So you don't know it was the defendant, then?" Meredith tried to bring this point home but she rowed against the tide.

"All I can tell you is that it was the defendant's gun that fired this bullet. I don't know who held the gun or who pointed it or who pulled the trigger. Like I said, that's police work." Chew let his irritation show through in his voice, and his posture, sitting up straight.

Meredith turned back to the table, sorted the documents a little, then said she had no more questions and thanked him.

"One moment," she said, turning around. " Excuse me, Your Honor, but I would like this witness to be available for further cross-examination."

"The witness will remain available. Do you have any problem with that Doctor Chew?"

"No, Your Honor." But his frown and look at Meredith said otherwise. City officials are always available. He knew that and didn't like the way she made an issue out of it.

"That will be all for this afternoon. The court is in recess until ten o'clock tomorrow," said Watson as she picked up the papers on her desk and started out.

Meredith turned to Rachel. "The last thing the jury is going to remember from this witness is that he does not know. That's doubt. We made some very good points today, Rachel, and we haven't even gotten to the police officers. They are the ones who will be more suited to our strategy."

But the jury got the picture. Rachel owned the gun that fired the bullet that went through the window, that crossed the street and killed Joshua.

Chapter 25

In the morning, Meredith wore another fashion statement suit. This time it was black. Rachel wanted to look at the back of the courtroom, hoping still to see Michael back there. When she turned in a slow measured movement, her peripheral vision caught that unmistakable bright red color of Sylvia Todaro's dress, and she stopped and looked back at the judge. She then looked sideways enough to notice the jury and saw that they were either watching her or looking to the back of the courtroom.

Berg called his next witness, Frank Sargenti, the head of the crime scene unit. The chief expert on the subject of the trajectory. The bullet, the gun, the trajectory, right on schedule. Rachel knew they'd leave Diane toward the end, to convince the jurors of jealousy. Then Tourville would show them how she'd hidden the gun, the true sign of guilt.

Either way. Guilt and jealousy. Jealousy and guilt.

Frank Sargenti came into the courtroom with his shoulders hunched. He wore a dark brown suit and yellow tie, both of which looked like he slept in them. His dusty shoes made an odd sound as he shuffled across the floor. He looked weary, lines of stress etched on his face.

Frank may not have looked the part, but he excelled when it came to doing his job. Over the years, Rachel came to have great respect for the man. But no love. Frank dealt with others as if they had somehow offended him. Or, he often acted as if others were getting in his way. There hid some dark source of insecurity inside him but no one knew what.

He took the oath and sat in the witness chair. He pulled his pants legs down.

"Would you state your position with the police department, please?" Berg said.

"I am head of the crime scene investigations unit."

"Would you tell us, please, Mr. Sargenti, what the difference is between your unit and the crime lab?"

"Yes, of course. They do analysis for us. We bring them what we find and they run a bunch of tests and tell us about the results or tell the others."

"Others, what do you mean?"

"Oh, sorry. I mean the other police units, the detectives, or the district attorney. Whoever needs to know."

"Thank you. Mr. Sargenti, your testimony in this trial is, if I may be obvious, about what you found at the scene of the murder, is that correct?"

"Yes, it is."

"Now, we know that the victim was taken alive to the hospital and died in the operating room. This was before your arrival on the scene, is that true?"

"Yes again."

"Given that the victim was not present when you inspected his apartment, were you able to determine the trajectory of the bullet that killed him?"

"Yes, we were."

"How were you able to do that without having the victim present?"

"We know the height of the victim, the place in the skull where the bullet entered, and the way the body fell."

"The height of the victim. You mean Joshua Todaro?"

"Yes."

"Did you measure it?"

"Yes, we measured the body in the morgue."

"So you made precise measurements."

"To the millimeter."

"And how do you know the way the body fell?"

"We discussed the matter with the paramedics who picked him up and put him on the gurney at the scene. They always make exact diagrams of the location and condition of the body."

"They do? Is that always the case?"

"Not necessarily. There are good paramedics and bad paramedics from my point of view. These were good paramedics and they did a fine job of identifying the location of the body."

"So what did you do with these measurements?"

"We knew from the paramedic report that the body was face down on the floor, and we knew where."

"You knew exactly where?"

"I wouldn't say exactly. But in this case it didn't matter."

"It didn't matter? Wait a minute," and Berg turned to the jury before he continued, "would you tell me why it doesn't matter exactly where the body was?"

"Of course. Because we did a laser trajectory from several possible positions."

"Hold on, Mr. Sargenti, I think you've lost us here. We need to slow down for a minute. Let's go back. How do you do a laser trajectory."

"We have a Hilti PD-30 laser range finder. You know what it looks like, it projects a red laser wherever you want."

"Just one moment," Berg said. "Let me show the jury what that is." He went back to his desk, bent down over his briefcase and pulled out a small red plastic device a little larger than a TV remote. He showed it to the jury, then pointed it to the ceiling. A straight red laser light hit the plaster. He turned it off and smiled over at the jury.

"So this is what you are talking about."

"Yes."

"Let me ask you something first, then I want to go back for more detail. Where did the laser beam project?"

"It projected out the victim's window across the street to Ms. McAlister's window."

"I see. You said you weren't exactly sure. How is that?"

"No, I didn't say I wasn't exactly sure, I said there was no exact measurement of where the body lay. We have only the paramedics diagram for that."

Berg raised his voice saying in a slow determined manner, "Then how can you be so sure, Mr. Sargenti, that the trajectory leads back to Ms. McAlister's office?"

"Because we exhausted all the possibilities. You see we know the angle at which the bullet entered the brain. We also know pretty darn close where the head lay on the carpet and how the body was positioned. We didn't take one reading or use the laser one time. We gave ourselves plenty of room for error, several inches in every direction. We assumed he was standing up as tall as possible, maybe he was hunched over a little bit. It didn't matter. In all cases, when we set up our equipment, at whatever height, up or down, left or right, it was the same. The red laser light pointed out his window over to Ms. McAlister's office."

Berg then went behind his table and brought out a large white chart with many red lines emanating out from the center and near the center. He went to the jury and put up an easel and put the chart on it, angled so that both the jury and Frank could see it. He went to the side of the chart and faced Sargenti.

"Mr. Sargenti, is this what you're talking about?"

"Yes. That panel shows all the laser trajectories that are compatible with the evidence we examined. You can see that all of them lead out from the head of the victim across the street to Ms. McAlister's window."

"Just to her office window?"

"Well, if you extend the laser trajectory far enough it will reach the moon. And when we made our trajectory, the window was without glass. Now, the door was closed, and certainly the trajectory itself runs through the window of the outside wall of the building and the window of the door out to the wall in the hallway. I can only tell you of the direction the bullet came from. That's what a trajectory is. It cannot tell you exactly where along that trajectory the bullet started out from."

"I see. Given all that testing and laser light pointing, what was your conclusion, Mr. Sargenti?"

"There was only one conclusion. The bullet that killed the victim came from the window in Ms. McAlister's office."

"Thank you very much. I have no more questions."

Judge Watson turned to Meredith.

"You may begin your cross-examination."

Meredith stood, looked at Rachel, then at the papers on her desk, and then went out front. She seemed to wait a good long time before beginning.

"Mr. Sargenti, did you do all these tests yourself?"

"Yes, of course, I had to. My chief thought it was very important."

"Your chief? You mean they told you what to do?"

"No of course not."

"What exactly were you told, Mr. Sargenti." She made a quick head turn to the jury and back. "I remind you that you're under oath."

He waited two seconds before answering. "I don't need reminding of that, thank you." He waited another two seconds, and appeared to think over what he wanted to say. "They told me, if you must know, that Ms. McAlister was a good detective for a long time." Sargenti looked over to Rachel and nodded to her. "Well, I've known her for a long time, they didn't have to tell me that. They said..."

"Yes?"

"They said that we should give her all the respect she deserves and make sure we do our job right."

He sure sucked Meredith into that one, Rachel thought. To try and make up for it, she walked back and forth a couple of times in front of the witness stand, posturing for effect. Rachel wasn't sure how it helped her cause.

"Let's go over your testimony for a minute. You said that you didn't have the body to work with, is that correct?"

"Yes, the paramedics had taken it away. This was the right thing to do. Saving a life comes first."

"You also say that all your tests on the trajectory were made on the basis of their drawings. Is that also correct?"

"Not completely. We did our own measurements of the body, of the location of the skull. Oh, yes. And we had one more thing."

"What was that, Mr. Sargenti?"

"We had the blood stain." He made a face, like he wasn't used to the subject or something. He must have been coached, Rachel thought.

"The blood stain?"

"The body, while it was on the floor, was still bleeding. Not a great amount, but some. We knew exactly where the blood was, of course, and we knew where the paramedics said the body was, and they matched exactly. The hole in the head and the blood on the floor. So we were quite certain that our measurements were correct."

All this detail about Joshua's death made Rachel nauseous. She pictured him there, reeling from the shot, falling to the floor, and the blood starting to flow.

The courtroom became very hot, and her skin felt prickly. She had to look down. She couldn't stand

Sargenti up there being so cold-blooded about Joshua. The jury started to look at her, and she knew they were making the wrong conclusion.

"The blood stain, was it tested?"

"Yes, of course. The DNA showed that it belonged to the victim, no question there."

Meredith looked to all in the courtroom like a soldier with a rifle trying to stop an oncoming tank.

"Let me ask you one last question, please. You said, I believe, that you don't know where the bullet trajectory started, you only know the direction it came from. Is that a fair assessment?"

"I'd say yes."

"And you also said that the red laser actually pointed out Ms. McAlister's door to the hallway and stopped at the wall on the other side of the hall?"

"I didn't say that exactly, but in fact, yes, it stopped at the wall. It wasn't going to go through it."

"Then let me ask you this, because the prosecutor didn't ask you, did the bullet not go through a window?"

"It presumably went through one, at least."

"Presumably?"

"Well, of course, when we arrived on the scene, the window to the victim's apartment was open and the window in the defendant's office was out. The glass to her window was on the floor or on the street."

"I see. Did you examine the glass?"

"We did, we took it into the lab and studied it." He made another face.

"And did you not find any evidence in the glass that it had been hit by a bullet?"

"I'm sorry, no, there was no way to tell that. When the glass broke, it fell a long way, it hit all kinds of surfaces and was in very many small pieces. You couldn't tell exactly which piece the bullet hit. Believe me, we certainly tried that, and it wasn't possible."

"You testified that the bullet came from Ms.

McAlister's office, is that right?"

"Yes."

"And you testified that your laser pointed went all the way past her office out to the hallway beyond it. Is that also true?"

"Yes."

"And you also testified you don't know where the bullet started it's trajectory. Correct?"

"Yes."

"So it could have started in the hallway, for example?"

"Yes."

"Thank you, no more questions."

Chapter 26

When Meredith came in the following day, she wore a navy blue suit nearly the exact same color as Rachel's. She had on the same white blouse, pearl earrings and Rolex. And the same smile. Rachel wondered if the jury noticed how uniformly she dressed. This morning, she had no compulsion to check the back of the courtroom to see whether Michael or Sylvia Todaro were there.

The judge came in, everyone stood and sat. The jurors took out their notebooks. A few had their pens ready to go. Judge Watson called on Berg to proceed.

Once more Berg turned to the bailiff and asked him to get the next witness. A few moments later Jim Barraza entered into the room. A very tall man with thinning hair and a long drawn-out, seemingly unhappy face, he looked at everyone in the courtroom as if he were surprised they were all here.

Jim looked at Rachel in exasperation, no doubt blaming her for making him speak in public. Normally he wouldn't be here because he would get one of his underlings in the coroner's office to do it. Another sign of the importance that the city placed on this prosecution.

Rachel would grant that he knew his work; he always double checked, and he didn't get things wrong very often. On any case when she depended on analysis from his office, she had always been completely confident.

He identified himself as the chief medical examiner of King County. The jury seemed duly impressed. They stared at him in unison.

Berg stood, holding his yellow legal pad before him. "Dr. Barraza you know the defendant, I believe."

"Is that a question?" Barraza replied, with a frown and a genteel smile. Not above invading the prosecutor's turf when he felt like it.

"Yes it is, Doctor. Do you know the defendant?"

"I do." Barraza, unlike Sargenti, avoided looking at Rachel.

"As the chief medical examiner did you examine the body of Joshua Todaro?"

"I did," he said, the perfect Mr. Laconic.

"Objection, Your Honor." Meredith got out of her chair, a little too fast.

Berg turned back and frowned dramatically.

"There's no laboratory report in evidence. This is hearsay," Meredith said.

Rachel hoped it sounded confusing.

Before the judge could even react, Berg raised his hand. "Sorry, Your Honor, a minor oversight." He had the report in his hand. "Permission to approach the witness?"

Watson nodded.

"I have a laboratory report on the autopsy of Mr. Todaro. Do you recognize it?" He handed it to Barraza.

"Yes, it's the report on the autopsy that I performed." He looked over at Meredith and raised his eyebrows, ensuring everyone knew this amounted to something trivial, and a waste of time. Then he flipped through the pages, moving his head up and down. Berg had it entered as an exhibit.

Way late in the trial, but Rachel didn't think the jury would make much of this kind of legal technicality.

Berg came and stood in front of the defense table. "You have a copy of this, do you not?"

Meredith, trying her best to look nonchalant, had to nod in agreement as the jury watched.

Berg smiled and went back to Barraza. "Can you tell us what you found that is related to this trial?"

"That he died of a gunshot wound to the head. Specifically, there was an entrance wound at the rear center of the cranium and no exit wound. There was extensive internal damage to the brain."

Meredith rose from her chair again. "Objection, Your Honor. Hearsay. Did the coroner, excuse me, the medical examiner, make that determination for himself? Or did he learn it from the medical staff at the hospital? If the latter, then it's hearsay."

Berg folded his arms across his chest, made a brief twist toward Meredith with a sigh, and then turned back to Barraza. "Did you read the report by Dr. Golden? The one detailing the massive hemorrhage that killed the victim?"

"Yes, I did."

Berg turned slowly toward the defense table and turned back. Did the jury buy this little dance? "Thank you." Then a nod at the jury before turning back to Barraza. "Although you read the report from the neurosurgeon, did you also do your own autopsy on Joshua Todaro?" Berg gave the defense table a quick glance.

"Yes I did."

At least Berg stopped the pirouettes for a while. "Will you tell us the relevant facts from that autopsy, Doctor, excluding information you yourself didn't determine?"

"The man was dead." A small bit of noise from the back of the courtroom.

Meredith shot up. "Your Honor, the witness is insulting the court, the jury and the defendant. And maybe the prosecutor."

Watson nodded at Berg, then waited several seconds. "Let's be civilized in this courtroom, please." The mildest thing she could've said.

Berg bowed slightly to the judge and returned to his

witness. "Would you please detail the results of the autopsy, Dr. Barraza? Was there a gunshot wound?"

"He had a gunshot wound in the back of his head."

Berg picked up a panel that they kept wrapped in plain brown paper. He nodded to the bailiff, who stood, went outside the courtroom and came back in with an easel. He handed the easel to Berg, who placed it prominently in the courtroom, to the right of the judge and the witness box, at an angle in front of the jurors. Jurors number six and twelve could've reached out and touched it. He then noisily took the paper off the panel and placed it on the easel.

The jurors saw a large full color blow-up of the back of a head with a hole in the middle of the skull.

"Dr. Barraza, have you seen this photo before?"

"Yes, I have. It's a picture of Joshua Todaro's head taken by our lab. It is the hole caused by the bullet that killed him."

Barraza had been left to the last of the expert witnesses, Rachel realized. So the jury would go away tonight with that image burned into their memory. The shock value hit home to the jury. Some of them couldn't even look at it.

This appeared to be a straightforward clinical picture. Scientific. Without lurid blood. The man lay on a cold marble slab. The bullet hole dominated the photo.

It looked like an execution. Now the jury started to look back over to Rachel and move their heads back and forth between her and the photo. Brilliant, absolutely brilliant. Leave the jury something they will never forget as long as they live.

Rachel felt their eyes burning on to her skin and into her soul. She couldn't look at them, she could feel the nausea gripping her. She held her hands tight together under the table. At this moment, she actually felt guilty. It didn't matter whether someone else killed him, she felt sick of his death, full of shame. No one could save her. She hadn't protected him. She had brought this harm to him. Who cared about the jury, the judge, the whole trial.

Berg continued with his well-prepared questioning. "Was there evidence of hemorrhaging?"

"Certainly, it was very obvious inside the cranial tissue."

"Were there any other traumas on the victim?"

Barraza put his arms across his chest and leaned back. "There were no other traumatic events showing up anywhere else on his body."

"So the report from the neurosurgeon stated that he died of massive hemorrhaging on the operating table, and you found evidence of the hemorrhaging during your autopsy, is that correct."

"Yes it is."

So Meredith's objections went nowhere, Rachel thought. Berg used them to pound the point home.

"And now, Dr. Barraza." Berg stood still for a moment. "Did you find any other substances in or on his body?"

"He did have substances from two different women on his body."

"Two different women?" Berg bowed his head and cocked it to one side as he spoke the word "different".

"Yes."

"Are you sure? Two?"

Barraza didn't answer, instead looking puzzled at Berg for questioning what he had just said.

Rub it in, don't want the jury to miss this one, Rachel sighed to herself. She put her hands under her thighs and held tight to the chair.

Berg recovered. "How do you know this, Doctor?"

"It's in the laboratory report."

"Going back, then, over the lab report." Berg focused on the jury, and paused, and turned back to Barraza. "How is it exactly that the laboratory report determines that there were two different women?"

"It's fairly straightforward. There are three different blood types."

"Three? I thought you said there were two."

"Of course, two women and then Mr. Todaro's blood type."

"Certainly, of course, I understand."

Berg walked over and stood in front of the jury and once more remained silent for a few seconds, making sure they knew they were going to be making the decision. Then he made a very quick turn and faced Barraza. "Doctor, one other question. How did you know that there were two women and not, say, three women?"

The courtroom remained quiet. The air conditioning blew air on everyone, like a cold never-ending whisper.

"That would be from the Barr Body."

"The Barr Body, Doctor? What would that be?"

They have this interaction down to a grandstanding science, Rachel thought.

"The Barr Body is a heterochromatic body found in the nuclei of normal females but absent in the nuclei of normal males."

"Excuse me, Dr. Barraza, but the word hetero-chromatic, is that important, does it mean anything, really?"

"Yes it does, but..." He put his hand under his chin. "Well, no it doesn't mean anything important. What is important is the Barr Body, found in the nuclei."

"I see," Berg said, smiling with a little bow. "Thank you. One less technical term is always welcome to all of us. But, this Barr Body, if it's absent in the nuclei of normal males, how do you know that we're dealing with normal males? Maybe one or the other is abnormal."

"It's one more test we do in order to be thorough."

"Yes, I understand." Berg turned to the jury. "So your testimony, Doctor, is that forensic evidence is conclusive that there were fluids from one male and two females on the body. Is that true?"

"Not exactly when you put it that way."

"Not exactly?" Berg put a finger on his tightened lips. "Hmm. Could you elaborate on that?"

"Of course. We took fluids off the victim's body, and found semen and blood. Of course the victim had been shot."

"I see. Is that it, Doctor? Is that all you found?"

"And also female fluids, like you get when you do a pap smear."

"So now that's everything?" Berg waited a second. "Is that the case? Blood, female fluids?"

"No, that wasn't all."

"What else was there?"

"There was hair, and lipstick, from a third person."

"Hair? What do you mean, hair? And lipstick." Berg looked long and hard at the jury.

"I mean we found a piece of human hair, and some lipstick on the body which were not from the victim."

"Could you tell us where you found them?"

Barraza shifted in his chair, as if it were some embarrassment to him, a doctor and experienced medical examiner. As rehearsed, no doubt, Rachel thought.

" The lower abdomen."

"I see. Did you do any further tests on the material found in the victim?"

"Yes, we did DNA testing."

Meredith shifted in her seat and touched Rachel on the arm, barely, so the jury couldn't see it.

"And what results were on the DNA testing?"

"We identified three individuals from the DNA."

"Three? You actually identified three individuals? Can you tell the Court please who those three individuals are? Do you actually know their names?"

Berg had a chair and a whip. And the courtroom became even quieter, if that were possible.

"One was of course Joshua Todaro himself, the victim."

"And the two women?"

"One of them was the defendant Rachel McAlister."

All the jurors moved their heads as one and looked with intensity at Rachel. Meredith put her hand on Rachel's, pressing hard. Berg looked over at the jury, then looked back at Rachel, paused, and then turned back.

"And the other woman, Dr. Barraza, were you able to determine who the other woman was?"

Barraza looked down at his fingernails, studying them, making everyone wait. He knew how to bring a point home. He raised his eyes to Berg, sighed, waited another second, then said, "Yes, I was."

Rachel felt her spine stiffen. She knew the medical examiner prepared to state Diane's name.

But Berg drew this out as long as he could. He knew the jury waited for a name, and he knew that Rachel suffered while she waited. "Before you go on to give us a particular name, Dr., could you tell us what methods you used to determine exactly who these three people were?"

"Certainly. For the victim we simply compared the DNA with DNA from another part of his body."

Berg, nodded, looked down, put one foot forward, then addressed Barraza again. "And the women, Dr. Barraza, how did you know what DNA to make a match with? Where did you get the DNA to use for the comparison?"

"We had lipstick and we had the hair and we had vaginal fluid."

"Yes, I think the jury understands that. We all understand you can get DNA from these materials. But what about the other DNA? Where did you find the other DNA to match with them? The DNA for their identity. That's what we want to know." Berg hammered this question home.

"From the police database."

Berg feigned surprise. "Police database? How could that be?"

For Rachel, this seemed too dramatic, theatrical even. But she noticed that the jury absorbed it all. They watched Berg, then, Barraza.

"It's nothing special. We run tests against the whole database. What we found was from the police department section of the DNA database."

Now Berg backed up a step. "So you didn't go looking for a suspect among the police."

"No. Not at all." Barraza shifted in his chair.

Rachel stared at Berg, although he did not see her. The defense, and Diane, had found this out very late in the investigation. But now Barraza is talking like the crime lab discovered Diane's DNA right from the beginning. They did it deliberately, and now they want to tell the jury that their thorough testing led to the discovery of the evidence. The evidence. The evidence before the jury. Meredith could not do anything about it. If she brought this up, it would just make the jury hear it over again.

"And, finally, Dr. Barraza, which DNA was which?"

"I'm not sure what you mean."

"The vaginal fluid, whose DNA was that?"

Some of the women jurors squirmed. Two of them turned their eyes to Rachel without moving their heads, as if they could hide their prurient interest.

"That was Rachel McAlister's."

"I see. And finally, Dr. Barraza. Tell us the name of the other person."

Again the moment of silence. Absolute silence in the courtroom. No one moved. The terminal silence surrounded Rachel and the air from the ceiling passed over her shoulders like a conspiracy of ghosts.

"The person whose DNA you found on the body of Mr. Joshua Todaro. The DNA of the hair and lipstick."

Berg rubbed his hands together and looked over at Meredith and Rachel, as if they had all signed an agreement and it was a done deal.

Rachel controlled her arms tight on her lap. Diane's hair. Diane's lipstick. The words burned into her chest.

Meredith sat up straight and put her hand on Rachel's arm. Rachel pulled it away. The jurors turned their chairs to face the witness stand. The whir of the air conditioning moved them all along to the arrival of truth. Even though Rachel knew what his next statement, she found it difficult to hear against the pounding of her heart.

Barraza, his restless dark brown eyes like an owl, turned his bony face out over the courtroom and then settled on Rachel as he spoke in a quiet, even tone. "Detective Diane Scanlan."

Diane? Did she really hear the name? The whole professional name? Out loud in the courtroom? Did the jury hear it? Rachel pulled away from Meredith and stood, knocking her chair over. It hit the floor with a loud thud. The judge gaveled hard several times. Rachel turned around to face Michael in the back of the courtroom. Michael stood and looked at Rachel with a face whose muscles were tight in a grim twist.

Rachel started to climb over the banister, but became dizzy. She couldn't tell whether she faced up or down, as if she twisted in the bottom of a pool. She put out her hand to steady herself. She touched only the air. She fell forward, landing on the floor. Her face felt hot and flushed. Before she could get up, the bailiff stood over her, holding her down while he called on his intercom for help. He kept her down until two more deputies arrived in the room. Then he let her up. The courtroom erupted in buzzing exclamations.

The judge stood up, leaned over the bench, hit her gavel hard again. Bam! Bam! She spoke sat the top of her voice. "There will be no outbursts in this courtroom!"

Rachel turned to Meredith. "This can't be happening." Her voice became louder as she spoke, her arms were flailing out wide.

It must have looked like Rachel wanted to hit Meredith. The bailiff came over and stood next to them. Rachel sat and buried her head in her hands. Suddenly she realized. Joshua, Meredith, Diane, all of them.

What had she done to deserve this? She turned to the jury and stared at them in defiance. What could they know? They had only a tiny fraction of the truth to help them as they returned her gaze. Their eyes looked back at her in amazement, even horror. Damnation.

Meredith stood. "Your honor, in view of my client's condition, I request a delay until tomorrow."

Berg stood as well and held out his arm in pleading. "Your honor, this can't be unknown to the defense. They were aware of this during discovery. The defendant is grandstanding."

"Your Honor," said Meredith, holding Rachel's arm, "my client is not grandstanding. Whatever the prosecution says, my client is obviously too upset to continue at this moment. If we are not allowed a recess so that she may gain control of herself, I think there will be grounds for appeal."

"I understand your situation counselor, and I grant your request. The court is in recess until tomorrow morning."

Rachel looked at Meredith, who now became a completely different person. As if Rachel had developed Alzheimer's and couldn't recognize anybody. She began to shake. She turned around and looked at Michael again but she saw this time Sylvia Todaro's head over her bright red fabric. Meredith touched Rachel's arm again but Rachel moved away and pushed the arm to the side violently.

The bailiff gently took hold of Rachel arms, walked

her out the door and back to her cell. The longest walk of her life.

It didn't take long for Meredith to arrive. She entered the interview room as if she were in a hurry. She began to talk in an excited voice, her eyes gleaming. "Rachel, I know you are upset. But this has become in fact an important moment for us." She held her hands up. "The jury had to see your true reaction."

"Well, they sure got it." Rachel's stomach churned and dizziness overtook her.

"You must understand this moment. The jury saw you as you really are. They saw your hurt and pain. They now have to be on our side."

Rachel put her hands over her ears. "Get out of here."

"My God, can't you see it? They can tell you are innocent."

Rachel looked up. "Get out of here, I said." She said it in a voice that rose up from the dark bottom of her soul.

"I'm going. You need some time to adjust. But I hope with some reflection that you will understand." Meredith left.

Rachel waited for the deputy, and walked with her the forty gray feet down the corridor to her cell.

Chapter 27

Nausea took hold of Rachel and she pressed the palm of her hand against her abdomen. She felt a sickness, loneliness, and absolute lack of control, and then a pressing weight in her chest. Even in war, when bullets were flying all around her, she controlled her actions and nothing could hurt her if she kept on going. But now she knew she faced an exit from this world alone. They had finally made her a target, hanging in the wind, for anyone to shoot at.

Rachel lay down on her back, eyes closed, arms at her side. What did she have left? Over and over, she heard Barraza saying Diane's name. She tried to think of something else, but only other names came to mind. Who did she have? No one. She dozed into oblivion.

The sound of the door opening awakened her as Amy walked into the cell and waited, her hand on the knob. When Rachel didn't move, Amy said, "Ms. McAlister, you have a visitor."

Rachel lifted herself up on her elbows and ran her fingers through her hair. "A visitor? I don't want a god damn visitor. Tell her to go to hell."

"I'm sorry, I'm just the messenger. Somebody must have gotten permission from the judge. That's not easy."

Rachel didn't reply. Did the so-called visitor lack the courage to come up? What, did Diane think she could talk about old times and it would all be over? "Tell me who it is."

"It's a Mr. Michael Scanlan."

Michael? Rachel sat up. What could he possibly want? The answer came to her quickly. Of course, he came here to apologize for Diane. As if that could make any difference. No negotiations could take place now. She sighed. She slumped. She shook her head. "All right," she said with a weary voice, "tell him I'll be down in a minute."

He waited for Rachel in the interview room. His hands were in his pocket, his head bowed, his eyes dark and subdued.

"How did you manage to get in here?"

"You have more friends around here than you think."

Rachel didn't say anything. She didn't have anything to say.

"It isn't true, you know." Michael shook his head back and forth but kept his eyes glued on her. "Don't believe it."

"Don't believe what?" Rachel looked down at her hands on the table.

"Diane would never do that to you. She wouldn't do it to me. She couldn't have."

Rachel took a deep breath, and waited for several long seconds. Then she looked up at him. "Right now you're the only person I believe in, Michael, in the whole world."

"You have to believe me. That's all we've got, that's all we have in this life."

"But there's evidence, Michael. You've known me for a long time. You know what evidence is."

"Evidence. No, there's no evidence Rachel, none. None at all."

She laughed a hard, bitter laugh. "Didn't you hear, weren't you there today? Haven't you been here the whole time? Oh, that's right, you guys all knew about it from the beginning. Maybe you shot him."

He stood, shaking with rage. "Rachel McAlister, what has gotten into you? How can you say something you know absolutely is not true."

She said nothing. She waited for him to leave, but he sat, still shaking. He stayed there, staring at her, saying nothing, just staring.

Rachel spoke almost in a whisper. She had only Michael, the last person on earth she could believe in. At least they hadn't brought any evidence against him. Her voice softened. "I didn't mean it. I don't know what to believe or whom. I have nothing left."

Michael held his palms up. "If there's anything on this earth that's true, you know that I am a victim as much as you."

"Yes, it's true, you and me."

"No Rachel McAlister, not you and me. You and me and Diane."

Hearing the name, she changed. The softness disappeared and her stomach convulsed. "Ah, you're forgetting the evidence. You know, the DNA."

He swiped the air with his hand. "Shit on the DNA, it's not true."

A wisp of hair fell across her eyes, and she flicked it aside with a quick jerk of her head. "How can you prove otherwise? There's a lab report. Crime scene."

He rubbed a hand along the back of his neck, trying to loosen the tension there. "Tell me, what about you? How can you expect me to believe that you're innocent? Why should I? Tell me why?" Michael said, his voice shuddering in despair.

She sat silent again. "I don't know."

He backed away, then pointed his finger at her. "No, you tell me, Rachel, why should I believe you? How many years have I known you? Tell me, how many?"

She folded her hands across her chest and looked down as if she were studying her ankles, trying to think of a response. She felt this tug between wanting to believe in him and not being able to accept anything. She let herself go for the moment. "Quite a few."

"Yes," he nodded in some sort of small triumph, "that's right, quite a few."

"I introduced you to Diane," Rachel said. She disappeared for a moment in the fog of a reverie. "It seems like a very long time ago now."

He fell silent again, looked at her, and his eyes misted over. Rachel couldn't look at him. She sat and stared at the floor.

"Rachel?" His voice resonated with warmth, in the belief that he had won her over.

"Yes?" She forced herself to look at him.

"Why did you introduce me to Diane?"

"My god, why are you asking me that?"

"Answer the question, Rachel. Go ahead, answer it."

"I don't know, that was so long ago. Quite a few years as you just said."

"Not so long ago." His face showed all sorrow. "Not so long ago."

She wet her lips, and swallowed, but her throat itched. "I don't know what you want from me."

Michael raised his eyebrows. His voice became more insistent. "Answer my question, will you? Tell me, why did you introduce me to Diane?"

"I still don't know what you're asking."

"I think you do. I want to hear it from you."

Her eyes were sharp and appraising. "Why? Is there something going on between Diane and you?" She toggled her head. "Well, I guess so, now."

"No, Rachel," he said with a sigh. "I love Diane, and we have two beautiful children. But I want to know."

"Know? I'm still drawing a blank." She spread her hands out.

Michael looked at Rachel in total frustration. "Why didn't you want me for yourself?"

Rachel looked back at him and couldn't think of anything that would be right to say to Michael. She couldn't believe what she heard. She sat in stunned silence in disbelief at the turn in the conversation.

He blew a short, hard breath out of his nose in exasperation. "Rachel, it's me. Don't tell me you have nothing to say."

"Michael," she said and then fell silent for a moment before she continued. "I wasn't ready."

"Ready? How many times did we go out together, you and Diane and me?"

She frowned and shrugged her shoulders. Her voice was dismissive. "I don't know."

His voice took on a tone of irritation. He had a point to make and she needed to hear it. "Yes you do. It's not a number. It's the time we spent. Did you never notice me looking at you?" He fought to remain in control of his emotions.

"Well, of course, all the time. When you're together with people you look at each other. Where is this going?" Her lips tightened.

"And did you ever dance with me?"

"Yes, we did." Now irritation became the prime quality in her voice. She sighed. "I did."

"And did you ever notice I had real feelings for you?"

"Yes, but not like that." She looked at him, waiting to see if he understood her meaning.

He shook his head. "But not like that. Hmm. How could you not know I had feelings for you?" He breathed heavily.

His eyes felt like needles pricking her skin. "You didn't say it, Michael." She felt so small and closed in on all sides.

"Well, I'm telling you now, Rachel McAlister, you broke my heart and it took years for Diane to put it back together again, and so you thought that you could fix Diane's depression and Diane's drinking and in the middle of it all I was the person you used. Do you know how many nights I lay awake thinking of you? Do you know how long it takes to get over that?"

Rachel fought back the tears, but they wouldn't stop.

"Well, let me tell you, Rachel, you're not going to throw all those years away and tell me that you believe the evidence against my wife. You might as well believe it against me. Or do you?"

She hung her head and the tears kept coming. "No, you know I don't believe anything against you."

He spoke in a low and guttural voice, quavering. "Then you tell me, you tell me right here and right now," he stopped for one second, "that you don't believe anything against my wife. I want to hear you say it." His voice rose and became firm. He held his finger high, his eyes blazing. "Say it, Rachel! Say it or I walk away."

Rachel looked at his eyes, his tears held back, the body shaking. What could she say to Michael? Here she stood, in a jail by a courtroom, looking at the end of her life and he told her that she, Rachel, messed his life up a long time ago. "Does Diane know any of this?"

"About my feelings for you? No, she never has known, and she never will. You will promise me that, too."

Rachel stood. Her eyes narrowed and she spoke in a resolute tone. "I promise, Michael." She nodded but her lips were a straight line. "I promise you. Because I will never see her again."

Stunned, Michael's face contorted as he searched for words. "But..."

Her voice broke like pure cut glass. "Just what part of betrayal don't you understand, Michael?"

"Betrayal?" He looked up as if the question came from a distance, then directed his gaze at Rachel. "Not Diane." He said it with absolute finality.

"Not Diane?" The anger in her voice rose. "You fool. Of course she knew about us. She must have known all along. That's why she had an affair with Joshua. Don't you get it?"

"No...she..."

"Oh, yes, Michael. Just to get me. Her revenge. You're an idiot."

He got up. "You stew in your own misery, Rachel. I'm going home to Diane and my children and my home. I am so much happier than you have ever been. You don't know how to trust your best friend." He left the room and slammed the door behind him.

Rachel covered her ears at the sound, then looked at her shaking hands. She felt a wound in her chest. She saw herself swinging from the gallows.

Chapter 28

The whole world changed. Rachel thought about how much time she had spent with Diane and Michael. She had given Diane her life back, and then became a parasite on that life. And Michael's.

It would never be the same again. Never. Now Rachel knew why she could never have a deep relationship with anyone. Because she pushed Michael into Diane's arms, when she really wanted him for herself, and didn't even know it. And she spent so much time with them, like a platonic ménage à trois.

She looked at Michael year after year and never saw what his eyes saw. Or felt what his heart felt. All the holidays, so many weekends, Thanksgiving, Christmas. Always with them. Babysitting their kids.

And she didn't think Diane had any idea either. She always had her arm around Michael, they were very romantic with each other. Maybe that's why Rachel did so well for the short time she was on the police force, dealing with crime and violence kept her own personal emotions in check.

And maybe Diane got it right. Rachel lost it with Gil Hamilton. She lost everything, starting with that event. Ted, as soon as he knew the location of her office, setting Joshua up across the street where Rachel couldn't help but see him. Joshua played the role of the perfect trap.

He probably waited in the dark until Rachel looked out the window and then walked innocently around in front of the window to make sure he got her attention.

At the very moment Rachel turned around to sit at her desk. She had no idea, he led her to the slaughter. He led them both.

Amy came again and brought Rachel to the interview room. Meredith stood waiting for Rachel outside, waiting to hear how things were going to continue. They both went in.

Meredith waited for Rachel to say something. She sat and motioned for Meredith to sit on a chair. For a very long time neither of them said anything. Obviously, Meredith needed to know where they stood. Rachel knew the truth, she had no real defense. No evidence to impeach. No procedures to impeach. No law to help her. The jury remained as her only possible defense. And that looked bleak.

She looked at Meredith. "What do we do now?"

"As difficult as this has been, I think it's going to help us."

"Help us?" Rachel said, incredulous. "In what way?"

Meredith waited several seconds before replying. She clearly wanted Rachel to believe she thought deeply. "I think the jury will be on our side now."

"What?" Rachel backed up a step, turned away and gave herself several more seconds before she replied. She, too, could be thinking deeply. But for her there still remained the suspicion of disingenuous talk by Meredith. "Give me a reason to believe that," she said with disbelief in her voice.

"It helps them to believe in you. They saw how surprised you were, how hurt and completely innocent you were. They saw today the real Rachel McAlister. We have planted the seed of doubt.

"You seem to be changing your strategy."

"No, this is still our strategy. Things look very different now to the jury. Up until this moment, it has been all about cold hard evidence, laboratory reports, analysis. We have introduced the human factor that will help this jury do what they want to do, which is acquit you. The jury is always reluctant to convict."

"You are losing me. I don't see any defense in this at all. We have other witnesses still to go, Ted Tourville. None of this changes that. Like you said, the gun the bullet, the window."

"Did you look at the jury today?"

"Yes."

"Did you see their reaction? They were shocked at what they saw. This is the opening we were looking for."

"Opening? There's no opening."

"The opening, listen to me again, is in the minds of the jury. It is very important now that you pay great attention to your body language and your attitude and what to look at. You must show anger at every person up there on that witness stand. They are telling lies."

"Are you going to prove that they are lying?"

"No, you are. The witnesses are lying because you're being framed. We don't know absolutely who it is, but we know it's happening. Let me ask you a question Rachel, and bear with me on this. Are you religious?"

"There you go. A miracle, that's the tool we need," Rachel said. She put as much disgust in her voice as she could. "This is as desperate as things can get, when you start asking questions about religion."

"No, I mean it, are you religious?"

Anger filled her voice. "Tell me why you're doing this."

Meredith spoke quietly "I know what they say about their faith, religious people, they say it's the evidence of things unseen. And that's what you have to project. What is unseen is how you're being framed, and the evidence is the way you look at the witnesses."

Rachel frowned and shook her head. "You know what, I don't know why I should go along with this." She raised her arms up and let them fall. Her words came from a hoarse voice. "I don't see how it's going to help me get through this trial."

Meredith raised her hands up as if to calm Rachel down. She sighed, "One more time." She stared at Rachel in silence for two seconds. "This is Ted's doing, right? We can't prove it. But think again about the jury."

"Not another one more time, please. I've had enough of those."

"Listen, Rachel. The jury does not want to convict you. They are human beings. You are not a child molester."

Rachel looked away. "You think this helps?"

"That's right. There's no blood all over the place. No torture. No serial killing. The whole thing is so clean. What matters is that the jury knows you're not a monster. They don't want to convict people like you. In their hearts they are searching for reasonable doubt."

"You make it all sound so pretty, Meredith. But you're not convincing me. And if you're not convincing me, then sure as hell forget convincing the jury." She blushed so hot she felt feverish.

Meredith folded her hands across her chest and stood straight. "All right, here we are, right here and right now. You are making me think...the way you're talking...the way you're giving up...you're making me wonder if you were framed. I know today was a total shock for you and the jury knows it was a total shock for you and the jury will not think you were framed unless you think that way."

"Do you doubt me now? This is where we end up? I'm on trial for my life and you start thinking about whether I was really framed or not?" Rachel felt heat rising up her back. Her cheeks felt flushed. She clenched her fists.

"Rachel, you tell me right now where you stand. You tell me how you want to proceed. I am listening to you, and waiting to hear what you have to say."

And what could she say? Meredith, to tell the truth,

appeared absolutely right. Rachel felt caught in a perfect frame. Only the hanging remained. Ted Tourville won. Joshua, Michael, Diane, they all had lost.

Meredith then turned and looked at Rachel. "Rachel, tomorrow morning, in court, everything will be different. We'll feel it. The jury will feel it. You especially will feel it. And you will show it. You wait and see. Get some rest. Tomorrow we begin anew." Meredith came over and touched her arm.

But Rachel did not respond. She just watched her leave. Begin anew. How could she take that? Anew? New what? And the strength for that came from—?

Chapter 29

The next morning in court Meredith had put on a dark blue pantsuit with a fine chalk line and a white blouse. A small diamond on a gold chain showed at her throat. And the polished wedding band on her finger. The women jurors looked at her. Rachel thought they watched with approval, but maybe she imagined it.

Meredith turned and put her hand on Rachel's arm. Rachel wanted to take it away, but didn't want the jury to see it. She kept herself from shaking her head.

Judge Watson arrived and stood at her desk, looking out over the room. The court came to order for her and quieted down.

"Mr. Berg," Judge Watson said, "you may continue with Dr. Barraza."

"Thank you, your honor." Berg turned and nodded to the bailiff, who left the courtroom and soon brought him in. Barraza walked up to the witness chair and sat.

"I remind you," the judge said, "that this is continuing testimony and you're still under oath."

Barraza looked at her in a moment of confusion. As if he didn't know how to give testimony.

She turned to the prosecution, looking out over her glasses. "You may proceed, Mr. Berg."

Berg stood and went out in front of his table. "Dr. Barraza, I want to go over something from your previous testimony. A day has passed, and I want to make sure we are all as clear about it as possible. Yesterday you

231

testified that you searched the police database for DNA match ups. Is that correct?"

"Yes, it is."

"Why would you go looking for suspects in the police department? That's not very reassuring to the average citizen of this town if you always look for police suspects, now, is it?"

"Now, that's not what it was like." They must have rehearsed this because Barraza acted out a grand melodrama, shaking his head back and forth. "We didn't go looking for suspects, not at all. We go through the police database sooner or later, because there are many policemen, detectives, crime scene investigators wandering all over the place. They can contaminate the evidence, or we can pick up some of their fluids, and we have to know that. It's routine, a precaution."

Rachel turned to Meredith and whispered, "Why don't you object, he already said this?"

Meredith leaned and whispered back into Rachel's ear. "There's something important, Rachel, he testified they can contaminate the evidence. I don't want to obscure that."

Rachel wanted to reply but then Berg went back to his desk and the room became quiet. He looked down at his legal pad, turned to face the judge, and absent-mindedly stabbed at it with his pen. "No further questions your honor." Looking at the defense table, he went around the desk and sat down.

Rachel kept her gaze firmly held on Barraza, hoping that the jury watched. Hoping that Meredith's strategy had some value.

"Your witness, Ms. Rawlings," said the judge.

Meredith stood, and went out in front of the defense table. She turned and looked at all the jurors, stood there a moment, and let them look at her, then turned back to Barraza. "Dr. Barraza, you performed the autopsy, is that correct?"

"Yes, I did." He spoke quietly, with assurance. He didn't give any sign that this question was old news to the courtroom.

"Did you do this alone, or with others?"

"I have some assistants, but I direct all the work, and I review all results."

"I see. You testified that the only trauma you found on the body was the bullet wound, is that correct?"

"Yes."

"Do you know of your own knowledge, sir, that he died of the bullet wound?"

"That was the only evidence I found."

"The only evidence? Were you there when he died?"

"No, I wasn't."

Berg leaned back in his chair and shook his head. The jury noticed.

Meredith continued. "Then you don't know what he died of, do you?"

"There was only the one trauma."

"Have you ever autopsied someone who was shot, but didn't die of the bullet wound?"

Berg leapt to his feet once more. Always on his feet. Always to drive a point home to the jurors. "Objection your honor, the defense is going beyond the evidence of this trial."

"Your honor, Dr. Barraza is presented as an expert witness, and I am merely exploring his expertise. And this is precisely about the circumstances of Mr. Todaro's death," Meredith said.

Judge Watson waited a moment, then said, "I agree. Your objection is overruled. You may answer, Dr. Barraza."

"Have you then, had an experience where someone died, but not of a bullet wound they sustained," Meredith repeated.

"Yes, of course."

"Could it be that someone died, say, from a drug

233

overdose, even though they were also shot."

"Yes, that's common enough. The streets are filled with such people."

Berg looked at his notes, as if the truth were somehow contained there. "Your Honor, please, the defense is taking this god knows where that has no relationship at all to the charges in this trial."

Judge Watson looked at Meredith and nodded. "Are you going somewhere, Ms. Rawlings?"

"Your Honor, the police report mentioned that cocaine was found on the person of Joshua Todaro, but the state has not mentioned any toxicology results. I am pursuing this cross-examination to that end."

Berg tried again. "Your Honor, no police officers have given any testimony, and there's no mention of any drugs in Dr. Barraza's testimony. She has no legal right to bring this subject up."

The judge looked at Meredith.

"Your Honor, this is the chief medical examiner for King County, who is testifying about an autopsy he performed. Surely, toxicology is part of what he does, even if the state does not ask him about it. I suggest that the objection on the part of Mr. Berg is out of order."

Judge Watson thought for a moment. "Mr. Berg, did you give the defense copies of the autopsy report?"

"Yes I did," he said with a lowered voice, but a head raised up to look the judge in the face, nodding in agreement.

"Well, then, I think the defense is entitled to ask questions about evidence, and the autopsy report is evidence. It may not be excluded. As an Assistant District Attorney, you know this. You may continue, Ms. Rawlings."

Having won this minor skirmish, Meredith looked straight at Barraza. "So this particular victim, Mr. Todaro, could've died of a drug overdose, and not of the gunshot wound. After all, there's no trauma with an overdose. Is that not true?"

Barraza started shaking his head even before she finished. "No, he couldn't have. There were no drugs in his system."

"No drugs in his system, are you sure of that?"

"Yes. Absolutely."

Meredith had done something brilliant, Rachel thought. Joshua wasn't taking cocaine. So it must have been planted on him, and that strengthened the argument that Rachel had been framed. Rachel hoped the jury saw the confusion.

"Then you didn't find cocaine in the toxicology test?"

"No."

"That's odd, don't you think, given that the hospital found cocaine on him?"

Berg, on his feet again. "Objection, without foundation. No evidence has been brought before this court."

"Your Honor, the medical examiner was requested to test for cocaine, and I have the right to ask about it."

The judge looked at Meredith, then gave Berg a quick little look of contempt.

Berg nodded, trying to keep on Watson's good side. "But her question isn't about the toxicology test. Her question is about what's odd. She is trying to get the medical examiner to testify about something that's not in evidence in this trial. There is no cocaine anywhere on the evidence table. The state did not present any evidence about cocaine because it isn't relevant." He looked at Meredith in a small triumph.

"Objection sustained. Please rephrase your question, Ms. Rawlings, or start in a different direction."

Meredith went back to the table and searched among the papers. She took a stapled set of documents over to the witness stand, looking at the judge as she did.

"Dr. Barraza, do you recognize this document?"

He took it and flipped each of the papers up and surveyed them. "Yes, these are the district attorney's autopsy request papers."

"If you look at the bottom of the second page, would you please tell us the request on the last paragraph?"

"It's a request to include testing for cocaine and other chemical substances."

Clever, Rachel thought. Watson sustained the objection, but the jury has learned that Joshua didn't do drugs. Unfortunately, Meredith took a long time getting to this point. And the whole point seemed meaningless. She wanted to shake her head but was able to control herself.

"We have heard the prosecutor state that there is no evidence on the table of cocaine. No evidence. No cocaine. But you had a request to test for cocaine. Did you ask whether there was cocaine involved?"

Barraza shifted in irritation. "No, I didn't. I..."

"Yes, go ahead."

"I did an autopsy as requested. That's all." He stared at Meredith in defiance.

He wasn't going to play her game, and there wasn't a damn thing she could do about it. "One last thing, sir. You say you found no other trauma to the body other than the head wound, is that correct?"

"Yes."

"Nothing, nothing at all, not any little bruises even?"

"No, there were no other bruises. Except those related to the surgery."

"What do you mean by that, Dr. Barraza?"

"I mean that there were extensive bruises around the area of the entrance wound, larger than a bullet would make. And where they inserted tubes."

"And how do you know those bruises were made during surgery, and not, say by someone who struck Mr. Todaro in the head?"

"Because they match the exact description of the actions the surgeon took in the operating room."

"So you can't exclude the possibility that someone,

who was in his apartment, and not across the street in the defendant's office, hit Mr. Todaro in the head, then shot him, and this earlier wound would have been masked by the actions of the surgeon?"

"No, I can't, but that's very speculative."

"Would you please answer the question that was asked? Can you exclude this possibility with absolute certainty?"

"No, I can't."

"Thank you, Your Honor." Meredith backed up one step, then slowly turned and walked back to the defense table, sat, and looked up, her arms folded.

Berg stood. "I have a question for the witness, Your Honor, if I may re-direct."

The judge acquiesced.

Berg moved out to the center of the courtroom, stood silent for a moment to force the attention of everyone in the courtroom. "Dr. Barraza, the wounds we are speculating about. That someone hit Mr. Todaro in the head. Compare those wounds with bruises made by surgery. Would they be the same?"

"No, they wouldn't."

"Can you tell us about the difference?"

"Yes, of course. The wound from being hit in the head is a blunt force trauma. There would be bruising on the bone as well as the skin. The bruises from a surgeon are small and delicate and superficial. They would not impact the skull itself."

"So, is there any reasonable doubt that the bruises in question are from the hands of a skilled surgeon?"

"None, whatsoever, in my mind. You can ask the surgeon himself."

Meredith stood. "Your Honor, that would be hearsay."

Berg turned to her. "You are right. But we don't have to ask the surgeon. We have the opinion of the medical examiner." He turned to the witness chair. "Thank you,

Dr. Barraza. I have no further questions, for now."

Watson looked at Meredith. "Do you wish to re-cross?"

"No. Not at this time, Your Honor."

Judge Watson turned to Barraza and excused him subject to later testimony, then recessed until the next day. Rachel decided that Meredith tried, but this last exchange didn't sound very believable. A couple of jurors frowned. And scribbled.

The next day. Two new witnesses. Detectives Theodore Tourville and Diane Scanlan.

Chapter 30

Alan Berg stood and declared "The state calls Detective Theodore Tourville." The bailiff walked to the back of the courtroom and opened the door. Ted Tourville came in so fast he looked like he had his ear to the door. The bailiff moved out of the way as the detective swaggered to the witness chair.

He wore a dark blue suit with a light blue tie and a starched white shirt. His back straightened almost to bending back as he stood for the oath. Then he sat down, put his large hands on the chair, turned to the defense table and looked at Rachel. Quickly, he looked over to Berg.

Rachel unconsciously fingered the bullet in her pocket. When she became aware of it, she took her hand out. Her throat ached and her heart beat faster as she looked at the man who had killed Joshua. She put her hand back in the pocket and wrapped it tight around the bullet. At least when Joshua had given her the bullet, he had not yet betrayed her. That's the Joshua she needed to hang on to.

Berg stood, then looked down at his yellow legal pad on the table, put his finger on it, then stepped forward to the evidence table. He first picked up the bullet, looked at it, put it down, then picked up the plastic bag with the gun inside and brought it over to the witness stand. He handed it to Tourville. "This is the defendant's gun. Is your signature on this evidence bag?"

Tourville looked at the bag then raised his head.

"Yes."

Berg went back to his desk and picked up a stapled set of papers and brought them back to Tourville. "Do you recognize this document?"

Tourville looked and responded. "Yes. It is the search warrant for the gun."

Berg entered the search warrant into evidence, then continued. "So you had a search warrant for the gun, and you obviously found the gun. Did you find it inside the defendant's home?"

"No."

"Did you find it inside the defendant's office?"

"No."

"Car?"

"No."

Rachel heard Berg cleverly list all the innocent places the gun could be found. Tourville had answered 'No' three times and did not change his demeanor. She looked sideways at Meredith, who paid no attention to her. Rachel bit her lip.

"Where did you find the gun?"

"In the back yard."

"In the yard. Where exactly?"

"In the corner against the back fence."

"In the corner?"

"Yes, precisely in the corner."

"Was the gun so easy to find, Detective?"

Tourville looked at his shoes and appeared to think for a moment about what he should say. Then he looked up. "We were very thorough. Another man searched in the back yard as well. We searched every inch. And we searched the perimeter first."

"Why did you do that?"

"Because there were bushes all along the fence."

"I see. Was the gun out in plain site?"

"No it was hidden by a thick bush."

Alarm bells went off in the heads of all the jurors.

240

They sat up and some leaned forward.

Meredith stood. "Objection, Your Honor, to the word 'hidden'. There is no evidence of that."

Tourville, experienced witness, recovered quickly. "I said 'hidden' because the gun was hidden from view."

Berg decided to help him out and at the same time ram the point home to the jury, all the while protecting his witness from the defense. "So you couldn't see the gun until you moved the bushes aside, is that true?"

"Yes."

"So you don't know who put the gun back behind the bush at the corner of fence. Is that correct?"

"Yes."

Berg went back to his desk and sat. He leaned back and folded his arms across his chest. He had countered the three earlier No answers from Tourville with Yes two times. "No further questions, Your Honor."

That ended Tourville's testimony. Short and sweet. Rachel felt the eyes of the jury on her and every one now understood: only a guilty person would hide a gun. Ted Tourville came across as the perfect cold witness.

Meredith began her cross examination. "Detective, where were you when the defendant's attorney arrived at her house the day you showed up with the search warrant?"

"Where was I?"

"Yes. Where exactly?"

Tourville hesitated. "I'm not sure I remember that precisely."

"I see. Were you inside the house or out by the fence in the back, or—?"

"I was—actually, I was inside the house."

Meredith looked at the jury, then back to the witness chair. "So you had entered the house prior to the arrival of the defendant's attorney. Is that correct?"

"Rachel had let me into the house."

Yes, Rachel remembered, she hadn't been strong

241

enough at the front door.

Meredith put on a smile of disbelief. "You mean you forced your way past her."

Rachel looked at the jury, to see if they were accepting Meredith's implication. Tourville had been too interested in getting in her house quickly before the lawyer could stop him. But before she could see any conviction in their faces, Tourville went on.

"We certainly did not force our way in. The door was open and we walked through the doorway."

Meredith had no success with Ted Tourville. It appeared just as Rachel understood from the beginning, that he had prepared himself, they had prepared him, and he showed himself too experienced in the courtroom. And also, too determined to look innocent. Tourville sat like Buddha looking at Meredith, waiting.

"Detective, you know the defendant, do you not?"

Tourville looked puzzled at the question, but then sat up. "Yes, I do."

"How is that?"

"Do you mean personally?"

"I mean in any way."

"I have been investigating this case."

"I see. I think we understand that. That's why you're on the witness stand, Detective, But did you know Rachel McAlister when she was a Seattle detective?"

He hesitated. Rachel wanted to think that Meredith was having some effect on him.

"I knew of her."

"You knew of her. All right. Let me refresh your memory, Detective." Meredith came back to the defense table and picked up a document. She took it over to Tourville. "Would you please read the title at the top of the page?"

He squirmed in his seat. Berg rose in his. "Objection, Your Honor, this document has not been introduced in evidence."

Meredith looked back at Berg and frowned, then turned to face the judge. "Your Honor, if you please, may I be allowed to continue the process of introducing this document in evidence?"

Judge Watson looked over her glasses at the prosecutor. "I think you are a little premature, Mr. Berg."

Berg sat and looked straight ahead, his face betraying nothing.

Meredith waited for Tourville.

He took his time. In a barely audible voice, he said, "It's a letter of reprimand."

Meredith held out her hand and Tourville gave her the paper back. "I introduce into evidence at this time, a letter of reprimand against Detective Ted Tourville."

Berg rose in place again and said in a loud voice, with that look of bewilderment on his face, "Your Honor, Detective Tourville is not on trial here. This has no relevancy whatsoever to this case. The document is not evidence and can't be entered as evidence."

Judge Watson looked at Meredith.

"On the contrary. This document, Your Honor, is a letter of reprimand to Mr. Tourville related to his unauthorized stakeout that led directly to the death of Seattle City Councilman Gil Hamilton."

The jury became excited. They leaned forward, eyes focused on Meredith.

Berg's face became red. "Your Honor, I must protest in the strongest terms." The jury turned toward him.

Judge Watson silenced him with her raised hand. The jury turned toward the bench. Her voice made it clear she wasn't pleased. "What is the nature of your objection?"

"Your Honor," Berg continued in the most respectful voice he could muster, "This is not relevant. The defense is trying to bring up something that does not relate to the evidence in this case." He turned to Meredith and stayed there, arms crossed.

Meredith looked at Berg, saying nothing for one second, then turned to the Judge. "Your Honor, Detective Tourville is a witness in this trial and..."

Berg interrupted her. "Your Honor, the detective is a witness to the evidence on the table, not to something a long time ago."

Meredith did not wait for the Judge to respond. "Your Honor, the defense has the right to challenge the credibility of the witness."

Berg did not wait for the judge. "Yes, of course, Your Honor, but only for the evidence in this case."

The judge looked at Meredith.

"Your Honor, both my client and Detective Tourville were present at the death of the city councilman. My client was there in response to a 911 call, the detective was not."

Judge Watson shook her head. "This document will not be allowed into evidence."

Meredith's eyes opened wide. "But Your Honor..."

The judge interrupted her. "I have ruled, Counselor. Whatever attitude the witness may have toward the defendant, it is hard to see how it changes the testimony he has given."

"Your Honor," Meredith said, "this will be grounds for appeal."

"That is your right. But for now," the judge turned to the jury, "the jury will disregard this evidence and the testimony of the witness related to it. I will include comments on this subject in my instructions." She turned to Meredith. "The defense may continue, but cross examination may relate only to testimony the witness has given on direct examination."

Meredith looked defeated. "Nothing further, Your Honor."

Berg stood. "May I redirect, Your Honor."

Judge Watson nodded to him.

Berg looked at Tourville. "Your testimony, then, is solely about the location of the gun when it was found?"

"Yes."

"The state has no further questions for this witness, Your Honor."

The judge and Rachel both looked at Meredith, who said "Nothing at this time."

The judge put her head down to examine something on her desk. Berg stood and said "Your Honor, the state requests a recess for the rest of this morning. In the afternoon, we will examine our final witness, Detective Diane Scanlon."

The name penetrated Rachel's skull as if it were another lethal projectile. The breath went out of her. She stared down at the desk, unable to react. Unable to think.

Whatever the witness list said, Rachel had not allowed herself to believe she would really see Diane, her partner in war and peace, on the witness stand.

Giving testimony for the prosecution.

The gavel rapped the judge's bench. "Court is in recess until 2 pm."

Chapter 31

When they were back in the interview room, Meredith put her briefcase on the table. She took out some papers, laid them down, and turned to Rachel. "I know this looks bad. But we can't give up."

"So, in the end, we have no strategy. You have no strategy, Meredith."

"No, not at all. You are too pessimistic."

"Pessimistic? What? All they have going for them is rock solid scientific evidence, and I'm pessimistic? There's no confusion here, Meredith, there's none. There's only the clear light of hell and it's shining on me. You said everything depended on Tourville. That was crap. And now Diane. So they can see the heart of my jealousy."

"I want you to listen to me. You haven't been on the stand yet."

"Me? On the stand? This is the new strategy?" She threw her hands up in the air and shook her head. "When did you come up with this idea? On the stairs?"

"No, I mean it. The jury has already seen you react strongly, they have seen, as I have, that you're completely innocent. Don't you see, you're my strategy because I know that the jury believes in you as much as I do."

"Stop it. Right here and now," Rachel said. "I know how to go on from here."

"What do you mean? I asked you if you had an

alternate strategy, and you didn't have one."

"Yeah, well I have one now." Rachel stared at her. She stood and folded her hands across her chest and waited. "I can go on without you."

"Without me? Are you crazy? You cannot go on without me." Meredith strode back and forth. "You need a lawyer, Rachel, you cannot go down there and start defending yourself now. You cannot do it! The judge won't allow it. Get hold of yourself. " Her voice got louder with each phrase.

"I've started to realize, I think my best defense now is that I've had an incompetent lawyer."

"No! Don't start blaming me now. I gave you the best defense possible."

"Not on your life. You didn't make any serious objections. You didn't hit any of those witnesses hard. You sure as hell didn't get one juror confused."

Meredith raised her voice and put a steel edge on it. "That's not my fault. What was I supposed to do, pretend there was no bullet, pretend there was no gun? Was I supposed to invent an alternate trajectory?"

"Something. Anything. Be a lawyer."

Meredith's voice became shrill. "No, don't put this on me. I gave you everything I had. I went over every word, every shred of evidence. I cannot work with nothing, and they gave me nothing."

Rachel put her hand on the table and swept the briefcase and papers on the floor. "Get the hell out of here!" She left the interview room and went back to her cell.

When she arrived inside, Rachel looked around the cell as the walls closed in on her from all sides. She slumped down at the foot of her bed, wrapped her arms around her stomach, and rocked slowly, as if she were trying to physically hold herself together. Then she stood.

She took four swift steps to the back of the room and

touched the wall, then reared back and hit it with the flat of her hand. It stung deep across her palm and fingers, she winced, but she wanted the raw pain. She did it again.

Rachel marched to the front of the room and stood at the door and pounded her head with her fists.

She walked to the back of the room and hit her head against the brick wall. God, is this how I'm going to die? Her adrenaline escalated. Sweat broke out on her forehead.

Rachel turned around and walked even faster to the front and her whole body crashed into the door, jamming Joshua's bullet into her thigh.

The sharp stab stopped her.

She knew.

The bullet.

He did love her after all.

The jagged edges of Joshua's bullet would save her.

Chapter 32

Rachel walked with strong purpose back to the interview room. Meredith had gone. She went out to Amy's desk at the end of the hall. "Do you know where my lawyer went?"

Amy looked at Rachel in exasperation. "Yes, I do. She's not far. She went to get a cup of coffee and said she would be back."

"Thanks." Rachel went back to her cell and called Meredith.

Meredith answered with a tired voice. "Yes? Are you feeling better?"

"Better? I don't think you're asking the right question. I have new evidence."

"New evidence?" Rachel could hear the disbelief in Meredith's voice. "What kind of new evidence?"

"Come up to the interview room and I'll tell you about it." Rachel listened to herself. She couldn't remember the last time she heard this much confidence in her own voice.

Not long after, Meredith entered the interview room, smiling but looking puzzled. "New evidence? Is that what you said?"

"Sit down and listen to me. Remember Chew on the stand? How easy it was to identify the bullet because it was so...I forget his exact words. He said it wasn't deformed."

"Yes, I remember that," Meredith said.

"So, think about it. The bullet in the evidence bag

supposedly went through Joshua's skull. It went right through the middle of the back of his head. It went through solid, hard bone. And before that it went through a windowpane. But there's no deformity." Rachel's eyes widened. She raised her eyebrows. "That's impossible."

"Meaning?" Meredith said, seemingly unable to draw the conclusion for herself.

Rachel looked at her. She bit her lip for a moment and cocked her head. Why did Meredith question this one ray of hope? Meaning, obviously, that the bullet in the evidence bag didn't go through Joshua's skull. Some other bullet killed him.

"So that means," Rachel continued, "somebody killed him and then replaced that bullet with one from my gun."

Meredith watched her in silence.

"That's the leap nobody has made," Rachel said. "The killer took the bullet out of his head." She paced up and down.

"So," Meredith said, watching her, but clearly not buying into this as new evidence, "what do we do, according to your plan?"

"Well, there's only one person who can help us now," Rachel said. "It's Dr. Chew. He's the only one. He said the bullet appeared perfect, so easy to identify. We have to confront him." Rachel looked at Meredith, who sat quiet for a long time. Rachel would have appreciated more support from her.

"I agree," Meredith finally said, nodding, her lips tightened. "You're right. This is a real chance. It is our only opportunity to challenge the evidence. It might not work, but it's worth a try."

"Like I said, I've got nothing to lose right now. Like I said." Rachel hesitated, then went on, in a louder voice, "It sure as hell ought to work. If he denies it, then we've got to get our own expert. It won't be hard to find one in

Seattle. But I have a feeling we won't have to. And I have one more thing to bring to your attention?"

"Good, what's that?" said Meredith. She seemed to be more on board now.

"Remember Dr. Golden, he said that the head was full of bone fragments."

Meredith spoke up. "He didn't say it was full of them."

"All right, don't get technical on me," Rachel continued. "The point is, the fragments were there because the bullet put them there. Bone fragments damage bullets. Barraza didn't mention that in his testimony. Of course not, he only answered questions that were put to him."

"Yes, well," Meredith said, standing up, "here is what we'll do. We'll go back and say that we want to re-cross Dr. Chew, for starters, and see what the judge says."

"Yes," Rachel echoed, "we'll see what the judge has to say about this."

At 2 p.m. the bailiff called everyone to order, and Judge Watson came in and sat, quietly, in her usual deliberate, dignified way, and looked out over the courtroom. Berg sat back relaxed, very smug. Meredith stood.

The judge acknowledged her.

"If I may Your Honor, I wish to examine Dr. Chew."

Berg jumped up. "Your Honor, the state has not completed its case. She had an opportunity to do this when Dr. Chew was on the stand. The defense can call Dr. Chew after the state has rested."

Watson raised her eyebrows, then turned from Berg, and looked at Meredith, smiled and waited.

"Your Honor, Dr. Chew is still available for testimony. Before the state continues with its case, we want to re-cross Dr. Chew. We believe it will change the entire direction of this case."

Berg's face turned red, he gesticulated, he glared. "Your Honor, I say again, we have but one more witness.

The defense can wait until this one final witness has given testimony. Then they present their case and can recall anybody they want."

Meredith maintained her composure. "Your Honor, Dr. Chew gave his testimony as a witness for the state. We must have the opportunity to cross examine Dr. Chew in that capacity. If this leads nowhere, the state can then go ahead and finish its case."

"If this leads nowhere?" Berg shook his head and threw his pencil down on the table. "Your Honor, this is either a fishing expedition or a stalling technique. The defense does not want to hear the testimony of Detective Diane Scanlan and they are trying everything to avoid it."

The judge waited for Meredith to respond.

"Your Honor," Meredith said, "the state cannot have it both ways. The state is trying to convict the defendant of murder. They only have one more witness. Recalling Dr. Chew is not going to delay much of anything."

Three minutes later, after Berg tried again to block it, Judge Watson told him to get Chew back on the witness stand. An hour later he appeared, the judge reminded him that he was still under oath, and he took the witness stand. He looked very puzzled.

"Dr. Chew," Meredith began, "I want to thank you for coming back to answer a few questions. I assure you we would not have done this if we didn't think it was important."

"I understand that," he said, nodding wisely.

"I don't think this will take very long, Dr. Chew."

He smiled and in a quiet voice said, "Take as long as you like. That's why I'm here."

Meredith looked at him, a little taken aback, then she seemed to realize how it looked and smiled back. "Let me ask you again about your testimony concerning the bullet. You testified, did you not, that the bullet in question, the one in the evidence bag," she walked over

252

to the evidence table and picked up the bag, "this one," she walked back and gave it to him, "this bullet, it's not deformed is it?"

"No, as I said, it's in very good shape."

"Dr. Chew, let me show you another bullet, if I may." Meredith came back to the defense table and picked up Joshua's jagged bullet, and took it over to the witness stand.

Chew looked it over. He bounced it up and down in his hand as if it were dice. He smiled and looked at the jury. "Pretty beat up."

"Yes it is. Thank you Dr. Chew. If you please, let me show these bullets to the jury and the prosecution." She took them back from Chew.

Berg began to get nervous. Meredith clearly intended to go somewhere dangerous with this and Rachel knew that he didn't understand where. A prosecutor's nightmare.

"Your Honor," Berg said, when Meredith showed him the bullets, "the bullet the defense counselor brought in has not been entered in evidence."

Judge Watson gave him a stern look.

"Your Honor," Meredith said, smiling at the judge, "if I may, I didn't say it was evidence. I have a point to make, that's all. I'm going to make a comparison. I want the jury to compare the bullet in evidence, the bullet the state says killed Joshua Todaro, with another bullet." A light seemed to suddenly go on in her head. "Yes, of course. My mistake, Your Honor. The defense enters this bullet in evidence for comparison purposes." She took it over to Berg, who waved her away.

Rachel thought he looked very foolish. And the jury noticed it.

Meredith took the bullets over to the jury box, and put them in the hand of the jury forewoman. "Please compare these bullets, take your time, make sure you see the difference, and pass them on. We'll wait until you have all seen them." She stepped back.

The jurors were clearly curious about this new set of events in the trial. It took some time for all the jurors to receive and inspect the two bullets and finally get them back to Meredith's hands. The jurors eyed each other. Then Meredith brought them over in front of Dr. Chew, and held them up, each in one hand.

"Do you come across a great variety of bullets, Dr. Chew?"

"Of course. It's my business."

Meredith raised her left hand with the evidence bag. "Can you explain to the jury how this bullet in my left hand, the one which is not deformed, nearly perfect as you said, how could it have gone through a window and a skull, and not be deformed?" She jerked the bag up and down several times.

"I didn't say that it did"

"You didn't?" She turned to the jurors to make sure they were paying close attention, then faced Chew and waited for his response.

"No, as I said, if I may remind you, all that I said was that the bullet was fired by a certain gun. I didn't say where the gun was at the time of the shooting, or what it's trajectory was, or where the bullet ended up. That wasn't my job." Chew found this a perfect opportunity to defend his own professional pride. He looked over at Berg with worry in the muscles surrounding his eyes.

"But you have seen so many bullets, Dr. Chew, tested so many, surely you knew that this bullet, the bullet in evidence, had only a small bit of deformity, so it must have gone through flesh but didn't go through bone."

"Why that's exactly what I assumed."

Berg came up on his feet. The jurors all turned in unison to look at him. The defense had delivered a surprise to the jury, and now Chew provided corroboration. Rachel could see that Berg feared he had wandered on to quicksand.

"Your Honor, this is going too far. This is not about Dr. Chew's testimony," he said.

"Please, Mr. Berg," the judge said, "let this continue. It's about the bullet, and you brought it into evidence." She nodded at Meredith.

Meredith went on. "Dr. Chew, may I ask what you meant when you agreed that the bullet went through flesh and not bone?"

Chew thought for a moment, then shook his head, causing his cheeks to wobble.

"I didn't mean anything. When I see a bullet, I can tell more or less what it has hit. In general. I assumed that this particular man was killed by a bullet to the chest, hit the lung or even the heart. Sometimes a bullet enters the brain, you know, through the exact center of the eye, or through the nose cavity. The bullet can in fact miss bone and go straight into the brain without being very much damaged."

"Thank you Dr. Chew. So, let me summarize what you have said. Is it your testimony that this bullet, the near-perfect bullet from the evidence bag, that it didn't go through bone?"

Meredith has finally hit home, doing her job as a litigator. After Rachel gave her the ammunition.

"No way."

"Then it couldn't have killed Joshua Todaro, is that correct?"

Rachel looked over at the jury. They were all at the edge of their seats and several of them were also writing in their little notebooks. The courtroom spectators stayed quiet, but the air was electric.

Berg stood once more. Louder, this time. "Objection Your Honor."

Judge Watson waited, then said, "What is your objection, Mr. Berg.?"

"Foundation, Your Honor. I object on the grounds that Dr. Chew gave no testimony relating to the death of

Joshua Todaro. He didn't sign the death certificate or do the autopsy." Berg lost his cool. His calm. His composure.

Meredith turned to Berg and raised a finger, and then looked at the judge. "That certainly is true. I have no more questions for Dr. Chew and I thank him for his testimony. "

Then she turned back to Chew. "Thank you, sir, for your testimony."

"Wait," she said before he could leave. "One more thing. And I promise this is the last question. About the autopsy report. Why did you not look at it? Would it not be relevant? Weren't you curious as to how the victim died?"

"No. For two reasons. Number one, I was asked whether or not this bullet was fired from this gun. That's all, and they wanted a report in a hurry."

"In a hurry, Dr. Chew? Did that not compromise your work?"

"No of course not. Not really in a hurry. I meant that they didn't ask me to analyze everything possible about the gun. They wanted it to be my number one priority."

"And the autopsy?"

Berg decided to lean across his desk this time to show he felt in control. "Objection, Your Honor, Dr. Chew did not testify about the autopsy."

The judge turned to Meredith and raised her eyebrows.

"I did not ask Dr. Chew about any evidence from the autopsy. I asked him why he didn't wait for the autopsy."

"Objection overruled. You may answer."

Berg sat, frustrated.

Chew also appeared to be frustrated. He continued. "My understanding was that the autopsy was going on at the same time. They wanted all this done before we started or completed any other work. Put everything aside and complete this analysis. Detective Tourville waited for it. The gun and the bullet."

"Thank you Dr. Chew. No more questions."

Chew looked at Berg. Rachel guessed he wondered what he would hear outside the courtroom after the trial.

The judge turned to Berg. "Do you want to ask any questions at this time, Mr. Berg?"

Berg grimaced, put his hands on the table, pushed hard and stood, seeming arthritic. He raised his index finger. He turned first to the judge.

"One quick question, Your Honor." Berg took a quick drink of water, picked up his legal pad and ran his finger down it. Then he turned to the witness stand. "Dr. Chew, how would you judge the quality of work you and your lab did?"

"Quality? If you ask me, I would say perfect and complete."

"Thank you for your testimony. No further questions."

"The witness may step down."

Chew shook his head back and forth, left the stand and went out the door in a hurry.

Meredith said to the judge "Your Honor, I must recall for testimony all the state's witnesses. Based on what Dr. Chew said, I think it's necessary."

Berg kept on standing. "Your Honor, I object strenuously. We cannot re-try this case again." He made a great effort, but he looked like the roof had fallen in on him. He knew he could not stop this whole re-cross. Everyone could see it in the judge's face.

The judge looked at him over her glasses. "I think we are going to have to, Mr. Berg. I will not allow this trial to be overturned on appeal because we denied the defense an opportunity. This is not a misdemeanor. Ms. Rawlings, are you sure you want to re-cross all of them?"

This time Meredith looked back at Rachel, who nodded. Now they were in the driver's seat. Electricity pulsed through the courtroom. A low-pitched hum came from the gallery. The jurors sat on the edge of their seats. "Yes, Your Honor, it's necessary."

Judge Watson hit her gavel hard down on the bench and waited for the courtroom to subside. "Very well, then. Tomorrow morning, Mr. Berg, have Dr. Barraza, Dr. Golden, and Mr. Sargenti ready for re-cross at ten o'clock in the morning."

"Begging you pardon, Your Honor," Meredith said, "we don't need to hear testimony from Dr. Golden."

"Why is that, Ms. Rawlings?"

"Because he said already he didn't know about the bullet. He cannot provide any more information."

"All right, then, Dr. Barraza and Mr. Sargenti." She banged her gavel. "At ten."

Chapter 33

Ten o'clock the next morning, everyone was in place. The judge signaled for Meredith to call her other witnesses back. She requested Frank Sargenti. He came in, less puzzled than Chew. Meredith had said there were four TV vans outside trained on everyone who entered, and Sargenti clearly wasn't happy with that.

He took the witness chair after accepting the reminder about his oath, and stared out at the defense table, not giving a damn what the jury thought of it. Rachel could see that he believed with absolute certainty that his testimony could resist all attempts to undermine it, and he wanted them all to know it as well.

Meredith stood just in front of him. "Thank you, Mr. Sargenti. I want to be absolutely sure, you know, as I have said more than once, this is a trial that affects my client's life directly, and I want to be as careful as possible. So please bear with me."

"Of course." Sargenti looked at Rachel again.

"You said that the trajectory of the bullet went from the victim's head across the street to Ms. McAlister's office. Am I stating that correctly?"

"Yes, you are."

Meredith picked up the evidence bag with the bullet in it and brought it up before Sargenti. She held it up high and pointed to it.

"And when you determined that trajectory, was the bullet in the victim's head, pointing away from Ms.

McAlister's office?"

"Certainly not. He was in the hospital, and you know that."

Meredith turned to Watson. "Your Honor, will you instruct the witness to reply to the questions and not attack the defense counsel."

Sargenti shook his head. Watson wagged her finger a little at Meredith. "You are overreacting, Counselor."

"Yes, Your Honor," Meredith said, acting surprised. She turned back to Sargenti.

"I do know that he was in the hospital. But we are making sure the jury understands all the details necessary for them to convict or acquit, do you not agree?"

Berg got out of his chair with some speed, but hesitated a moment before speaking, as if he knew he looked a bit in a hurry. "Your Honor, this is a court of law and we all know the reasons why we are here. It is not necessary to assume the jury is ignorant."

Watson threw up her hands and lay back in her chair.

Meredith looked over at Berg and spoke to him. "This is not about the jury. I was merely clarifying to the witness why I am asking all these questions. Because he has already testified, I want him to understand that we are looking for more clarity. We are not trying to repeat testimony already given."

The judge sat up and looked to heaven for relief. "Please help us all and go on, Ms. Rawlings." She waited for Berg to object to that, but nothing came from him.

Meredith continued, "Would you then also tell me, for the benefit of the jury, Mr. Sargenti, what is the exact connection between the trajectory of the bullet and Ms. McAlister's gun?"

Berg spoke without moving. "Objection Your Honor, no foundation."

Meredith looked at him and smiled. She took a little

walk in front of the witness stand, posturing for the jury. "Well, then, I withdraw that question. Let me put it this way, Mr. Sargenti. Is there any direct connection between the trajectory, all the trajectories in fact that you showed us on your panel, all the red lines? They all start out at the victim's head. How do they end up at Ms. McAlister's gun?"

Berg remained silent, but he shuffled some papers around on his table, and turned and talked to his aide. Rachel knew he did it in the hope the jury would read it as a sign they shouldn't pay any attention. She could also see it also as a sign that he lost confidence in his testimony.

"They don't," Sargenti said. "I didn't say that. If you recall, what I said was that the trajectory went as far as the hallway wall."

"Please bear with me. The trajectory of the bullet you traced. Do you know that it was the bullet removed from the victim's head?"

Sargenti looked puzzled for a moment and screwed his mouth up. "No, I know it was the trajectory which led out from the brain."

"So, you know there was a trajectory, but a trajectory of what, Mr. Sargenti?"

Sargenti sat silent thinking. "It was the trajectory of a bullet."

"But how do you know that the bullet of your trajectory is the bullet that killed the victim?"

"I don't. It is a hypothetical trajectory based on the wound. It's a trajectory from the bullet hole, not the bullet inside the head." He said this last sentence with more assurance, like Chew before him reassuring everyone of his own competence.

"So you cannot, Mr. Sargenti, with your evidence, connect this hypothetical trajectory in any way with my client's gun?"

"Not me. I never said I could. No one asked me, and

if they had, I would have said it's not what I do." For the first time, he showed some concern. He took out a handkerchief and wiped some sweat from his brow, even though there didn't seem to be any.

Rachel knew the important and potential impact of this point. For the first time everyone knew with certainty, and more importantly with emphasis, that they could connect the bullet to the gun but they couldn't connect the gun to Rachel. Here and now the possibility of reasonable doubt came out in this trial for the very first —explosive— time.

"Thank you very much, Mr. Sargenti."

" You may step down," Judge Watson said, "unless Mr. Berg has some re-direct."

Berg's face displayed his frustration and fluster. He shook his head and threw his pen down on the table, and looked sideways at the jury to see if they were watching him.

Meredith spoke in a voice that showed greater confidence. She stopped, stood straight and looked to the judge. "We need to cross-examine Dr. Barraza again."

Berg turned to her with his mouth down. "This is going too far." Then he opened his hands wide and spoke to Judge Watson. "Your Honor. Dr. Barraza has already testified in complete detail to everything he knows. To every question, I am going to object that it's been asked and answered, and I will be sustained every time."

Rachel knew that Berg wanted to stall. For the first time, a sense of hope filled her heart.

Meredith listened to Berg, then her voice rose. "Your Honor, it's clear now," she said with loud emphasis on 'clear', "that the state has no way of connecting the evidence to my client. But I expect the same courtesy for my client as the state has received. Dr. Barraza testified about the death of Joshua Todaro, and we have the right to hear him testify on the new evidence we have produced."

Berg, on his feet, whining. "Your Honor, please, there is no new evidence." He said it in very melo-dramatic fashion, as if it pained him.

Meredith stood turned toward the bench. "Your Honor, it is not exactly a new piece of evidence. I give you that, but it is a new way of looking at the evidence, and it does prompt new questions for the medical examiner as it did for the other technical witnesses."

Judge Watson didn't hesitate. "I agree with the defense counsel, Mr. Berg. Please have Dr. Barraza come in for further testimony."

A few minutes later and Barraza reappeared in the witness chair, no happier than the others. His eyes shone in anger at both Berg and Rachel.

Meredith stood before him. She did not have the two bullets. She did not need them anymore. "Dr. Barraza, when you did the autopsy, did you have the bullet that came from my client's gun to use in the lab?"

"No, of course not." This time he spoke with arrogance.

Let him have his pride, Rachel thought, it didn't matter anymore to her.

"Of course not?" Meredith said, cocking her head to one side. "Why do you say it so emphatically?"

"Well, because I did an autopsy," Barraza said. "My job was to certify the cause of death, which was undeniably a hole in the poor young man's head. That I did to perfection. I could tell it was a gunshot wound, not a knife wound, not a blunt force trauma, as if it were a club of some sort. The victim did not fall off a cliff."

"So you didn't actually tie the bullet wound in the victim's head to the bullet in the police evidence bag."

"No, I did not. Not directly, at least."

Meredith acted surprised. "Not directly? How is that?"

"I specified in my report, if you read it, what caliber of bullet was compatible with this wound. You know," he said, sounding flustered for the first time, "what caliber of bullet could have entered the opening in the skull."

"I see," said Meredith. She put her hand up to her mouth and held it there for a long moment, then let both arms drop. "The caliber of bullet. What caliber was that, Dr. Barraza."

He looked at Meredith as if he hated her. "It's in the report." He almost yelled it out.

"Ah, yes." Meredith, at last, dragged this out for the benefit of the jury. She looked over at Diane, then came over to the table and picked up the report and brought it to Barraza. "Would you read to the jury what caliber it was?"

Barraza didn't wait. "I don't have to," he said. "It could have been one of several."

"Several?" Meredith said. "How many?"

"Look, it depends, German or American. Nine millimeter, or 40 Smith & Wesson. From my point of view, inside the body, they are all pretty much the same. They all do the same lethal damage, depending on the velocity."

Meredith looked quizzical. "Velocity? Why do you say that?"

Barraza looked irritated at having to explain himself. "This bullet did not exit the brain. That means that it did not have enough velocity. No doubt because it went through a window across the street before hitting the victim."

This is interesting, Rachel thought. Barraza knew all about the circumstances of Joshua's death, while Chew knew none of them. If Chew had been as thorough in the beginning, they would never have come looking for her.

"Thank you, Dr. Barraza. So let me finish by asking you, do you know which bullet actually made the hole in Joshua Todaro's head? Did you ever see that bullet?"

Barraza put his head down and made a long sigh, then looked up at Meredith and over at the jury and gestured widely in frustration. "No, I didn't."

Oh, Rachel heard herself breathe in fast, so Barraza hadn't been so professional and complete as he could have been, either.

Berg stood and tried to put Meredith on the defensive. "Your Honor, this has gone on too long. The defense attorney will take all day bringing up irrelevant testimony about nothing."

Meredith turned to Berg. "On the contrary, Your Honor, the prosecution itself is making irrelevant statements. This is testimony that is relevant to this case. More than that, it is directly relevant to why we asked for re-cross of the witnesses. No one actually examined the bullet in the victim."

Meredith and Berg both stood there, looking at each other, white heat in their eyes, arms across their chests.

Rachel saw that Berg, for the first time, understood that his case lay in jeopardy. She also saw Meredith for the first time truly fighting for her client's life.

Judge Watson raised her hand, then thought better of that, and instead stood and surveyed the courtroom before speaking. She put her hand on the gavel, and looked like she intended to raise it up and bang down hard, but changed her mind. She spoke slowly and seriously. Rachel could see the judge's intent. In her courtroom she maintained control. Over everyone.

"We will not have arguments in place of closing statements. Both of you, in my chambers, now. Including the defendant." Watson moved toward the back door.

Berg moved toward the judge. "Your Honor, the defendant should not be part of this conversation." Clearly he did not like the implications of this.

Judge Watson turned back halfway and looked at him over her shoulder, clearly angered at this affront to her authority. "On the contrary, Mr. Berg, I think she should be. And she will be." She nodded in rhythm with each syllable. Then she turned to the bailiff. "Let's do it the other way around. Please excuse the witness for a moment, then escort the jury to the jury room. And the spectators out of the courtroom."

This made things more serious. The jury surely thought that it would take a long time to resolve this problem, and it didn't look good for the prosecution. For the first time Rachel believed she really had a chance to get out of this. She felt an impulse to turn around and see if Michael still sat in the back of the room, but she resisted. The wrong impulse could cause problems now. She needed to maintain self-control.

Berg sat in frustration. The bailiff went to the jury and motioned them to stand up and file out to the hallway to the jury room. Then he came back and made sure all the spectators were out in the hallway.

Judge Watson watched them until they were all out of the room and the door had closed. She looked at Meredith. "I want you to tell me exactly what you think you're doing. We are not going to have an informal debate in front of the jury."

Before Meredith could answer, Watson held up her hand and turned and looked at Berg. "And then I want you to tell me exactly what your objections are. Now begin, Ms. Rawlings."

Meredith took a long, deep breath. "It is very clear, given the testimony of Dr. Chew, that there's no connection here at all with my client. None whatsoever."

Berg opened his eyes wide, and with a stiff back and neck turned slowly to Meredith, his usual show of surprise. "You have got to be kidding. After all this testimony? From experts, I might add."

Meredith ignored him and looked directly at the judge. "It is certainly clear that talking to Dr. Barraza will not change his testimony one way or another. And I must admit it was the same with Mr. Sargenti. But that's the whole point." Meredith opened her palms wide. "It does not come together."

She put her left index finger on the top of her right thumb. "Number one, if you ask the surgeon, he didn't look at the bullet."

Meredith moved to the index finger. "Two, if you ask the medical examiner, he didn't look at the bullet."

She moved to the middle finger. "Three, if you ask the crime scene investigator, he didn't look at the bullet."

Meredith moved to the fourth finger. "And four, the bullet in evidence can't possibly have killed Joshua Todaro because it didn't go through his skull. We all saw the picture made by the coroner of her skull. And then Dr. Chew looked at the bullet but didn't look at the victim. No one informed him how the bullet entered the body. And I'm sure he didn't ask, either. He made assumptions. They all did."

She dropped her hand. The jury should have heard all of this. Rachel couldn't have said it better herself.

Meredith, increasingly sure of herself, continued. "They all made assumptions. It is obvious the police department thought this was a done deal from the very beginning. So here we are, Your Honor, I believe you must give a directed verdict of acquittal because there's nothing here in all the evidence presented by the state to connect my client to this victim. The bullet in the evidence bag did not go through bone. It did not kill Joshua Todaro."

The judge turned to Berg. He shuffled in his chair, then stood and put on an air of frustration as if this were all the ravings of a lunatic.

Rachel could see that deep inside, he knew that his entire future career hung on the line today in this courtroom.

"I disagree," Berg said. "Whoever shot Joshua Todaro shot him from McAlister's office, that's beyond dispute." A tape of this conversation for his peers to hear would've been very damaging to his career, Rachel said to herself.

Watson frowned, cocked her head, and looked at him out of one eye. "Excuse me, Mr. Berg, a person with the name of Whoever is not on trial here. I want you to tell me exactly how you think you tied this evidence to the defendant. And I don't mean any old evidence. I mean the evidence that killed the victim. Go on. Let's hear it. I don't see where you have introduced any such evidence into this courtroom. Unless you have it up your sleeve."

Berg waited a moment, opening up his hands and looking up as if he were getting his answer straight from heaven. Then he looked around at Rachel, Meredith, and Judge Watson, as if that gesture would make the truth come out. "The trajectory is clear."

He made it up as he went along, desperate, probably thinking about the scene outside with the reporters or when he gets back to the office and has to face them all, Rachel thought. His boss and the mayor and the commissioner and all those who made it out to Broadmoor on that cold night when the councilman died and Tourville hid in the bushes. Berg appeared to be thinking hard, trying to come up with something that would save this trial and save his career.

"No, absolutely not," the judge said. "The trajectory does not lead to Ms. McAlister here, it leads to the moon as Mr. Sargenti said so poetically. Unless you can place Ms. McAlister exactly at the trajectory at the time the gun fired the bullet down that trajectory. Can you do that, Mr. Berg?" She paused, lifted up her palms, widened her eyes, and cocked her head to one side. "Without the bullet that went down that trajectory?" Watson leaned back in her chair and chewed on the stem of her glasses.

"Your Honor, we can place her in the room."

Rachel spoke up. "I beg your pardon? There has been

no evidence about that at all. None of the witnesses has testified to my whereabouts. None. They had my gun, they didn't care about anything else."

Watson now frowned at her. "You haven't been called as a witness, Ms. McAlister. Please don't interrupt."

Meredith stood. "Apologies on behalf of my client, Your Honor. She will refrain in the future. The jury is not here, so she naturally assumed she could speak."

Berg studied his hands, then spoke with a strained forcefulness. "This is obviously not a suicide."

At this moment, Rachel felt a little sorry for him. It had to be difficult for a lawyer trained in legal argument and used to winning all the cases to come up with words that don't help him at all.

"That's right," Meredith said. "But that does not make a connection to Ms. McAlister."

"She's the one who heard the gunshot!"

Meredith's voice showed excitement. "Oh, come on, Mr. Berg, it would not matter anyway. You cannot connect it to my client."

Rachel had to give it to Meredith, she could argue well when things were going in her favor. Berg fumed.

The judge leaned forward. "Mr. Berg, the bullet you put into evidence is not the bullet that killed Mr. Todaro. It is clear that some other bullet killed the victim, and you don't have that bullet. You don't have the trajectory either. There is a missing bullet and a missing trajectory and there's no evidentiary connection with Ms. McAlister." The judge stood and looked as if she intended to make a pronouncement. She looked at Berg.

Berg had his head down and thought hard. Then he raised his head as if he had made a discovery. "If this is not the bullet, then the other one must be embedded in the wall. That would also be from McAlister's gun."

Rachel thought back to Joshua's apartment. No, there would not be a bullet there anymore. Tourville would have removed it the first day of the investigation.

The judge practically fell back in her chair in a sign of exhaustion. "For God's sake, Mr. Berg, don't tell me that you're now going to go back and look for more evidence. Wouldn't that make a nice precedent. Every time the state loses it will keep on going like the Energizer bunny until it finds more clues."

She pushed herself up to her desk and said, "I don't think so. You are where you were back when you started this investigation, Mr. Berg. You had probable cause to consider Ms. McAlister a suspect, but here and now there is considerable reasonable doubt about your evidence. I now understand clearly that any reasonable group of men and women would acquit the defendant."

She surveyed all of them. "I am going to issue a directed verdict of acquittal."

"Your Honor!"

"No, Mr. Berg, let me make myself completely clear. You have no case. This trial is over."

"Your Honor, people have been convicted even without the body."

Watson leaned back and laughed. "Not in my court-room, Mr. Berg. Not here. And certainly not in this case."

Her voice became more animated. "It is my judgment here and now that any reasonable jury would be required to acquit this defendant. Therefore I must issue a directed verdict of acquittal."

She looked over at Meredith. "If I have a motion."

Meredith stood and looked at Rachel with a forced smile.

"Your Honor, the defense introduces a motion that you issue a directed verdict of acquittal."

Berg stood and started to raise his hand and say something, but Watson cut him off.

"Mr. Berg, I am assuming the fact finding role of the jury. You cannot connect the crime to the defendant. Ms. Rawlings, your motion is granted."

The judge stood again and frowned, raised her eyebrows and pushed her hair back, leaned on her desk and turned to the bailiff.

"Have the jury return to the courtroom, please. And visitors   as   well."

Chapter 34

The bailiff walked over to the hallway door and disappeared for a moment. Then the door opened and the jury slowly filed back to their seats, trying to avoid stumbling while they strained hard to read the faces of Meredith, Berg and Watson.

The back door opened and spectators began filing back in. They were all talking excitedly. The courtroom sounded like the street.

The judge waited patiently for everyone to be seated, stood leaning on her desk and looming over the courtroom until she got the complete quiet she wanted. Then she stood straight, and took her time making the announcement. She gave her undivided attention to Rachel. "I will issue a written ruling in the morning. For now, all charges against the defendant are dismissed. Ms. McAlister, you are free to go."

She then turned to the jury. "Thank you for your service. Based on the evidence submitted by the State, I will prepare a written directed verdict of acquittal."

Then she addressed the courtroom. "If you will all excuse me, I have work to do." She slammed her gavel on the desk while looking at Berg.

Shocked silence permeated the room. No one moved, until after half a minute they realized what Judge Watson had done, and began filing out. And then the room filled with excited conversation and wagging heads.

Rachel felt Meredith's hand, again, on her shoulder. She turned around and Meredith hugged her and she shook and held Rachel as tight as she possibly could. Her flowery perfume didn't fit this occasion. Rachel let her hold on for a while, then strongly pulled back.

Meredith put both hands up to her face and began wiping her eyes, then got a tissue off the table, and buried her face in it. Then she said, "Rachel, you don't know how happy I am for you. I always had faith that this would turn out right for you."

Rachel had not heard her before with this warmth in her voice. "No. Joshua alone gave me the idea that saved my life. I believe he gave me that bullet for my protection, and he is protecting me now."

"Rachel, look, I have a few things to clean up. Then let's go away, you and me, somewhere where we can be alone, talk things out. What do you say?" She put her hands together as if she prayed to—who knows what.

"Meredith, if I have learned one thing from all this, it's that I don't even know my own self. I need to spend a few days thinking about my situation. Then I'll give you a call. For now, thank you for your time. I'm sure I'll be able to get enough money out of my house to pay your bill. For now it's just my head trying to clear itself." She saw Meredith stuffing a final stack of papers into her briefcase and heading out past the bailiff's desk. She never looked back.

Outside the court building, Rachel looked over the throng of reporters and cameras below her on steps and sidewalk. All the cameras, all the microphones were pointed at her. She wondered at all the shades of green on the trees up and down the street. A memory floated up of the last time she had to face cameras, standing on different steps, responding to questions about the killing of Gil Hamilton. She ought to feel differently this time, but she didn't.

She held Joshua's bullet tight in her hand. A bullet

saved her this time, but a different bullet took her Joshua away. Four bullets in this case. The one in her hand. The one that killed Joshua. The one submitted in evidence. And the one the crime lab used to connect to her gun. But only one that mattered.

She leaned next to somebody's microphone. "I have nothing to say except this. The Seattle Police Department is the finest in the world. I am proud of the time I spent with them. The whole city should be proud of them. But now, thank God, they have better things to do, and I want to get on with my life."

A young woman in a bright green sweater and jeans shoved a microphone right up to her mouth. "Do you feel vindicated, Ms. McAlister?"

Rachel looked at her and out at the crowd watching. "No, I don't feel vindicated. I have no need of vindication. And Joshua Todaro's killer is at large. Until he's caught, none of us will rest."

Chapter 35

Rachel arrived home, unlocked the front door and went in. "Irene?" Nothing. She said it again louder.

"Oh, hell! Oh, hell!" Antoinette perched on a dining room chair. "Haa. Haa." Irene, following her usual practice, had spread papers on the seat to keep it clean.

Irene's voice suddenly sounded from behind. "I'm sorry, I was napping for a few minutes."

Rachel gave her a big smile. The scent of smoke on Irene's clothes made Rachel want to say something, but she'd given up on that a long time ago. Irene had been splayed out on the sofa, looking like she had been awakened from a nice dream, still in her bathrobe, slippers and curlers. She closed her bathrobe tight and she came over and gave Rachel a big hug. That didn't fit for Irene and her British reserve.

"I'm sorry, I guess I got used to having the house all to Antoinette and myself."

"They tried to stick it to me but they couldn't, Irene. I'm too tough for that. You've had it all to yourself for a long time."

"And I have taken very good care of it, too. I didn't let anybody in upstairs, and only came up myself once in a while to make sure everything is all right. It's been so peaceful and quiet." She stood up, went and put her finger out. Antoinette hopped on. They walked toward the back of the house.

"I'm going downstairs. Don't forget to lock the door."

Then she stopped and turned back to Rachel. "Are you back home for a while?"

"No, I'm going up to my cabin for a couple of weeks."

"You taking anyone up there with you?"

"Not on your life. I really need to be alone. To think things over."

"Good for you." Irene waved, then turned back and said, "I'll be downstairs if you need us. Me."

"I'm leaving my cell phone here," Rachel said. "It'll just be me and the bears. If the house burns down, don't bother calling me. I need some time to do nothing, let all this sink in. I won't even do any planning for the future. Who knows, maybe I won't even want to continue my work after I get back." Then she thought for a moment. "Sorry, Irene, I didn't mean to unload on you."

"Well, I will take care of everything like I usually do. You know you can rely on me."

"Yes, if there's any one thing I can rely on, Irene, it's you. I'll be getting a few things together and be out of here. Do we have any wine in the refrigerator?"

"Yes, but nothing good, I'm sure."

"All right. I'll then be on my way."

Rachel went out to the kitchen and took out a bottle of Chateau St. Michelle Riesling, opened it, lifted the bottle to her lips and felt the cold stream all the way down her esophagus. She took out some roast beef and ate it practically in one bite. Then she went to her bedroom, put the cell phone on the dresser and felt an immediate sense of relief, as if she had already gone far away.

She put a few things into her suitcase, and came back downstairs and went out the door without saying a word. She drove toward I-5 and relaxed.

But when she saw the turnoff to 244th, she felt an irresistible tug that made her make a turn south toward Holyrood Cemetery.

Once there, she stopped and bought a bouquet of

roses. She went to God's Acre, through the white arch, and walked down the long, narrow aisles to Joshua's graveside. There were dead flowers in a vase. She pulled them out and tossed them in a trash can, then carefully put her flowers in.

Rachel stood still for a moment, alone, quiet, remembering. Cold air from Puget Sound swept past her up to the green hills and over to Lake Washington but the delicate fragrance of the roses kept her close to him. She touched the cold concrete of the tombstone and traced his name with her finger. The roughness of the stone pierced her heart with the reality of his absence.

A flurry of memories flew past her mind of Joshua in the hospital, in bed, in the kitchen together making dinner, a kiss at the nape of her neck, his cheek when he hadn't shaved. Her chest tightened and she sat in front of his grave, put her hands over her eyes and began to cry. "I'm sorry, Joshua. I failed you."

She stayed a minute longer in silence, took a tissue out of her purse and cleaned her face. Then she got herself up somehow, walked up past the row of family chapels, found her car and drove out to the freeway again. A beautiful clear afternoon, the sky blue, she headed north out of the city.

Rachel followed I-5 up to the lake, intending on turning east on 542 after Bellingham and on to Mt. Baker. Sometimes two hours can go by in a hurry. Past Everett, Washington is a different world. Rachel just wanted to leave Seattle behind. She had a strong temptation to keep on going up to British Columbia. A temptation. But her parents had bequeathed her the cabin at Mt. Baker, and she went there when she really needed to feel their presence.

Rachel pushed down on the accelerator.

Something in her rear view mirror caught her attention. A silver Chevrolet. She didn't think anything special about being followed by another car for long distances, not on the main highway to Canada. But this car caught her eye. Brian Phillips drove it. Or someone who looked like him.

Maybe he followed her, maybe not. She certainly needed to know. The trial lay behind her, but suddenly she didn't feel like a free woman. Did he follow her because he still thought she had killed Joshua? Because he wanted to make sure she got her punishment? Or did he simply plan to finish the job? And why Brian Phillips?

She had only one way to find out. If she left the road, he would have to do the same or wait for her to come back.

Instead of turning right onto 542, she kept going on I-5. The sign to Bellingham Golf and Country Club came into view. She made a slow turn off to the right and on to Meridian Avenue and into the club. Brian followed her off the freeway but kept on going on Meridian. Now it didn't seem so smart to leave her cell phone back home.

The sign said straight ahead for the clubhouse. A half a minute later, she pulled up to a dramatic north woods building, a very natural oversized log cabin with golf carts out front. Beyond the clubhouse she saw a putting green surrounded by majestic towers of dark green fir trees. Several players were lining up their shots, and two men were getting into a cart, deep in animated conversation. She looked around for a silver Chevy, but didn't see one.

She followed the road as it wound around the putting green and led back out. When she got back to the highway, she looked around again, but could not see a silver Chevy. She figured it had been just a coincidence, someone who resembled Brian. Maybe. She needed one more proof to make sure.

When Rachel got to the freeway, she didn't turn north toward the cabin, but turned back south. As she made the turn into traffic, she looked in her rear view mirror. One car behind she could clearly make out the head of Ted Tourville in a black Ford Taurus. So they were working in tandem, Rachel thought. As usual, they were careless.

Ten minutes later, she passed the big Skagit Valley Casino sign and took the next exit. She pulled up to valet parking, and took her sports bag, taking her time, giving a tip, looking around, so Tourville and Phillips wouldn't miss her. She waited and watched while the attendant drove her black Audi A4 away.

Once inside the casino, she went to the front desk, took more time talking to a clerk, and signed up for a room for two nights, just in case Tourville decided to use his badge to get information.

Rachel picked up her bag and walked toward the casino. Shiny trinkets in the sundries store caught her eye. She went in, walked up and down the aisles for several minutes, picking objects up and examining them, before she bought some Ray-Ban sunglasses, extra large and dark. She tried them on in a mirror, using the occasion to survey the hallway outside the store as best she could.

If Ted or Brian were there, they were careful to remain hidden. Then she bought a dark red Skagit Valley College knit beanie and hooded sweatshirt.

A blackjack table had two open seats. Rachel took one of them and dropped twenty dollars and left. Then she stopped at some slots before she went to her room.

Once inside, she called Enterprise in Bellingham. An Avis desk dominated a corner of the lobby of the hotel, but she didn't want Ted to see her renting a car. The woman at Enterprise said they could have the car out front in less than an hour. Rachel gave the woman the necessary information, then told her to have it brought behind the hotel outside the kitchens. "Yes, of course. In one hour, max," the woman responded.

Rachel then called room service and asked about kosher food. That wouldn't be a problem. But what if she wanted to see the conditions down there, talk to the chef, and make sure the guy who prepared the food followed kosher practices? "Of course", came the response. "Come on down to the basement. We are more than happy to accommodate you."

Leaving her room, Rachel carried her luggage down to the end of the hallway to the stairwell, and followed it all the way down to the basement. She walked past the fitness center, the pool, and the laundry room. Just beyond that she spied the kitchen. She pushed open the swinging doors and saw, twenty feet ahead of her, a door to the outside. Passing racks of pans and dishes, she made her way to the door.

"Oh, Miss, hello. Are you here to inspect our kitchen?"

Rachel turned around. A smiling young man with a dark beard dressed in a starched white chef coat and American flag skull cap looked at her. "Yes," she said, "I'm sorry, yes, it was me, but it will have to wait. Is that okay?"

The young man nodded. "Of course, any time. Just give us some notice if you're coming right at dinner time."

"Thank you, I will, I promise." Rachel smiled, picked up her luggage, and went outside.

A few minutes later, Enterprise showed up, and with a couple of signatures she released the brake on a white Ford Econoline cargo van. As she went out and past the front of the casino, wearing her glasses, her hair tucked under the beanie, she saw both vehicles, Brian's Chevy and Ted's Ford, parked at the entrance to the casino. They would be in there quite a while trying to find her.

Soon Rachel headed north again on I-5. A mile past Bellingham, she turned on to Mount Baker Highway and the final few crooked miles up to Lake Kendall. She kept her eye on the rear view mirror as she left the north fork of the Nooksack and entered into Columbia Valley. She left the highway on to Kendall Road, straight arrow up the valley to the lake.

One last look in the mirror assured her that no one else followed her on the road. She turned right onto Overland Trail facing Lake Kendall. A hundred feet on she reached the cabin. Tall fir trees kept it nice and cool in the summer and offered great beauty in the winter when they were covered in snow.

Rachel parked the van along the side of the gravel in front of a large fir. She opened the garage doors wide. In the middle the snow blower lay on its side, beginning to show rust around the edges.

An image of her dad floated before her, trying hard to get it started, cursing, and finally getting it out and blowing a pathway around the house and to the street. She moved it to the side to make enough room for the van.

She looked out to the side of the house, past the large green lawn, to the bench overlooking the small finger of a lake, a very big pond, really, thirty yards wide and half a mile long. No one ventured out this early evening.

The wind whistled quietly all around her, letting her know that it knew she was here. Safe. Home with mom and dad. The sounds of birds, three different songs or more, added another welcome. Smelling the fir needles that crunched under her feet as she walked, she headed down the gravel path. The air felt chilly.

Not fancy as Mt. Baker cabins go, but nice families have cabins on either side, and all three dated from the time when you could still get an affordable cabin on the lake. A one story house but with a great sun room out back facing the water. The most beautiful sunrise in the world, if you're in the mood to get up early, or a great place to relax with a glass of wine and watch the mood of the light change as darkness takes over the little lake in the evening. A roaring fireplace after a morning on the slopes, or a long walk or climb in the forest. Paradise.

No lights on in any of the houses. Good. They're not nosy neighbors and all she would have to do is say the word and they would leave her completely alone.

Her parents left it to her long ago and many a time, it had been her sanctuary. Diane and Michael and their kids used it every year for skiing, and in the summer the kids dove off the tiny pier. It's where both Sean and Shannon learned to swim. If something happened to Rachel, this house would have gone to them. Until Joshua came along and her dreams had changed. But now she didn't want to think about it.

The solemn quiet of the scene always shrouded Rachel in peace. She could look out at the water and think she had the lake and the mountains to herself.

Rachel walked along the side of the house. The blue garbage can lay on its side. She picked it up, put it up against the wall and kicked it hard in place. Then she continued out to the lawn, over to the gravel section where a bench waited for someone to relax and forget their cares and enjoy the view. If they could.

She sat, stretched her arms along the back, closed her eyes, and listened to the quiet forest, then she watched the ripples in the water follow one another restlessly to the bank. She heard the wild chirp of birds, and the humming of the breeze in the towering pines. Rachel breathed deeply in and then out several times, filling her lungs with the fresh air. Every time she exhaled, she felt the foul courtroom air leave her body like a devil being exorcised.

Her dad had built this bench, and used the experience to try to teach her carpentry, but he couldn't get her interested, tomboy though she had been. He and Rachel's mom had retired to a condo near Sacramento, and memories of her childhood home gradually disappeared. Rachel's strongest memories were here.

She took her shoes and socks off, rolled her pant legs up and stepped out into the lake and waded slowly out a few feet. The cold mountain water sent a thrill up her legs and spine. She fell backwards and floated. She didn't care, she let the water cover her body and swam a few strokes as well as she could.

For a moment she lost her breath, but she stayed in the water until she didn't think she could feel her body any longer, then gradually got used to it. Rachel swam for two, maybe three minutes more, and then got out of the water.

She took the key out of her wet pocket, opened up the back door of the cabin and went in. She looked out the window to make sure she had privacy, then took everything off, leaving her dripping clothes on the floor of the sun room.

Her parents again invaded her thoughts, as she remembered them putting down the old rug in the small living room. In the corner of the kitchen she saw her mother at the sink, cutting up vegetables. Sarah McAlister, unsubstantial, looked at Rachel and smiled, as if to say she loved her and that everything would be all right.

A sudden gust of wind outside caught her attention. Rachel turned around to watch a large swath of small leaves like burnt snowflakes drop down in chaos from the roof and swirl around on their way down to the grass.

Rachel went into the bedroom and found some old clothes in the closet and the dresser and put them on. Nothing like old jeans and a Pendleton shirt to make you feel at home.

The sun had gone down beyond the mountain, gloom taking hold, so she turned the lights on, and got the hot water heater started. She couldn't find any wood around for the fireplace. She wished she had thought about it on the way up. Instead, she got the little heater out of the closet and plugged it in. The house wasn't very cool, but after the swim, the hot air coming out of the heater felt very good. In the small kitchen area, she plugged in the refrigerator and closed the doors. Then she noticed all the small puddles across the floor, found a mop and cleaned them up.

That's the kind of activity that seemed right just now. Bumming around for a week, maybe two, doing the bare minimum to keep the place civilized, spending most of her time walking around the lake or the woods. Or getting the rowboat out there and getting long, slow exercise.

Thinking what Michael told her, although she had no idea what to do about it. Old memories and new ones competed to shove her in some direction. Trying to figure out how she ended up in this situation.

And much as she didn't want to, she knew she would keep going over and over in her mind how she might have done things differently with Joshua. Perhaps she might even try again to make contact with his sister, find out if she wanted to harbor such angry feelings forever toward her.

Someday she would want to bring closure to all of this, but that day lay a long way off. She couldn't even think about dealing with Diane. And without closure on Diane, she couldn't deal with Michael.

But first she felt hunger pangs, so she got in the van and went back down the road a few minutes to the Village Market, stocked up on wine, although Gallo was what she had to settle for, and things to make sandwiches with. She watched for someone following her. No one.

Chapter 36

As Rachel braked in front of her cabin, and pulled into the parking spot, she looked out ahead and saw a car in front of the tree. A green Camry. Just what she needed, neighbors showing up uninvited. Or maybe stealing someone else's parking space. Rachel looked around but saw no one. She pulled up next to the Camry. It didn't belong to anyone she knew.

She got out of the van and looked around, but all the houses visible were dark. The empty Camry looked like a rental car, although she didn't see a sticker. She went around to the van and opened the passenger door and took out the bag of groceries, then decided to put the car in the garage.

She put the groceries back, pulled out, and slowly edged it into the garage. She locked the car, and went out around to the front of the house, and opened the door and reached in to turn on the light.

Before she could reach the switch, even with the cold wind going past her from outside, she inhaled the sickly sweet fragrance of roses. She turned the light on.

"Rachel!" Meredith stood there, in front of the kitchen table, with a bottle of sparkling wine in one hand and two champagne glasses in the other, filled and ready to drink. She wore a tight-fitting black velvet outfit with a black Nike jacket and had her usual wide white smile, posing innocently as she leaned against the table. Even her running shoes were black.

She had pulled back her hair and tied it in a ponytail, her head covered with a black baseball cap. She looked like a spotlight shone on her in the center of the room, with the bright effervescence of the sparkling wine in the glasses. The brown hair glistened beside her neck. "Are you surprised to see me?"

Rachel left the door open wide and felt the heat of the room in front of her. She felt her spine stiffen and her jaw tighten. "What are you doing here? How did you get in?"

"Don't you see, Rachel? I brought champagne, so we can celebrate." Meredith lifted the bottle in the air.

Standing still, Rachel waited a few seconds then shook her head, looking around the room and finally, slowly, back to Meredith. She lowered her head so that she looked up at Meredith from the top of her eyes. Another cold breeze hit the back of Rachel's neck. The low rumble of a car passing by mixed with high squeals from the squirrel outside the house.

"Didn't I tell you that I wanted to be alone for a while?"

"Well...yes... but I didn't think you meant all by your lonesome." Meredith began to frown, and then smiled again. "You know, no reporters. I thought you meant the two of us."

"I drove up here by myself. A long way," Rachel said, her eyes widening in disbelief. "There is no two of us."

Meredith opened her arms wide, still holding the bottle and the glasses. Then she shrugged her shoulders. "But you were so rattled after the verdict." She took a step sideways, then stopped. "You didn't know what to think. I thought I was doing what you wanted...okay..."

"And you followed me all the way up here, Meredith? I didn't see you following me. Something is definitely wrong here."

"Oh, Rachel, Irene told me. She was worried about you being all alone up here."

"Bullshit."

"No not at all. But that's not the issue here, Rachel. And I'm sorry."

Meredith carefully let the bottle and glasses down by her side and slumped, then straightened up again, spilled a little champagne on her pants, and brushed if off with her hand.

"I tell you what. I don't want to spoil your little retreat." She said this so sincerely, with her smile, her mouth open to show all her white teeth, but the eyes didn't quite match. "Why don't we have a glass of champagne together, then I will go down to Bellingham and stay at the Holiday Inn or something. You can call me when you're ready."

The groceries were pulling on the muscles above Rachel's elbow. Coming in the room a step, she shoved the front door closed with her foot. The room became warmer. She put the bags on the kitchen counter, then inhaled deeply.

Turning around and folding her arms in front of her, Rachel said, "Listen, you need to let me be by myself. I'm not ready for celebrating. I want to settle down, get over the trial. Partying is not the way to do it. I can't be by myself if you're a few miles away waiting for me."

Meredith backed away. "All right. You don't need to get so upset." There seemed to be, Rachel couldn't be sure, a genuine nervousness in her voice. Or something. She leaned over and put the champagne and glasses on the table and then turned back to Rachel. "I'll go back to Seattle right now. In fact I'm going back to Los Angeles if that'll make you happy. I can see this was a mistake. I didn't mean to upset you. Will you call me when you feel better?"

"It will be a long time." Rachel picked Meredith's car keys off the table and handed them to her.

Meredith came over as if to hug her, but Rachel backed far away. Meredith took the keys, buttoned up her coat, and walked fast over to the door.

She opened the door. Then she turned back and looked with sadness and said, "I am sorry, Rachel. I misread you. Don't hold it against me, please." She left, closing the door solidly behind her.

Rachel parted the curtains and watched her go out to the car. Meredith opened the door, then looked back over at the house, saw Rachel at the window, and shrugged her shoulders.

Rachel listened for the sound of her car disappearing in the distance, but could hear only the wind in the trees. She waited another ten seconds, and then went back in to the kitchen.

She put the bread on the corner of the counter, and the groceries in the refrigerator. She uncorked the wine, turned around and leaned against the counter. The champagne bottle and the two glasses were brightly lit in the center of the table.

The odd mix of Chablis and champagne hit her nose. She put the cork back into the wine bottle, put it down and picked up one of the glasses. She looked at the champagne bottle. Krug Grande Cuvee. Did she think that would impress me? Rachel thought. Meredith started to seem bizarre.

But still, the wine appeared to be good stuff. Rachel took a glass and watched the little bubbles fizz up to the top, then drank the whole thing down. She poured the other glass out. It would be a while before she got back to the champagne, Grande Cuvee or not. Rachel picked up her Chablis, uncorked it again, and started to take a drink when the room started spinning. She felt gripped by nausea, dropped the bottle, and saw the floor coming up and blanked out.

When she woke up, she found herself on a chair, her head feeling like it had been broken in half. The objects in front of her were blurry, but were starting to clear. Rachel started to get up, but couldn't move. She saw her arms and legs bound with duct tape. She strained, first her arms, then her legs, trying to pull herself back and forth, but couldn't move anything. Meredith stood in front of her.

"What are you—" Rachel said.

Before she could finish, she saw Meredith's fist swing in toward her. It hit her cheek so hard Rachel thought she must have broken a bone. The pain jarred her whole head.

Meredith stuck her face in front of Rachel and twisted it up in a nasty snarl. "Thank God, Rachel? Thank God you're alive? Is that it?"

"Y... Yes, I mean..."

Meredith took a gun out of her pocket and put it on the kitchen table. "Looks like yours, doesn't it? But it's not. Maybe you already know that."

And again her hand swung around. She slapped Rachel's head to the other side.

"No, Rachel, hate God you're still alive." Meredith spit the words out like they came straight up from the bile inside her.

She reached over to the table, picked up a syringe and turned it in her hand, then put it right in front of Rachel's face. She pushed up and watched a little fluid jump out of the needle. "A little something to make you sleep, Rachel. Don't worry, it's only ordinary sleeping pills dissolved in water. Something a suicidal person would take."

She put the syringe back on the table, opened the door, and disappeared for a moment and came back with a small portable propane tank. She left it on the floor in front of Rachel.

"See, there, for you."

"What? What is this?"

"You will find out soon enough. More or less."

"I don't understand. Why are you doing this?"

"Are you that stupid? Don't you know?"

"No, I don't."

"Who killed Joshua Todaro?"

"I don't know."

"You stupid woman. I killed him."

"You?"

"Me. Did you think it was Detective Tourville? Stupid."

"I..."

"Did you suffer, Rachel? Did it break your heart?"

Rachel's heart pounded.

Meredith held out her left hand. "See? See the ring?" she said with a diabolical smile. She spoke in a sympathetic voice. "I'm so sorry, you never got to wear it." Then she spoke it with pure poison on her tongue, raising her voice. "Now I'll wear it while you rot."

"What ring?"

"You know, the one Joshua was going to give you. He didn't because I'm wearing it. I took it, Rachel, right off his precious architectural model. You don't deserve it."

Rachel's heart almost gave out. She thought of Joshua going for the ring and not finding it. She strained against the tape, but could not move. Her heart pounded against her chest. To learn that not only had Joshua not betrayed her but that his murderer stood in front of her, she couldn't grasp it.

Meredith went to the window and looked out. She turned back to Rachel and said, "You are all careless. How easy it was to steal Diane's lipstick and get a hair, too." Then she came back close to Rachel, her eyes wide with hatred. "Why did you kill Gil Hamilton?"

"Gil Hamilton? He...somebody...shot at me. I shot back. It was an accident."

"Accident? No, it was not an accident for me." Meredith held her fists tight against her head. Her eyes widened and her voice hardened. "He was my lover! He was the father of my child!"

"There was a whole inquest."

"Did you hear me? There was no inquest for me. They let you off." She began to shiver as she spoke. "They let you off, Rachel. They let you go free." She stood for a moment directly in front of Rachel, eyes burning, still shaking.

Then Meredith stood still, seeming to gain control of herself. She walked over to the front window and looked in both directions. Then she turned out the lights, and waited in the dark, standing quiet. She came back and stood in front of Rachel. "Nobody needs to know we're here."

Meredith looked down at the floor, concentrating, then at Rachel's face. "You know what, Rachel, it was the second worst day of my life. When they let you off. The worst day was when I lost our baby, Gil and mine. Do you know what that's like? Do you?"

"N...no I don't."

She leaned closer to Rachel's face, her mouth twitching as she spoke. "Did you think you were going to get away with it?"

Rachel moved her head back, but Meredith moved with her. "What?"

"What? What? Is that all you can say? Huh?" Meredith's spoke in a voice that neared grunting. "Let me tell you, it was never going to happen. Never."

She groped in the dark for the syringe and found it, pushed up a little spray again, and felt for Rachel's arm.

Rachel tried to make her voice convincing and serious. "Meredith, they will know, they will see the mark."

Meredith stood straight. "Give me a break, it's just a little pin prick. They won't look, it's sleeping pills. Sleeping pills and liquor and some carbon monoxide. Maybe a little propane at the end for effect. Don't worry. When you're asleep, I'll remove all the evidence of duct tape." She looked at Rachel with eyes filled not only with hatred, but also with insult. "Did you think I was that stupid?"

Rachel struggled and felt her muscles straining against the tape, but couldn't budge her arms or her legs. Twisting, she tried to tip over the chair, but couldn't get enough leverage to do it.

Meredith looked at her and spoke in her own soft, concerned voice. "You know, I was going to tell you all this before they put the drugs in your veins in the execution chamber." Meredith toggled her head back and forth. "In the chamber, in the car, what difference does it make."

"Meredith..."

Meredith's voice changed to a hard rage. She shook her head. She took hold of Rachel's hair and pulled her head back. "I'd rather tear your intestines out."

She took a small bottle out of her pocket and opened it up. Joshua's Knize Ten. She started to sprinkle it all over Rachel's body. "Here you can smell and smell and smell. Think of him. He doesn't smell like this anymore."

Meredith poured some on Rachel's face. The cologne made Rachel dizzy. Meredith emptied the bottle on Rachel's clothes, then with an athletic swing, threw it against the wall. It hit with a hard thud and clattered on the floor.

Meredith made a wide sweeping move with her arm and slapped Rachel across the face. She moved her face closer, leaned over and started to put the syringe in Rachel's arm.

A shot rang out and the sound of glass hitting the floor came from the window on the right. Cold air streamed into the room.

Meredith fell on top of Rachel and dripped blood from her chest. She rolled over and fell with a thump on the floor, stopping next to the propane tank. Her head bobbed back and forth once. Her eyes closed, opened and stared, then closed again. The syringe had stuck in her thigh.

A moment later the door opened, the light came on, and Diane Scanlan walked into the room, arms out straight, gun tight in both hands, sweeping left and right. She let the gun fall to her side, knelt down and felt Meredith's neck, then stood and removed the duct tape from Rachel's arms and legs.

"Diane...how...what?"

"Are you all right? That's quite a bruise on your cheek." Diane focused her eyes and put her hand softly up to the cheek, but did not touch it. She looked at Rachel for a response.

"All right? Yes, thanks to you."

"Excuse me," Diane said, raising her finger. She went to Meredith and stood over her and dialed her cell phone, then waited several seconds.

"Yes, this is Seattle police detective Diane Scanlan. I shot someone in the act of attempted murder...I think she's dead. She doesn't seem to have a pulse, but you never know...49 Kendall Road, on the lake...myself, Rachel McAlister the intended victim, and Meredith Rawlings, the woman I shot. Rachel is the owner of the house. She's been beat up, but I don't think it's serious...I guess she was hit on the cheek with something hard. No blood... My badge number is 1266. You're going to send paramedics and the sheriff, right? Good. Of course, we'll wait right here. 206-555-9275. Here? There's no phone here." Diane closed her cell phone and put it in her pocket.

"There's an ambulance coming from St. Joseph," she said, "it won't take it 15 minutes to get here. I don't know how long the sheriff's department will take."

Diane walked over to the table and picked up the bottle of champagne, turning it as if to study the label.

Rachel knocked the bottle out of her hand. The champagne flew across the room and hit the front wall, then fell to the floor and broke into shards with the broken glass from the window. The wine bubbled over the pieces.

Diane backed away and stared wide-eyed at Rachel.

"It's drugged," Rachel said.

"Thank you for that, but I don't think I was going to drink any of it," Diane said, smiling now and raising her eyebrows. Then she frowned and scrunched up her nose. "You smell like a perfume factory. What's going on?"

Rachel laughed. "That was her. She dumped a bottle of Joshua's cologne on me." She stretched her arms and legs. "But tell me, why did you come up here?"

"Because you didn't answer your phone. I called Irene and she said you left your cell phone at home."

"Yeah, that's true. If I needed to make a call, I planned to go down to the Village Market. So why?"

Diane studied Rachel's face, then looked up and thought for a moment "Think about it, Rachel. First I was framed..."

"The same as me," Rachel interrupted. She returned Diane's gaze and felt as close to her in this moment as she had during the battle in Afghanistan. "And I was too much a fool to accept it."

Diane put her palm up and shook her head. "Then Berg was going to put me on the witness stand against you, even as a hostile witness." She turned and looked at the body on the floor, then came back to Rachel. "But you know what? Meredith wouldn't talk to me. I tried several times. That really got to me. I knew something was wrong there. When I called Irene and she said you'd come up here alone, I just had to come to talk to you. I went first to Meredith's apartment, to insist on talking to her, to find out what I could from her. To confront her. But she wasn't there. So...it wasn't hard...I just broke in. Inside I found her picture, Rachel. Standing next to Gil Hamilton. She was clearly pregnant. Then I knew I had to get up here. Just in case. I had to let you know."

Rachel looked down at Meredith, on her side, eyes closed. The siren drew closer to the house. A vehicle moved across the front lawn and stopped. Two deputies stepped out of the car. One came to the door and pushed it open. The other peered through the empty window frame.

Rachel and Diane both had their hands in the air, holding identification up.

The deputies' eyes widened as they looked past them.

"Unhh," came a grunt from behind them. Rachel turned around and saw Meredith leaning on her elbow, blood oozing over her jacket. She tried to open the propane with one shaking hand while she flipped a lighter on with the other. Rachel took one step and flew horizontal several feet over to Meredith, landing on her, knocking the lighter away and pounding her fist on Meredith's head. The unlit lighter fell with a metallic clang to the floor.

Rachel rolled over and turned the propane off.

Meredith lay still, eyes staring lifeless at the ceiling.

One of the deputies knelt, checked her neck for a pulse, looked at them and said, "Now she's gone."

The other deputy put his gun back in its holster. "That was pretty close. Are you okay?"

Diane and Rachel looked at each other and then nodded in agreement.

Rachel put her hands around Diane's head. "You never cease to amaze me. There's always a good cop around when you need one."

She pulled Joshua's ring off Meredith's finger, looked at it, and grasped it tight in her fist. She closed her eyes and felt his presence. Then she put it on her own finger. She now had the ring and Joshua's bullet and that was better than only memories.

Chapter 37

Rachel's hair blew in her face as the cool wind swept through the cedars and firs on the shore of Lake Union. Red geraniums were artfully arranged against the green and brown of trees to the side of the Joshua Todaro Portage Bay Conference Center. Rachel, Diane and Michael waited for Mayor Janine Jordan to begin the laying of the cornerstone.

"You guys look wonderful in your uniforms," Michael said. Rachel and Diane exchanged glances, both in their military dress blue, with their Silver and Bronze stars prominently displayed.

"Yes, you do," came a woman's voice behind them.

The voice sounded familiar, but Rachel wasn't sure. She turned around.

Sylvia Todaro, smiling, moved toward her, hand outstretched. Rachel moved closer to shake Sylvia's hand, but then Sylvia opened her arms wide and enveloped Rachel in a long, warm embrace.

With Sylvia's arms around her shoulders, Rachel closed her eyes and breathed in Joshua's presence, and his love. When they parted, Sylvia also kissed Rachel warmly on the cheek. Rachel saw tears flow down Sylvia's face, but then they disappeared in the blur of her own tears.

"Thank you," Rachel said. "I can't thank you enough. You don't know how much you have moved me by coming here today." She wiped her tears away.

"No, I must thank you," Sylvia said. "I misjudged you so thoroughly." Her voice came from emotions deep inside her.

She kept her hands on Rachel's shoulders and she moved her head with deliberate slowness from side to side. "I know you meant so much to Joshua. If he was going to have a short life, I am happy he had the last few months with you. Rachel, you gave him the only true happiness he knew in his life. You must forgive me for not understanding."

"Oh, no," Rachel said. She took Sylvia's hands in her own. "We gave each other happiness, and now I know, whenever I will see you, I see him in your eyes. And feel him in your heart. You and I will always have to be close."

Sylvia embraced Rachel again, saying, "That's important for me, too," and then pulled back, but kept hold of one of Rachel's hands as they turned to where the mayor stood.

Mayor Jordan came up to them and shook hands with Rachel, Diane and Sylvia. "Thank you for coming." She looked around. "It's a beautiful day, isn't it? That's only appropriate for a setting as stunning as this one." She looked at the crowd and began the ceremony. Her remarks were short, and received polite but prolonged applause.

As the mayor started to push the dedication stone into the opening, Rachel stepped forward and said, "Please, wait a second." The mayor stopped and looked at Rachel, but turned to the crowd, smiling. A quiet murmur began to circulate as people turned to look at one another.

Rachel looked down to her hand, fingers extended, stared at them, waited a long time, then removed the engagement ring and held it between her thumb and forefinger. She looked over at Sylvia, at Joshua's eyes. Sylvia nodded in solemn and heartfelt agreement. Rachel leaned down and placed the ring inside the opening for the stone. "Thank you," she said, as she stood and looked at the mayor, and stepped back.

The mayor, her hands on her cheeks and eyes wide in sympathy, said "Certainly," and waited for Rachel to move farther away. Then she pushed the dolly flush with the opening. Two aides came up and helped her slide the stone until it lined up flush with the wall. The crowd started sustained loud applause.

Rachel linked her arms with Diane and Michael, and lowered her head. A few yards out in the bay, a fireboat set off a high spray and the crowd increased their applause.

After the celebration, Rachel, Diane and Michael, along with Sylvia Todaro, headed back up to the parking lot, to go to Rachel's home for long conversations, reminiscences about the past, and uncertainty for the future.

As they started to get into the car, Rachel noticed a face in the crowd, no longer grim, but watching her. She saw the face of Ted Tourville, standing next to Sandra, his wife. He moved toward her. She observed him a long time, noting the sincerity on his face but not trusting him. She walked to meet him.

He offered his hand and a sincere voice. "Rachel, I offer you my apologies. I'm sorry for everything that happened. Maybe someday I'll be able to make it up to you."

Rachel looked down at his hand and shook her head. "You know what, Ted, you'll never make it up to me. This day has brought closure for me, about Joshua, about my future. But not about you. Ever. I've learned to be careful about who to trust. And who not to." She waved good-bye to Sandra as she turned back to the others.

Sylvia came up to the three of them, Rachel, Diane, and Michael. "Please," she said. "Come over with me to my house. I live on Bainbridge Island now. It would mean everything if you spent time with me today. You can all fit in my SUV, and I'll bring you back tonight." She looked at them in turn, smiling, waiting, with clear humility and sincerity. Especially, she looked at Rachel.

The three of them turned and looked at each other, but left it for Rachel to decide. And she didn't hesitate. "I think it's a very good idea. Joshua would want it very much for me."

Heading across Puget Sound, they stood on the deck of the ferry *Tacoma,* facing the waterfront as the ship churned out into Elliott Bay. The Public Market sign, spelled backwards from their view, receded in the distance. Three seagulls flew past and then soared upward, and she felt the motion of the birds as if they were taking her away. Rachel touched Diane on the shoulder. Diane turned with a smile and rested her hand on Rachel's and held it there for several seconds.

Then Rachel returned to the view of the waterfront. She knew that someday, wherever she is, there will be another thunderstorm, and lightning in the sky and she will remember back to that evening on Pike Place and imagine Joshua across the street watching her from his window. Once more, the bullet in her pocket bit into her leg. She took it out and turned it over in her hand, then put it in her purse. Later, she could find a place to keep it.

There will be, someday, another love as great as his. But she knew in her heart she would never have to settle for anyone less than him.

Acknowledgments

I want to thank Samantha Marshall, M.D., John Howsden of the Fremont, California police, and Myles Sorensen. Thanks to Tory Hartmann, Roy L. Jackson, Joyce Krieg, and Pat Nipper for professional reviews And early on, reviews by Becky Levine and Richard Burns. And thanks to Paulette back in Idaho for putting two bullets on the table one day. Most of all, thanks to Charleyne, my wife and collaborator.

www.ingramcontent.com/pod-product-compliance
Lightning Source LLC
Chambersburg PA
CBHW020946260626
47169CB00006B/1838